"Luke's bachelor party is tonight...if you're not doing anything, stop by."

"Stop by?" Bailey asked, staring incredulously at Ethan. "To Luke's boys' night?" She hung out with the guys all the time, but a bachelor party?

"Yeah, why not?"

"Well, for one, I have Victoria's bachelorette tonight. A wine and cheese at the Brookhollow Inn." The poker and beer was so much more appealing.

"That sounds awful. Why would you go to that?"

Bailey shook her head. "Because I'm a woman, and women go to boring bachelorette parties and talk about you guys, while you guys have all the fun and forget we exist."

"Huh." Ethan's eyes narrowed as he studied her.

"What?"

"Nothing," he said with a shrug. "I guess I just never really see you that way. As a woman, I mean."

Dear Reader,

Real-life love stories happen in many different ways, but one of my all-time favorite stories is when a friendship develops into a different kind of love. In *What A Girl Wants,* it was so much fun exploring what could happen when the hero begins to see his best friend, the heroine, in a new light. Two people who know each other's secrets, who share a common history and who respect and appreciate each other can create the biggest spark when one or both are awakened to the awareness that maybe there's something more....

Of course the real pleasure of these stories lies in the mystery of the pathway from awareness to happily ever after. I hope you enjoy reading Bailey and Ethan's journey to love as much as I've enjoyed helping them overcome the odds to get there.

Hugs,

Jennifer

HARLEQUIN HEARTWARMING

Jennifer Snow

What a Girl Wants

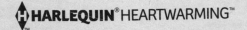

Recycling programs
for this product may
not exist in your area.

ISBN-13: 978-0-373-36664-4

WHAT A GIRL WANTS

Copyright © 2014 by Jennifer Snow

This edition published by arrangement with Harlequin Books S.A.

For questions and comments about the quality of this book, please contact us at CustomerService@Harlequin.com.

® and TM are trademarks of Harlequin Enterprises Limited or its corporate affiliates. Trademarks indicated with ® are registered in the United States Patent and Trademark Office, the Canadian Trade Marks Office and in other countries.

Printed in U.S.A.

JENNIFER SNOW

has been writing fairy tales with happy endings from a very young age, and she is excited to be sharing her new small-town contemporary series with Harlequin fans. Living in Edmonton, Alberta, with her husband and three-year-old son, she is dedicated to creating lasting, heartfelt romances that readers can share with those they love. Visit www.JenniferSnowBooks.com.

Books by Jennifer Snow

HARLEQUIN HEARTWARMING

Acknowledgments

Thank you as always to my family, my agent, Stephany Evans, and my editor, Victoria Curran—whose encouragement and support make it possible for me to realize this dream.
Also, a special thank-you to Richard Hynes of the St. John's Regional Fire Department and Trevor Zawaski of Edmonton Fire Rescue for their much-appreciated assistance in my research for this book.

CHAPTER ONE

FEW SIGHTS IN Brookhollow, New Jersey, were as jaw-dropping as the scene taking place in front of fire station number five: fire truck washing day. Watching five of the twelve firefighters, shirtless and a little sweaty, soaping up and hosing off the big red engines was by far the highlight of any summer's day in the small town.

Cutting the engine of her cherry-red Kawasaki Ninja, Bailey Sheppard removed her helmet, letting her dark hair cascade over her shoulders. She swung her leg over the bike and, tucking the helmet under her arm, unlatched her tool kit from the back of the motorcycle. Squinting in the bright, early-morning sunlight, she weighed her options. Should she attempt to enter through the open bay doors or go around to the side entrance?

Knowing she'd never make it through the front bay doors where the men were working without getting drenched with the freezing water, she jogged unnoticed around the big brick building. The dousing would be refreshing, but her dark blue coveralls with her name embroidered on the left front pocket would take forever to dry, even in the blazing August heat.

A long line of women waited at the door and Bailey hid a smile as she approached. It was almost nine o'clock on the first Friday of the month, the day the fire hall provided free blood pressure and cholesterol screening. The Bishop brothers, Jim and Ethan, had set up the free program after their grandfather had experienced a series of strokes the year before. Like many seniors in the community, he'd neglected to visit the local medical clinic regularly, and his high blood pressure had gone undetected.

The fire hall's staff was continually looking for ways to give back to the community. While there were always a few women, young and old, waiting to be checked at the free screening, today there was quite a lineup. Bailey suspected some of the blood pressure results were going to be a little higher than usual. Brookhollow's local heroes were as handsome as they were brave. Having grown up with them in the small New Jersey town of less than ten thousand residents, she'd dated most of them at one time or another throughout their junior high and high school years, all except Ethan Bishop—the one she wanted.

Pushing through the west door to the fire hall, she entered the main office where the fire chief, Ken Clarke, sat behind his desk. An open box of doughnuts was within arm's reach and white confectioners' sugar covered his top lip. Quite a contrast to the image of his twentysomething self still hanging on the wall with the rest of the staff photos. New shots of the twelve-member crew were taken yearly. Well, everyone except Ken, who preferred the image of his younger self.

He stood as she approached. "Hey, Bailey, you here to get your heart racing—" he pointed to the shirtless men washing trucks outside "—or checked?" With a grin, he nodded toward the fully uniformed men running the free clinic. With two of the fire trucks outside, they'd transformed the big open bays into a makeshift medical facility.

Derek Johnson, the newest recruit, handed out the prescreening questionnaire and waiver to a group of sitting women who were waiting the required five minutes to allow their heart rate to settle before testing. Mark Adams took blood pressure readings in the fire hall's dining area several feet away. He waved at her.

"Neither," Bailey said, smiling as she leaned her hip against the desk. "Why aren't you outside helping?"

Ken shook his head. "My days of six-pack abs and bulging biceps are over, I'm afraid. No one wants to see this out there." Rubbing his large stomach, he shuddered.

"That's the truth," Mark called from his post, where he secured the blood pressure cuff around Mrs. Norris's arm.

The older woman, the owner of Ginger Snaps, the bakery on Main Street, shot Chief Clarke a look that suggested he was past his prime, though Bailey suspected Ginger Norris was at least ten years his senior.

"You looking to get assigned nightshift duty, Adams?" Ken warned.

"You can't. I've had nights for three weeks now. Tonight is my first one off and the beginning of a rotation of days." Mark removed the cuff and recorded the reading on a wallet card for Ginger. He handed it to her and accepted her hug, before gathering her purse and jacket for her.

"Are you sure about that?" Ken asked, checking the rotation schedule on the pegboard behind him, which was covered with pictures of his grandchildren. To say he was a proud grandfather would be an understatement.

"Positive."

"Darn," Ken muttered. "Well, that doesn't prevent me from putting you on bathroom duties."

"You already put Craig on bathroom duty for pouring salt in the sugar dish in the lunchroom last week, remember?"

Bailey watched the scene with unconcealed amusement. The men were always pulling pranks on each other at the fire hall and Ken was often on the receiving end. It was all in good fun and the guys knew they'd pay for it with extra shifts or unwanted responsibilities. Injecting some fun into their routine helped to break up the monotony of quiet days and ease tension whenever there was a real emergency.

"Anyway, I'm not here to check out the guys," Bailey said, though it was an added bonus. "I'm here to check on truck number two." The ladder engine was rarely used, causing the hydraulic fluid lines to clog and making it untrustworthy in the event of an emergency. While most buildings in Brookhollow were no more than two stories high, some of the newer structures in the downtown business sector were four stories or more.

"Great timing. The hydraulic motor didn't work last week during a routine test." He motioned behind her. "There's Ethan. Get him to show you the problem with the rotating gear on the motor."

Bailey held her breath as she turned to face her best friend. He was in full uniform, on clinic duty. She wasn't sure whether to feel relieved or disappointed. Relieved, she decided, yet… She cleared her throat.

"Hey, you. How's the arm?" She nodded toward the small hand-shaped purple-and-yellow bruise visible on the inside of his strong, perfectly smooth left biceps, just below the firefighter crest on the sleeve of his dark blue shirt.

Ethan's broad smile revealed perfect, straight white teeth and a deep dimple in his left cheek. "It's fine. You don't really think that move you pulled on me last night actually worked, do you? I was just playing along… for the sake of the class."

"Yeah, sure. That's why you looked ready to cry when I wrenched your arm behind your back?" Bailey taught a weekly self-defense class at her brothers' gym and mixed-martial-arts—MMA—club, Extreme Athletics, and Ethan had volunteered to act as the attacker for demonstration purposes.

"I told you—it was all for show. Besides, I'll do anything I can to get you closer to your trip to Venice."

It had been his suggestion to charge for the self-defense class, knowing she'd been saving money for the trip to Italy. Her parents had honeymooned in Venice years before and her mom had told Bailey stories about its beautiful scenery and culture when she was growing up. She'd always wanted to go and decided it was time, but having just bought the garage from her uncle Doug the month before, funds were limited.

"Well, your injuries are definitely appreciated."

"Come on, I'll show you the problem with the truck." Ethan led the way to the ladder truck in the last bay. "So where's your sidekick today?"

Bailey followed him to the engine. "Are you kidding me? Nick would never be up this early. He works in the shop from about ten to three-ish three days a week…and even that's too much." Doug's son, her cousin Nick, had started to work in the shop that summer after dropping out of the computer program he'd been attending at the New Jersey Institute of Technology the previous year. He knew nothing about mechanics and had even less interest, but Doug had insisted that he apprentice with her that summer. She only prayed he planned to return to school in the fall. Her cousin was a great guy, but having him around the shop proved to be more work than help, and he certainly didn't enjoy being there.

"Probably a good thing. You said yourself, the guy doesn't know a wrench from a screwdriver," Ethan said with a shake of his head.

Climbing up onto the roof of the fire engine, she studied the hydraulic motor. "So what's wrong with this?"

"The rotating piece of the motor—it won't shift left to right."

"Probably just a fluid buildup in the lines."

"If you say so," Ethan said with a laugh. "You're the expert."

"Ethan, quit flirting with our mechanic and get over here," Mark called.

Bailey paused and glanced at Ethan.

A slow teasing grin spread across his face. "Are we flirting?" he asked loud enough for Mark to hear.

Bailey played along. "Well, if the biggest flirt in town thinks so…"

"Very funny, you two," Mark grumbled, nodding toward Sheila Mason, who awaited her turn for the blood pressure check, her cell phone to her ear and her sandaled foot tapping against the concrete floor.

Bailey frowned. "Mrs. Mason is here?"

"Yeah, she's helping Victoria plan the wedding. I wouldn't be surprised if her blood pressure is a little high."

Sheila Mason's daughter, Victoria, had returned to Brookhollow eight months before to buy out Legend's, the local sporting-goods store, on behalf of her client, Play Hard Sports. She'd not only acquired the store, but also rekindled the flame with her former fiancé, Luke Dawson. Bailey could understand Sheila's anxiety. Her daughter had called off her first wedding twelve years ago just two weeks before it was to take place.

Turning her attention to the engine, Bailey fiddled with the rotating gear just as her beeper chimed on her hip. The fire-hall phone rang seconds later and Ethan dived for it. "Fire hall five…Yes, no problem…South of exit forty-eight," he said, repeating the information flashing on her pager. Grabbing her tool kit, she climbed back down as he replaced the receiver.

"Car stranded on I-95?"

"Looks like we're heading in the same direction," he confirmed.

ETHAN'S CELL PHONE vibrated against the console of the fire truck and he barely heard the familiar ringtone above the wail of the sirens as he sped along the highway toward exit forty-eight. His gaze flew to the call display and his grip tightened on the steering wheel. The Miami number flashed on the screen for a torturous five rings before the call went to voice mail. Emily wouldn't leave a message. She never did. Yet lately the calls from his ex-girlfriend were becoming more and more frequent…as were the text messages that simply said she needed to talk. Yeah, well, the time for talking had long passed.

"Her again?" his brother and coworker Jim asked from the passenger seat of the engine. He'd just finished washing the truck when the call had come in and had offered to go along as the other men were busy running the clinic.

"Yeah," Ethan mumbled, avoiding Jim's expression. One he'd seen too many times over the past six months since his long-term girl-friend, Emily Parsons, had dumped him and left Brookhollow to follow a big corporate executive from Play Hard Sports to Miami. Greg Harrison, the vice president of sales, had arrived in town to train the new store managers and Emily had caught his attention and interest. For weeks, all Ethan had heard was Greg this, Greg that, and while he wasn't normally a jealous person, he'd suspected Emily was interested in the man who'd driven into Brookhollow in his Audi R8 and designer suit.

So when the executive had offered her an opportunity to join the management trainee program to become a corporate trainer, Emily had jumped at the opportunity. That hadn't surprised Ethan. Emily had always talked about leaving Brookhollow to live in a big city, but he wondered how much of her decision had been based on the job offer and how much on her new boss.

"Why don't you ever answer it?"

"I've got nothing to say to her." In fact, he had a lot to say, but he preferred to take the high road. Emily had made her choice, and while her decision to end a ten-year relationship on a whim had made him angry, there had been nothing he could do about it when she was standing right there in front of him. He doubted he could talk sense into her when she was in sunny Florida, living the life she'd always claimed she wanted.

"I can think of a few things to say. Can I answer it next time?" Jim drained the contents of his iced cappuccino and set the cup in the holder.

"There's no point, Jim. Nothing we say will bring her back." Ethan checked the rearview mirror and noticed Bailey's tow truck speeding along in the lane beside him.

"Is that what you think I want?" Jim scoffed. "Tell me *you're* not crazy enough to want that."

Ethan remained silent. His brother didn't get it. Jim and his girlfriend, Jill, had only been seeing each other for two years. They were sickeningly in love and Jim had never had to experience the pain and humiliation Ethan had suffered. Emily's leaving had shocked him, along with almost everyone else in town. Sure, things hadn't been great between them for a while, but they'd still loved each other. At least, *he'd* still been in love. And to leave him for a man she'd known less

than a month was a blow to his ego, difficult
to recover from.

"Oh, come on, man. She ran off the first
opportunity she got."

"Yes, I'm aware of that." And his family
hadn't allowed him to forget. They expected
that his anger over the situation should help
to erase the pain and longing he felt for the
woman who'd been a major part—maybe
even the biggest part—of his life since high
school. His sister, Melody, was probably the
most understanding, having lost her husband
two years before in a car accident, but even
she thought that he would have moved on by
now. And for the most part, he thought he was
doing well. At least, until the phone rang and
it was her. Not answering her calls when he
longed to hear her voice was torture.

The phone chimed with a text message and
he reached for it.

But Jim got to it first. "We need to talk?"
he read aloud.

Ethan sighed. "That's all she ever says."
Above everything else was a nagging curiosity about what she obviously needed to say
to him. He wondered how long he could remain strong and continue to ignore her. Admittedly, his resolve was weakening. Angry

or not, he missed the life they had created together. He had liked knowing where he was headed—his job was solid, one he enjoyed and did well, and his relationship had been comfortable, secure.... Maybe that had been the problem. Emily thrived on new and exciting, changing jobs every few months. He wondered how long the new Play Hard opportunity would keep her happy.

"Do you think she wants to come back?"

Ethan denied himself that hope. "I don't know."

"Would you take her back if she did?"

The million-dollar question. He hesitated before saying, "I'm not an idiot, Jim."

"You're not answering the question."

Ethan snatched the phone away before Jim could answer the text, which he knew he was aching to do, and slid it into his shirt pocket. He pulled the truck to the side of the highway behind an old rusted red Volkswagen Jetta and jumped down onto the gravel. He positioned two traffic cones in the inside lane, forcing the oncoming traffic to take the outside lane, as Bailey's tow truck pulled in front of the Jetta and she climbed out, clipboard in hand.

"I'll be here if you need me," Jim called

from inside the truck, reclining the seat and shutting his eyes.

"You're not even going to get out of the truck?"

"It's a simple backup call. I only came along to get out of clinic duty."

Ethan shook his head as he closed the truck door. It amazed him how their work ethic differed so drastically. Jim was four years older, yet he'd never shown any interest in advancing his rank at the fire hall. Ethan had worked hard, proving himself to his senior coworkers and landing the position of captain by the time he was twenty-four.

He approached Bailey at the front of the vehicle where she was speaking to a short, frazzled-looking bald man. "I'll just need your driver's license and your credit card… and I'll have you hooked up and ready to go in just a few minutes. Feel free to sit in the truck to wait. The air-conditioning is on and it's much cooler in there."

The man disappeared inside the cab of the tow truck and Ethan waited until he was out of earshot before saying, "This car has to be at least thirty years old." He leaned against the bumper to watch her work, and the metal frame creaked in protest.

"That thing looks about to fall off," she warned as she put the tow dolly's coupler in open position by lowering the locking lever all the way down and inserting the locking pin to secure it in place.

Good point, he thought as he stood. "So, before I forget, we're holding Luke's bachelor party at the fire hall tonight—poker, darts, beer, the baseball game.... If you're not doing anything, stop by." Bailey was a regular at their weekly poker games, much to the dismay of the other guys, whose wallets she emptied.

"Stop by? To Luke's bachelor party—the ultimate boys night?" She sounded incredulous as she inserted the electrical plug from the dolly into the switch on the back of the tow truck. That way the brake lights and turning signals on the dolly would work while en route to the shop.

"Yeah, why not?" He knew Luke wouldn't mind. Bailey had always been like a third, less-annoying sister to the groom-to-be, and she kept his ancient, rusted-out truck on the road.

"I have Victoria's bachelorette party tonight. A wine and cheese in the backyard of the Brookhollow Inn." She crisscrossed the chains and connected them to the eyelets on the bumper of the car.

"That sounds awful."

"You're telling me."

A loud boom sounded and they both swung around to see smoke and flames coming from the hood of the Jetta.

Great, the piece of crap car was on fire.

Quickly, he pushed Bailey toward the guardrail on the side of the highway and said, "Stay right here!" Then, running to the truck, he rapped on the passenger door to get Jim's attention before grabbing a jump line of two lengths of forty-four-inch hose and a nozzle.

"What happened?" Jim asked, joining him.

"That car should never have passed its last road-safety inspection," he muttered as he grabbed his coat and self-contained breathing apparatus from inside the fire truck. Nothing annoyed him more than accidents that could have been prevented. This car was long past retirement and posed a safety threat.

He secured the mask in place before advancing toward the car, spraying the flames that had spread around the base of the vehicle. The last thing he wanted was for the flames to spread to the tow truck. Bailey had just purchased the wheel-lift truck the month before after buying the garage from her uncle. She loved that four-wheel drive almost as much as she loved her motorcycle. It would serve as her primary vehicle in the winter months.

Jim grabbed the Halligan bar to gain access to the fire under the hood. Hurrying, he pierced a hole in the hood and used the tool to pry it open. Moving closer, Ethan sprayed a stream of water, extinguishing the flames.

After a thorough walkabout and once satisfied that the fire was completely out, he put the tools away and approached Bailey while Jim filled out the report inside the truck. "You okay?" He rubbed her shoulders, noticing the goose bumps on her forearms, despite the heat waves radiating from the highway.

"Yeah… That was just so sudden."

The car's owner had jumped out of the tow truck and run some twenty-five yards away while his vehicle was consumed by flames. He joined them now, shaking slightly.

"My car," he said, wide-eyed as he stared at the charred mess.

"It only takes a small spark to ignite into major flames," Ethan told him, then turned once more to Bailey. "I think you should unhook the car. That thing is a hazard. You don't want it in your shop." Who knew what else was wrong with that wreck? In his professional opinion, it was a chance too risky to take...not to mention his personal concern as her friend.

"What? You won't tow it?" The man looked frantic at the thought of being stranded on the side of the highway any longer.

"I seriously doubt there's a whole lot Bailey can—" Ethan started, but Bailey interrupted.

"Of course I will."

Ethan shot her an annoyed look and lowered his voice. "I really don't think it's a good idea, Bailey."

"I appreciate your concern, Ethan, but it's not your decision to make. We both know Uncle Doug would never leave this car stranded."

She was right, and while he wanted to argue, he knew his words would fall on deaf ears. Bailey had been on her own since she was seventeen. She'd lost her mom to cancer at twelve, and she'd been desperate to escape her family home where her father and two overprotective brothers had driven her crazy. Listening to the advice of others was not her strong point. She insisted on doing things her way. That stubborn independence was one of the things he liked about his friend, unless he was going up against it.

"Fine, it's your shop." He shrugged, but he couldn't resist taking a jab at her. "Oh…and be sure to have fun tonight," he said with a smirk as he hopped back into the fire truck.

ARRIVING BACK AT the shop fifteen minutes later, after dropping the frazzled Mr. Huntley at the Brookhollow Inn for the evening, Bailey wasn't surprised to find the door locked and no one around. Nick wouldn't be there unless he had to be. She let herself in and picked up the mail on the floor. Flicking through the envelopes, she was happy to see payments for work completed last month.

Her uncle had run the shop on an invoicing system for the town locals. Only out-of-towners were required to pay at the time of delivery and even then he accepted personal checks. When she'd taken over the bookkeeping and accounting side of the business several months before, there had been many outstanding, unpaid invoices. In a few short weeks, she'd collected on almost all of them and the shop's finances were in much better shape. Unfortunately the surplus in revenue had been one of the reasons her uncle had been able to talk her into giving Nick the job as her apprentice that summer.

She pushed through the swinging door that led to the bays where two vehicles awaited paint jobs. Might as well get them ready for pickup and parked outside before bringing in the Jetta. Though she wasn't sure what she could do to fix the old car. She'd try her best, but she suspected it was headed for the junkyard in town.

Sighing, she tied her hair back into a ponytail at the base of her neck, tucking the strands beneath her collar. Detail work was her least favorite job. She'd rather be under the body or peering under a hood any day.

Approaching the workbench where all the paint supplies and air-brush color cans were, she noticed several detail brushes in containers of warm, soapy water and six or seven spray cans in the trash under the desk. Had Doug come by and completed the work himself? Since retiring, he sometimes came by to tinker with a vehicle or two. Bailey suspected he was going crazy at home with nothing to do. However, she couldn't remember the last time the older man had taken on any paintwork, claiming his less-than-rock-steady hands and less-than-perfect eyesight couldn't be trusted anymore.

Bailey flicked the light switch on the wall to see the vehicles more clearly. Checking the work order, she approached the first one. A Toyota Corolla brought in a few days ago by Mrs. Norris. There had been body damage to the left side of her front bumper after she'd hit a newly placed concrete divider in the grocery store parking lot. Inspecting the bumper, she was shocked to see the expert paint job. Doug could claim he wasn't as good as he used to be, but his work rivaled hers any day. The second vehicle, a Ford Focus that belonged to Dr. Carson, the local pediatrician, was done with the same precision and care. Bailey felt herself relax. One less thing to worry about.

ETHAN STRAINED UNDER the weight of the three cases of beer he balanced on his forearms as he continued to wait in the long line at the liquor depot. The beer-can-shaped clock hanging above the register revealed it was six-thirty. The men would be arriving at the station in less than an hour. The blood pressure and cholesterol screening had gone on past five o'clock, putting them a little behind in their bachelor-party preparations. Each month there seemed to be even more women in Brookhollow coming to the free clinic, and today he'd even caught a few getting in line for a second time in one day.

He loved his involvement with the local fire hall and its contributions to the town. His father was the head of the police department in Brookhollow, and his older brother, Jim, and he had inherited their dad's sense of pride and responsibility for the community. As kids they'd spent a lot of time at the police station and the fire hall, learning about the trucks and the duties of the fire chief and crew. As soon as they were old enough, they'd signed on to become firefighters.

The line moved, creating an empty space on the conveyor belt, just as his grip slipped from the side of his load. *That was close.* As he set the beer down and rubbed his aching forearms, his eye was caught fleetingly by a blonde disappearing at the far end of the store's middle aisle. Emily? His mind raced, but his feet remained frozen to the floor as he leaned around the end of the register to try to catch another glimpse. *Don't be ridiculous,* he told himself. She'd just called a few hours ago from Miami. *Just pay for the beer....*

"Just a second," he told the clerk as he moved past the other customers waiting in line behind him. "Go ahead and take the next person." Quickly he made his way toward the center aisle. "Emily?"

The woman turned immediately and smiled when she saw him. "Ethan, hi. How are you?" Emily's younger sister Kimberly rushed forward to hug him.

He swallowed the lump in his throat and wiped his sweaty palms on his jeans before wrapping one arm around her in a brief hug. The sisters wore the same perfume.

"Hi, Kim. Sorry, I thought you were..."

"Emily. I know. I've been getting that a lot since I highlighted my hair." She tossed the wavy golden locks over her shoulder. "Sorry," she said with a sympathetic smile.

Ethan flinched, hating that look. It had been the only way anyone had looked at him for months after Emily had left, and he'd felt uneasy to be on the receiving end of sympathetic smiles and gossipy whispers.

"No, don't apologize. I should have known anyway—Emily always wore her hair straight...." He coughed. *Not doing a great job recovering here, man. Get a grip.* "Anyway, how is she?" He closed his eyes and shook his head. He was hopeless. "I mean you. How are you?"

Kimberly gave him a knowing look. "She's good...I think," she said with a shrug as she reached for two bottles of merlot from the shelf. "I mean, she hardly calls, but she texts me every few days.... She was just offered a promotion to the senior management team—corporate trainer, I think." She paused, her expression sheepish. "I'm sorry if all of this is hard to hear."

"No," Ethan lied. Of course he was happy that she was doing well, wasn't he? "I'm glad she's doing okay. How's everyone else?"

"My parents just got back from a Caribbean cruise and I've been accepted to the media-design program at NYU for the fall semester."

"Wow, Kim, that's great." He really meant it.

"Thank you. You know, that invite to dinner always stands. With or without Emily, you'll always be part of the family."

Ethan shuffled his feet, avoiding the sympathy in her ocean-blue eyes—Emily's eyes. Just one of the features the sisters shared.

"Tell your folks I said hello...." He wasn't ready to commit to anything with the family just yet. And though he suspected Kim might be genuine in the offer, he wasn't sure Mayor and Mrs. Parsons would be as comfortable seeing him. Part of him believed they held him responsible for the relationship breakdown. Who knows, maybe they were right. His unwavering commitment to life in Brookhollow hadn't made Emily happy. "And maybe think about changing that hair color, huh?" he teased.

"I promise to think about it," she said, struggling to grab another bottle of wine from the rack.

"Here, let me help," he offered, picking up the extra bottle. "Having a celebration tonight?"

"Victoria's bachelorette party at the B and B. Actually, it's a bridal shower, but they're calling it a bachelorette party to make it sound more fun." Kimberly followed him to the counter.

"Well, then, allow me." He waved Jim's credit card in the air. "Consider it a gift from the best man," he said as he took the wine from her and added it to his own items on the counter.

CHAPTER TWO

JIM PROPPED OPEN the west entrance door of the fire hall with a brick as they carried the cases of beer into the fire hall later that evening. He plucked the receipt from the top case and shot his brother a questioning look. "What's this wine on the bill?"

"I ran into Kim Parsons at the liquor depot. She was picking up wine for Victoria's bachelorette party. I took care of it.... Rather, you took care of it."

Ethan shut the back door of the Jeep. His brother, Jim, had been friends with Luke Dawson since grade school and he knew, despite his grumbling, Jim had been honored when Luke asked him to be his best man.

"Last time I send you to get the booze," Jim huffed as Luke's truck pulled into the driveway of the fire hall. The old clunker rattled and gurgled as Luke cut the engine and a dark puff of exhaust escaped the tailpipe.

Ethan watched in amusement. "What happened to his new truck?" Owner of a successful architecture firm that had contracts in New Jersey, New York and Boston, Luke had bought a new Ford F-250 just before Christmas, but whenever Ethan saw him, he was driving that old beater.

"Victoria is using it. As long as Bailey keeps reviving that thing, he'll keep driving it," he said, nodding toward the truck where Luke was trapped inside, struggling with the door handle.

"Must be love," Ethan said. "So explain to me why Luke and Victoria are holding their prewedding parties so early. The wedding isn't for another month." His brother's longtime best friend had gotten engaged for the second time to his childhood sweetheart on New Year's Eve and the wedding was scheduled for the Labor Day weekend.

"Luke's out of town a lot working on that restaurant in Boston for the next few weeks. His crews are under a tight deadline for a grand opening the first weekend in September. This was really the only time we could do it, and holding it at the fire hall made sense because I somehow got stuck on night rotation this weekend." He turned as Luke entered, a case of beer under his left arm. "Hey, man. You weren't supposed to bring your own drinks," Jim said, taking the beer from him and putting the bottles in the cooler filled with ice near the poker table.

"My mother says you shouldn't go anywhere empty-handed. Hey, great setup." Luke scanned the transformed fire hall. A poker table stood ready to go, stacks of multicolored chips at each place. A dartboard hung on the wall and the scoreboard had each of their names already written in white chalk. The old tan leather sofa and matching recliner had been moved to the side of the room and a small flat screen was set up on the coffee table. The first inning of the baseball game lit up the screen.

"Make yourself comfortable. I'm going to run out to get the pizza and wings before my shift starts," Jim said, grabbing his truck keys from the hook on the wall near the door.

Ethan glanced at the clock on the wall. "Your shift started five minutes ago."

"Yeah, but I'm usually fifteen minutes late, so technically I've got ten minutes," Jim said as he disappeared out the side door.

"Can't argue with logic like that," Luke said.

"Brother or not, I'm going to have to start

writing him up." Ethan shook his head. "Anyway, ready to get wild and crazy?" he asked, slapping Luke on the back.

Luke laughed, suppressing a yawn. "As long as we're done by ten. I'm exhausted."

"Working a lot these days?" Ethan stocked the small bar fridge with extra beer, removing bottles of water and Gatorade to make more space.

"Around the clock. This restaurant chain I'm working on has me commuting to Boston three or four times a week. And then I'm helping Vic plan the wedding...." Luke pulled out a chair at the poker table and sat. He reached for a chip and flicked it between his fingers.

"I thought women loved to do all the wedding planning themselves?" Ethan opened a beer and handed it to Luke. "A game of darts before everyone else gets here?"

"Sure." Luke headed over to the board and took out the darts. "Oh, don't get me wrong. When I say helping, I mean acting as a buffer between our moms." He handed Ethan three red darts, keeping the blue ones.

Ethan gestured for him to throw first.

Aiming carefully at the bull's-eye, Luke released the dart with one easy, smooth motion. It landed in the black zone just millimeters from the center.

"Nice," Ethan said, positioning himself for his turn. "But I thought your mom and Mrs. Mason were getting along again." When Victoria had called off their wedding years before, it had created a feud between the mothers, one that had lasted over twelve years, but the couples reuniting last Christmas had brought the two women close again. Ethan threw his dart, landing it square in the bull's-eye.

Luke let out a low whistle. "Impressive."

"We have a lot of downtime," Ethan explained.

"Our mothers are getting along, until there's a decision to be made about flowers or cake…." Luke shook his head. "I swear they call Victoria at least four times a day. Then, of course, she calls me."

"Women. I don't know how you survive."

"Hey, I'm just grateful she agreed to marry me—again. I'll do whatever it takes to get her down the aisle this time," he joked. "She left me once—twice actually…." he corrected, releasing his last dart. "I won't be letting her go this time." The dart missed by a mile and he turned to Ethan. "Sorry, man, I didn't mean…"

"Don't worry about it, really," Ethan said, tossing his final dart and reaching for his beer.

"You know, Victoria still feels partly responsible for the whole Emily thing. She says so all the time."

"What?" Ethan shook his head as he removed his darts and wrote the scores on the board. "She shouldn't. Emily leaving town had nothing to do with her."

"Well, if Play Hard Sports hadn't come to town…"

"Look, tell your pretty fiancée she has enough to worry about with running the bed-and-breakfast and planning the wedding. Besides, if it hadn't been the executive from Play Hard Sports, someone else would have caught Emily's eye eventually. She hadn't been as committed to our relationship in the months before she left." Ethan shrugged. "Victoria did a good thing. I know better than anyone about the positive impact that Play Hard has had on the community."

He was the first to admit that the big chain store had improved the town's sports facilities, paying for an extra rink at the hockey arena and maintaining the soccer and football fields.

"Yeah, but you've also taken the biggest hit on your personal life because of it." Luke took a sip of his beer and waved to John Bentley, a member of their bowling league, who had just entered the fire hall.

"Ah, it's been six months. I'm done feeling sorry for myself."

His cell phone chimed in his pocket with a new text message. Bailey's familiar ringtone. He opened it and read Get me out of here. "It's Bailey."

Luke turned to look around the room. "Hey, where is she?"

"At the B and B."

"Oh, man, didn't anyone tell her she's welcome here tonight?" Luke said. "She took a bunch of my money last weekend playing pool. I was kind of hoping to get some of it back at poker."

"Or lose even more."

"Good point."

"Thanks for your help cleaning up, Bailey." Rachel Harper, coowner of the Brookhollow Inn, carried another load of dirty dishes into the newly remodeled kitchen of the bed-and-breakfast. In the past six months, Brookhollow's historic landmark had undergone a complete makeover thanks to the new ownership team of Victoria Mason and Rachel Harper. The main common areas and guest quarters had been freshly painted and the original hardwood floor refinished. The chipped stained glass windows had been replaced with large bay windows, complete with a window seat and lined with small bookshelves for the enjoyment of their guests. The living quarters had been transformed into a home for the Harper family of mom, dad and five kids.

The dishwasher was already running with a full load, so Bailey stood at the double sink washing dessert plates. The stack of plates, cups and cutlery piling up on the granite counter seemed never ending. The turnout had been even better than expected—Victoria Mason was well liked in Brookhollow.

"No problem," Bailey assured her.

Victoria entered the kitchen with several empty wine bottles gathered in one arm and a big garbage bag of discarded wrapping paper from the shower gifts, which were now stored inside the gazebo in the yard. She tossed the bottles into the blue recycle bin and dropped the bag near the kitchen door. "Thanks, Bailey," she said, reaching for a dish towel and a handful of cutlery.

"Hey, you're not supposed to be cleaning up after your own party," Rachel chided, taking the dish towel from her. "Go sit. We've got this."

"I'm not arguing." Victoria surrendered the towel and slumped into a wicker chair at the table with a yawn. Glancing at her watch, she gasped. "What? Nine-thirty, that's it?" Her emerald-green eyes were wide with disbelief. "We must be getting old. The sun's not even completely set and I'm done."

"We're not old, we're responsible," Rachel defended, abandoning the dishes and joining her at the table. She reached for a half bottle of white wine and said, "Bailey, come sit. Have a drink with us. We'll finish cleaning up in the morning." She poured herself a glass of pinot grigio and took a sip before handing the bottle and an unused wineglass to Victoria. "I'd forgotten how much I missed wine."

Bailey dried her hands on a dish towel and pulled out a chair at the table. With the fire hall off-limits to the female species that evening, she really had nowhere else to go.

"Wasn't I right about that breast pump?"

Rachel's sister-in-law, Lindsay Harper, entered the kitchen with a bowl of veggie straws and dip.

"Yes. I never used one with the other children, but it's been a lifesaver this time with the girls." Rachel's eight-month-old twins, Abigail and Mackenzie, were the most recent addition to the Harper clan.

Bailey glanced between the women, almost afraid to ask. "Breast pump?" It didn't sound like something she wanted to know about, but she suspected she was about to get an education.

Victoria handed her the bottle of wine. "Don't worry, I knew nothing about mommy life eight months ago, either." She turned to Rachel and Lindsay. "And you know what, ladies, I think we should allow Bailey to live in her wonderful breast-pump- and vomit-free oblivion a little longer. I'm actually dying to hear about her exciting single life."

"Definitely a better topic," Lindsay agreed, climbing onto a kitchen stool at the counter and reaching for a carrot stick.

"What do you mean, Lindsay? You're single, too, and I'm sure you have better stories," Bailey said, desperate to take the attention off herself. Lindsay, a nurse at the medical clinic in town, was known for her serial dating and late-night partying. While Bailey refused to date just anyone, hoping to find the right person, Lindsay adopted a different approach. The voluptuous blonde believed you had to kiss a lot of frogs before finding Mr. Right.

But Lindsay just shook her head. "Not lately. My shifts at the clinic have been crazy. All I do is work and sleep. So come on, let us live vicariously through you."

Bailey stretched in the wicker chair. "Sorry to disappoint you, but I've got nothing to report."

"That can't be true," Lindsay protested. "You're always with the men. I know for a fact you have a VIP card to the fire hall."

Not tonight.

"And weren't you dating Jonathan Turner for a while?" Rachel asked.

"Yeah, that didn't work out." Jonathan was a great guy, but they had very little in common. He was bookish and serious and she was a grease monkey who loved loud music. Their three weeks of dating had confirmed one thing for sure—compatibility was key to a successful relationship.

"Why not? Jonathan's gorgeous and so

sweet," Victoria said, standing and pouring a cup of coffee.

The phone rang on the wall and she checked the caller display as Rachel reached for the cordless on the table. "Don't!" Victoria said.

Rachel froze.

"It's my mom," Victoria explained. "Since leaving here an hour ago, she's texted me three times about different types of fabric for the wedding dress. I'm ignoring her."

"Understood," Rachel said, letting the phone ring. "Although, Vic, you really do need to make a decision about your dress. I know the B and B and your position on the New Jersey tourism board have kept you busy this summer, but you need to take some time to focus on you for a bit. All of the other wedding details have been sorted out, except that one. Your mom is a fantastic seamstress, the best in town, but even she can't perform miracles."

"I know, I know. It's just every time I think I've decided on a style, I see something else I love even more…. I just want to look perfect, you know?" Victoria waved a hand and turned to Bailey. "Anyway, back to Jonathan…."

"Um…we're just too different," Bailey said

with a shrug. "I mean, he spent most of our date trying to convince me that my motorcycle is too dangerous and that I should buy something safer." Bailey knew she was more vulnerable on a bike, but in a small town like Brookhollow where traffic was minimal, the bike was often the only vehicle on the road, especially in the early morning when she started her shift at the garage.

"He was concerned about you—that's a nice thing," Rachel pointed out.

"There were other things, too—he said the UFC was barbaric." She just couldn't date someone who didn't like the Ultimate Fighting Championship. She watched it all the time, knew all the fighter stats and even trained in mixed martial arts with her younger brothers at Extreme Athletics.

"Again, not exactly an invalid point," Victoria pointed out.

"Either way, it's important for me to date someone with similar interests, but then most of the guys in town just see me as one of them." A no-win situation. "In fact, they even invited me to Luke's bachelor party tonight."

The women gasped and exchanged looks. "What?"

Victoria sipped her coffee and Rachel toyed

with the edge of a paper napkin. Even Lindsay held her tongue.

"Come on… What?"

"Well, I guess we all just figured you had your pick of them," Victoria said.

"Yeah, I mean, look at you." Lindsay stood and tugged an old elastic band from Bailey's hair. The loose, dark waves fell around her thin shoulders. "Look at this beautiful virgin hair. I'd kill for these thick, healthy strands." Lindsay's voice was filled with pure jealousy as she examined Bailey's hair. "Nope, not a split end to be found, despite using elastic bands." She dropped Bailey's hair and crossed her arms.

"And you're in great shape, too. I'd kill for your flat tummy," Rachel said, frowning as she touched her own stomach.

"I guess I'm just waiting for the right one, that's all," Bailey said. The challenge had never been finding someone interested in her, it was finding someone who could hold her interest. She wanted someone who made her laugh, someone she could have fun with but who also understood her need for independence and admired her strength. She wasn't prepared to change who she was just to fit someone else's idea of the perfect partner.

"Okay, well, if you aren't seeing anyone, who have you been texting all night?" Rachel asked. "I saw those smiles, and it definitely wasn't a female friend."

Wow, these women were observant. She waved a hand. "Oh, that was just Ethan."

"Ethan, huh?" Lindsay pulled out the chair next to her and sat, leaning her elbows on the table and resting her chin in her hands. "Tell us more about that dreamboat."

"You two are awfully close," Victoria said, then added quickly, "not judging."

No, just interested in gossip like everyone else in town. "There's really not much to tell. We're friends…and lately I've served as a shoulder to cry on," she said wryly.

"He has to be getting over Emily by now." Lindsay refilled her glass, emptying the bottle.

"I don't know about that, but he's not moping around town as much anymore."

Silence filled the room as all three women stared at her expectantly.

"What?"

Victoria finally spoke for the three of them. "We're just wondering when you plan on asking him out yourself."

Bailey hesitated. It wasn't that she hadn't

thought of it since Emily had left town, but to hear it suggested by others…

"Didn't you just say you wanted a guy with similar interests?" Victoria asked. "Personally, I think you two would be perfect together."

"Don't say you haven't thought about it," Lindsay insisted.

These women were relentless. "Ethan's a great guy and I like him…as a…"

"If you say brother, I'll die," Victoria interrupted. "I've met your brothers. Ethan couldn't be more different than Brandon and Jordan. Those two are big and burly and tough…."

"Hot in their own way," Lindsay chimed in.

"But not Ethan hot," Rachel interjected.

"Agreed," Lindsay said with a nod.

These women were insane and they wouldn't ease up until she confessed. "Fine, I'm attracted to him, but who in this room isn't?" Bailey countered.

Victoria's lone hand shot up, then she slowly lowered it. "He's a firefighter, it's the uniform. I may be getting married, but I'm not blind." She took another sip of her coffee, then added, "Don't tell Luke I said that. Poor guy is terrified that I'm going to back out of this wedding again and take off to New York while he's out of town. As if I'd be that stupid again." Her eyes took on a faraway, dreamy look.

"Anyway, I think you should make a play for him," Rachel said with a definitive nod.

"No way." Bailey stood. She had to get out of there before they suggested that they call him right now and ask him out for her. A little too much wine had been consumed that evening.

"Why not?" Lindsay asked.

"He'd never go for it." There. The truth was out. The main reason she would never gather the courage to ask Ethan out was her fear of being rejected. The same reason she hadn't approached him years before and had stood by while Emily had asked him to prom. It didn't matter, though. Ethan had only ever seen her as a friend, and with or without Emily, that didn't seem to change.

THE NEXT DAY, Bailey arrived at the shop to find four vehicles parked in the lot and a frazzled-looking Nick behind the service counter. Not quite eight o'clock in the morning and the shop was busier than it ever was. That couldn't be good news. Joining him on the other side of the counter, she quickly stashed her motorcycle helmet under the desk and unzipped her leather jacket in the humid heat of the unair-conditioned shop.

"What's going on?" she asked, recognizing the annoyed, impatient faces on the other side. They'd all been in earlier that week to pick up their vehicles after repairs. All four had been worked on by Nick.

He stabbed the enter key and moved the mouse anxiously around the Corvette-shaped mouse pad, staring at the frozen computer screen. He muttered under his breath as he moved away from the computer. "Stupid thing is frozen again and it won't let me bring up last week's work orders."

"Let me try," she said, shrugging free of her jacket and approaching the monitor. A new computer system was on her list of upgrades, as soon as possible. The dinosaur program they were currently using was more trouble than it was worth. "Sorry about the wait. Please help yourselves to coffee."

Nick cleared his throat behind her. "We're out."

Bailey swung around. "How is that possible? I asked you to pick some up yesterday...."

He shrugged. "Forgot."

Of course he'd forgotten. Why was she surprised? She couldn't count on him for anything. How was she supposed to train a guy who didn't want to learn and had no interest in the family business? The work orders popped up on the screen and she scanned them quickly. All four were basic oil-and-filter changes. Well, luckily whatever the issues were, they should be easy to fix.

She turned to the first two people in line. "Please drive your cars into the bays. I'll have you out of here in fifteen minutes." As they moved away from the counter, she told the others, "Give us half an hour and you'll be on your way, as well."

The angry expressions disappeared as they took seats in the small waiting area.

A half hour later, Bailey wiped her forehead and fanned herself with a newspaper as she updated and closed off the work orders on the computer. Glancing up at the sound of the chime above the door, she saw Ethan enter the shop. She loved how he looked in his firefighter's uniform. It wasn't just the clothing, it was what the uniform represented—bravery, courage, strength, compassion and heart. His sense of duty and loyalty was admirable. Then there were those smoky dark eyes. She busied herself with the work order for the Volkswagen Jetta.

"Hey, Ethan, what brings you by?"

"It's inspection time again," he said.

"Aren't you supposed to give us a heads-up?" she asked, glancing around the shop. They'd been extrabusy that morning, so some things weren't as organized as she would have liked them to be before an inspection.

"We did. Chief left a message with Nick yesterday."

"You know that doesn't count," Bailey said as Ethan scanned the shop. "We had a crazy busy morning, so go easy on us this time, okay?"

"No."

Friends or not, she knew Ethan took his job seriously. Inspections were a yearly occurrence, and he always found something not up to code. She knew his intentions were good, but she wasn't looking forward to having to make any expensive updates at the moment. Heck, she still hadn't changed the ownership sign out front.

Taking out his inspection checklist, he started at the door, examining the exit signs and lights that were required to be illuminated when the building was occupied. "You know this extinguisher is too high, right? The handle height should be between three and five feet. This is at least five foot one...."

Bailey cocked her head to the side. "It's in the exact same spot as last year."

Ethan hesitated. "I really should insist on lowering it," he said before signing the inspection tag with his initials and the day's date.

"Thank you for letting it slide." Her voice held a note of sarcasm. Ethan could be so uptight about these things. She doubted one inch higher would make that big of a difference in the event of an emergency.

Heading toward the back, he pushed through the shop door and tested the emergency lighting. "Have you given any more thought to that sprinkler system I suggested?"

Bailey shrugged, "I mentioned it to Doug, but since I just bought the place, I don't think it's quite in the budget at the moment."

Ethan clenched his jaw. "I really hate that I can't insist on it. I should be able to enforce the new building codes," he said, shaking his head.

The building had been constructed in the sixties and the standard codes at the time hadn't required a sprinkler or ventilation system for the permit. Unless upgrades were done, the fire department couldn't apply the new codes so that the shop failed the inspection. "Look, I promise to check the sprinkler thing out myself, okay?"

"Promise?" he asked.

"I just did," she said as he disappeared through the swinging door toward the bays in the back of the shop.

The bell chimed again and Bailey was surprised to see Victoria coming through the front door of the garage, wedding planner stuck under her arm and her cell phone cradled between her right ear and shoulder. Bailey waved in greeting and Victoria rolled her eyes, gesturing to the phone.

"Mrs. Dawson," she whispered, covering the speaker with her left hand.

Bailey nodded her understanding. Victoria and Darlene were more acquaintances than friends. As the head of the social committee in town, Luke's mother was sure to be very hands-on with the wedding preparations. She suspected Victoria had very little to say about her wedding, between Mrs. Dawson and her own mother weighing in on each decision. Grabbing a box of motor oil, Bailey stocked the metal racks along the wall, listening to one side of the conversation.

"Yes, Darlene, that's fine. If you think the pale pink Gerbera daisies work better in the bridesmaids' bouquets instead of the dark fuchsia ones, please go ahead and make the switch, as long as Pearl is okay with it... No, I'm not sure what Luke's favorite flower is...."

Bailey hid a smile. Luke, local architect and business owner, didn't strike her as a man who would have a favorite flower.

"Okay, thanks, Darlene. I appreciate your help." The words sounded forcibly polite even to Bailey's ears.

Victoria disconnected the call and shook the phone. "Wow!" she said as she approached. "Forty-three minutes of that, just to decide between two shades of pink.... I'll be happy once this wedding part is over and the house renovations are done." She let out a deep breath. "Sorry, I'm through venting. Hi, Bailey." Her shoulders visibly relaxed and her smile was now genuine.

"What brings you by?" Outside, Luke's new Ford F250 sat parked on an angle, taking up two stalls. Victoria wasn't the best driver in town. Twelve years living in New York

City hadn't provided her with much driving experience. "Is something wrong with the truck?"

"Besides the fact that it's huge and I can't park it? No, it runs like a dream. I really wish Luke would drive it when he travels for work," she said. "You have to stop fixing the old one so well."

"I'll try." Luke's other truck was at least thirty years old and Bailey knew he kept it for sentimental reasons, but she wasn't sure how much longer she could keep it in running condition. "Believe me, I've told him a million times that the truck won't last forever."

"One can only hope. Anyway, I'm actually here because I need your help with something else."

"Okay," Bailey said, reaching into the box for the last two bottles of oil, and aligning them on the shelf. She broke down the carton and tossed it onto the stack of other stock boxes near the door, scanning the shop for Nick. Nowhere to be found—how unusual. Biting back the annoyance she felt at his relaxed work ethic, she asked, "What can I do for you?"

"I need you to be a bridesmaid in the wedding."

Bailey's mouth gaped. "I'm sorry, what?" She couldn't have heard right.

"My cousin Adele was supposed to be back from her mission trip to South Africa in time for the wedding, but her grant from the university was extended until the end of September. The dress was made to fit her and, well...you're just the right size. If I have to ask my mom to make a new one or even alter that one, she's going to kill me."

Bailey stared at the bride-to-be, a good excuse eluding her. The last thing she wanted was to be in a wedding party and stand in front of the whole community in a dress... holding a bouquet of flowers. She'd be forced to wear makeup and do her hair...and be in the photos. The mere thought made it difficult to breathe. She remained silent.

Victoria looked desperate as she moved closer. "I know it's a lot to ask and it's really short notice, but please."

"Wouldn't you rather a family member or a close friend? What about your friend Heather from New York? She looks tiny in those photos you have on Facebook of the two of you."

Victoria shook her head. "Weddings are not exactly Heather's thing. If she wasn't such a close friend, she'd never even have agreed to attend, and her work schedule at Clarke and Johnson is busy—the way mine used to be—so I can't rely on her. Besides, Luke has always thought of you as another sister. I know he'd be thrilled if you agreed to do it."

Bailey hated to disappoint Victoria and Luke, but weddings weren't exactly her thing, either. They always made her sad when she saw the mother of the bride looking on as her daughter said the vows. Even if she did find someone she wanted to spend her life with, her own mother wouldn't be there to be part of the wedding, not in the physical sense, anyway. She had been hoping to skip the ceremony and just attend the reception if at all possible. "There has to be someone else."

"Bailey, it's either you or Lindsay, and I can't ask her for obvious reasons…."

Bailey nodded her understanding. "She'll try to steal Luke away at the altar. Yes, I get that, but…"

"Bailey, please. It would mean a lot to both of us." She cocked her head to the side. "You get to keep the dress," she said in an attempt to persuade.

"That doesn't really sell it for me, Vic," Bailey said with a laugh. She owned one dress, a black knee-length formal that worked for both funerals and weddings. She hesitated. "Fine, okay, I'll be your bridesmaid, but I'll warn you now—I have no idea what I'm doing."

"Neither do I. Don't worry, Reverend Miller said he will walk us through everything at the rehearsal the day before. Thank you, Bailey." Victoria looked relieved.

"Sure."

"So I told my mom you would stop by sometime tomorrow to try on the dress… just to be sure."

Bailey shook her head. Victoria had really assumed she would say yes. "Okay."

"Great, thanks again, Bailey." Her cell phone beeped with a new text message and she sighed as she read it. Turning the phone toward Bailey, she asked, "Do you know the difference between these two flowers?"

"Amaryllis and hyacinth," she read. "I wouldn't even have known they were types of flowers. Sorry, Vic."

"No worries, you've done enough," she said as she typed *amaryllis* into Google search on her cell phone.

Ethan reentered the front of the shop. "Hey, Vic. How are the wedding plans coming along? All set for the big day?"

Victoria's eyes narrowed.

He held up his hands in defense. "Forget I asked." Turning to Bailey, he handed her the inspection report.

She scanned it, noticing several fail marks, including the extinguisher. "Hey, I thought you were going to let the extinguisher position slide?"

"Changed my mind," he said, placing a yellow tag on it. "Are we still on for the UFC tonight?"

"How can you switch back and forth from mean fire inspector guy to my good friend like that?" She placed her hands on her hips.

"Easy—both guys care about your safety. Eight o'clock at the fire hall?"

"Wouldn't miss it," she mumbled, tucking the report into a drawer.

Victoria watched his disappearing figure before turning to Bailey. "So are you making any progress with that one?"

"What?"

"With Ethan. Come on, don't tell me you're not completely in love with him. Whenever he's around your eyes look excited and your cheeks turn red."

"That obvious, huh?" And she thought she'd been doing a good job hiding her true feelings. "Think anyone else knows?"

"Yes."

"Do you think *he* knows?"

"I figure you're safe there. He's completely oblivious. Is he really still pining over Emily?"

"Unfortunately." How was she supposed to make a play for a man who refused to get over his ex? "I swear, he's making himself miserable on purpose. He still listens to her CDs in his Jeep, even though he hates country music and always complained about having to listen to it before. There are photos of them everywhere in his place…." She shook her head. It annoyed her that he didn't seem to be making an effort to move on.

Victoria frowned. "I guess I don't get it. Granted, I didn't know Emily as well as the rest of you, but in the two months that I saw them together, they were always fighting. What exactly is he holding on to?"

"The past. The way they were in the beginning. The truth is, they'd been growing apart for years, and then once Emily met Greg Harrison from Play Hard Sports, that was it. Anyway, you can understand why I'm not about to put myself out there, especially since he's always thought of me as one of the guys." She hated that saying. So she liked to work on cars and enjoyed sporting events and beer? She was still a woman. A woman who was much better for him than Emily had ever been.

"I guess you'll just have to open his eyes," Victoria said.

"How?" If the bride-to-be had any suggestions, she was more than willing to try them. After over a decade of believing that the man she loved was off-limits, she'd be willing to make a play for him if she thought she actually had a chance.

"Sorry, that's where you may have to talk to Luke. He was the one to open my eyes to the possibility of love…but I remember it had something to do with a mistletoe kiss." She smiled, obviously lost in the memory of it.

"Well, it's August, Victoria, and unless you know where I can find some mistletoe, I may have to come up with a different plan."

CHAPTER THREE

"Wow, DID YOU see that takedown defense? That guy is insane." Mark Adams used the sleeve of his shirt to twist the cap off a beer.

Inside the fire hall, the four men on duty and their friends had dragged every available chair to crowd around the thirty-six-inch television to watch the Saturday-night ultimate-fighter fight. Eight men and Bailey. Cold leftover pizza and wings from Luke's party the night before sat on the table, and once again, Bailey was annoyed that she'd missed the celebration. At least here with the guys she wouldn't have been forced to admit her feelings about Ethan. Not admitting to them had made them easier to ignore.

"There's no way that takedown defense should have worked." Sitting on the couch, Ethan extended his long legs out in front of him and raised his arms above his head.

Bailey tore her eyes away as his shirt rose, exposing his abs. She could blame it on the women the night before, but in recent months, she'd been finding it increasingly hard to conceal her long-repressed feelings for him. Without Emily around as a reminder that Ethan was unavailable, every time she looked at him, all she saw were the gold flecks in his chocolate eyes or the deep dimple in his chin or the six-pack under his shirt. Those things hadn't escaped her notice before, but now it was near impossible to push the feelings of attraction away whenever she looked at him. And after watching him put out that car fire the day before...

She forced her gaze back to the television. "It totally works," she argued, watching the slow-motion replay at the end of the fourth five-minute round of the champion match for the light heavyweight title.

"Prove it," Ethan said, jumping up and turning to her in challenge.

"I think Sanchez just did," Bailey scoffed, leaning around him to see the television screen. She took a sip of her diet soda, fighting to calm her raging pulse. Any other time, dropping him on his butt in front of the guys would be fun, but now the idea of physical contact made her heart race.

"I think he just got lucky."

"You're serious?"

"Yeah, come on, bring it on." He danced sideways from one foot to the other.

The other men encouraged her.

"Come on, Bailey. Show him how it's done," Jim said, taking his wallet from his back pocket. He pulled out several bills and turned to the other men. "You guys want to place bets? My money's on Bailey."

Bailey stood as the men placed their twenties in a pile on the coffee table. Eyeing the stack as it grew, she reached into the pocket of her jean shorts. "My money's on me, too," she said, tossing two ten-dollar bills onto the pile, then she rolled the sleeves of her favorite UFC shirt.

"You really think I can't take you down?" Ethan's eyes shone with amusement.

"You do remember that both of my brothers train mixed martial arts, right? Aren't you afraid I may have picked up a skill or two?"

"You may have me on skill, but I am a little bigger," Ethan said, moving the coffee table to the side to make room for his attack. "Ready?"

"Let's go." Bailey got into defensive position as he approached.

Grabbing both of her arms, Ethan moved

in closer. Bending quickly, he grabbed for her left leg.

Ah, a single-leg takedown. How many times had Brandon taught her to defend that one?

As his hand wrapped around the back of her knee, Bailey rotated her hips to the left, quickly switching position until she was now behind Ethan in a mount position. Freeing her leg, she straightened, forcing him off-balance, taking control.

The others whooped and hollered.

Removing her hand from his shoulder, Ethan turned to face her, towering over her, head down, nodding slowly. "Not bad," he said, but in one swift motion he swooped her off her feet, slowly dropping her toward the floor.

Caught off guard, Bailey clutched at his shirt and stopped just inches from the concrete floor. Ethan hovered above her, a firm grip on her arms, holding her in place. Staring up into his eyes, she saw the amused look on his handsome face and felt her pulse quicken and her cheeks flame. Pushing him away, she scrambled to her feet and turned to the others. "That doesn't count—you all saw I had him first." She pointed to Jim.

"Hey, my money was on you, I'm not arguing," Jim said with a laugh, handing over her portion of the winnings as the last round of the fight began.

Reclaiming her place on the sofa next to Ethan, she struggled to calm the pounding in her chest. It was just Ethan. So what if he was hot, fun, exciting…still brooding over his ex?

The sound of the guys cheering interrupted her thoughts. The fight had ended and the current champion had his arms raised in the air. His opponent was out cold on the mat inside the octagon. Crap, she'd missed the knockout.

"Did you see that?" Ethan exclaimed, turning to face her.

She forced enthusiasm into the lie. "Yeah, amazing." So were his dark eyes, full mouth, solid chest…. She took a breath and stood, needing to put some distance between them. Opening the bar fridge, she took out a bottle of water and gulped its contents, aware of those mesmerizing eyes on her. She was in trouble; there was no more denying it. She was in love with Ethan, and without Emily standing in the way, there was nothing stopping her from going after what she'd always wanted.

ETHAN STOOD AND stretched. "Okay, guys, I think that's it for me. Thank you for stealing my money. Good night." He checked his watch. A little past one o'clock. Everyone else had taken off after the fights, but he'd stayed to play cards with his coworkers on duty that evening. He was spending a lot of his free time at the fire hall these days, which only reminded him how much time he'd devoted to his relationship with Emily. His shifts at the fire hall and coaching his nephew's soccer and hockey teams just weren't enough to keep him occupied. The days weren't the challenge; it was the lonely nights.

He grabbed his wallet and keys from the table and waved as he left the hall. Taking the steps two at a time, he jogged upstairs to his loft-style bachelor suite. It had been a long-standing tradition in Brookhollow for the captain of the fire team to live in the apartment if he or she was single. While it essentially meant he was always on call, he loved his nine hundred square feet and the fact he was only seconds away if he was needed in an emergency.

Inside, he kicked off his shoes and headed straight for his upstairs bedroom. He was exhausted after the late night and early morning. He just hoped that his inability to keep his eyes open would mean a good night's sleep for a change. In the six months since Emily had left, sleep had constantly eluded him. He wished that for just one night, the last thought he had wouldn't be of her. Removing his shirt, he tossed it into the corner laundry basket as his cell phone rang on the bedside table.

Oh, come on, it was almost one-thirty in the morning. She couldn't possibly expect him to answer. He sat on the edge of the bed, rubbing his forehead. What was he supposed to do? He reached for the phone just as the emergency alarm sounded downstairs. Dropping the ringing phone onto his bed, Ethan bounded back down the stairs and out the front door of the apartment without even stopping for his shoes.

Inside the fire hall, the men had rushed to the duty racks. Derek's face paled as he listened to the call from dispatch. "Yeah, okay. Yeah, two units are on it." He motioned for the other men to suit up.

Ethan grabbed the report as it came over the machine. The familiar address in bold, block letters on top of the emergency reporting page caught his attention. Doug's Motors.

Grabbing the report, he ran toward the duty racks and grabbed his boots.

Derek approached and grabbed the report. "What are you doing? You're off duty."

"It's the shop, man. I'm coming." Ethan slid his jacket over his bare shoulders and grabbed his gear.

Derek followed behind him toward the unit. "I think you're a little too close to this one...."

Jim jumped into the passenger seat of the first response vehicle. "He's right, Ethan, you're out. Your emotions are running too high right now."

Ethan ignored him and jumped into the driver's seat of the truck. "Any fire in Brookhollow would be close for any of us. Now let's go."

"Ethan, I'm not speaking as your brother, but as a member of this squad. I think you should sit this one out."

"As captain, I respect your opinion, Jim, but on duty or not, I'm leading this one."

Jim looked about to argue, but Derek said, "We're wasting time, guys."

"Fine, but for the safety of everyone involved, you're on pump only," Jim insisted.

"No, you're faster on pump. I'm going in."

"Only if you can get a grip."

Ethan just nodded as he flicked on the emergency lights and sirens and tore through the bay door into the street. His thoughts ran wild—the garage, Bailey's shop. His hands shook on the wheel and he tightened his grip in an effort to steady them under Jim's watchful gaze. He forced a calming breath. Jim and Derek were right. He was a little too close to this one and he needed to keep a clear head. Not only did Bailey depend on him keeping his focus and his safety training in mind, but his team, as well. One of the many benefits of small-town life was that everything was close, and at this hour of night the streets were deserted, but as the speedometer reached forty, Jim shot him a look.

"I said, get a grip." His brother's voice was stern.

Ethan slowed just a fraction as the big truck made a right off Main Street onto Vermont Avenue and the shop came into sight. Thirty-six seconds later—it felt more like thirty-six minutes—they pulled into the lot, followed by the wailing sirens of the ladder truck behind them. Thick, dark gray smoke billowed from the side bay doors and he could see flames through the shop's big front window.

"Okay, let's do a 360." He motioned to Jim as they jumped down from the first truck. The perimeter check was important to locate the fire and confirm that no one needed immediate rescue, as well as identify any possible hazards to their own safety. A propane tank or any flammable waste materials near the building could cause serious problems. He wasn't taking any chances with his team.

Jim nodded his understanding as he put on his self-contained breathing apparatus and followed Derek around the side of the building.

"Back door is locked, preventing access," Jim called over the radio to Derek and Mark as Ethan secured the nozzle of the hose on the back of the truck.

Bailey always kept the back door dead bolted at night. Even in a town as safe as Brookhollow, she didn't take chances with her clients' vehicles.

"Is there an internal sprinkler system?" Derek asked.

"No." Why hadn't he insisted that Doug install the proper security measures years before? Without a doubt the damage this fire would cause could have been eliminated or at least reduced had a system been installed to respond to the first signs of smoke or flames. There was nothing he could do about it now. "Check for open windows and doors," Ethan said.

"Small open window on the left side of the building," Mark confirmed.

Thank God. An open window eliminated several possible dangers in a situation like this one. An airtight space had the potential for a backdraft or flashover when a firefighter had to force entry. The last thing they needed was an unexpected explosion increasing the danger level.

"Parameter check complete," Jim announced. "Several discarded car engines and an old battery have been transferred off the premises."

Ethan tried the front door.

"Front door is locked. I'm breaking in." He grabbed an ax and shattered the thin pane of glass in seconds.

Derek and Jim joined him with the hose line, and all three dropped to their knees to crawl under the heavy blanket of thick, dark smoke that made it impossible to see past several feet. The emergency lighting through the back of the shop and the illuminated exit signs were their only source of light.

Ethan stood as he reached the swinging door to the back bays and peered through the small window. The Volkswagen Jetta in the middle bay was completely engulfed in a violent orange blaze and the flames extended to the surrounding walls. He scanned the area and his pulse quickened at the sight of spray-paint cans lining the shelves just inches above the reach of the flames. That wasn't good. In another minute those cans would start to explode. Pushing the door open, he stood back and motioned the other guys through, pointing to the burning car.

Jim and Derek moved closer and opened the nozzle on the flames.

When the fire was mostly contained, he said, "Bulk of the fire is knocked down. Let's create a cross draft of air flow. I don't want any airtight areas and we need to get this thick smoke out of here to secure the remaining area."

"All clear," Derek reported.

"Windows are all broken out," Mark said.

"Heavy smoke only, no more flames." Ethan gave the final all clear and a collective sigh of relief could be heard over the radios. Jim shut off the water access and disengaged the hose.

Great, now for the hard part, Ethan thought as he scanned the charred walls and ceiling above the bays. The sound of Bailey's motorcycle approaching made him sigh. He'd hoped to do this without her watching.

FRANTICALLY, BAILEY CUT the engine on the bike and pulled off her helmet.

"What happened?" she asked, approaching Ethan, who was exiting through the broken glass in the front door.

The sound of crunching glass under his boots made her cringe, and she stared blankly at the burned shop with its broken windows and melted bay doors.

"I was just here a couple of hours ago." She'd stopped by the shop on her way home from the fire hall and noticed that Nick had left the back door wide open. Nick… She'd bet almost anything that he had something to do with this. Why had she agreed to let him work in the shop for the summer? Anger mixed with her shock and confusion.

Ethan met her gaze, but hesitated.

"What are you not telling me?"

"The fire was started by a short circuit of that Volkswagen Jetta's battery cable."

The disabled car on the highway. Her knees

weakened and she placed a hand to her stomach as a wave of nausea made her dizzy. She'd brought the car in…disregarding Ethan's advice not to. This wasn't Nick's fault; it was hers.

"You okay? Here, sit." Taking her arm, Ethan guided her to the back of the fire truck and gently forced her to sit. "Take a deep breath." His voice sounded far away.

"We're about to start the overhaul." Jim's voice came over Ethan's shoulder radio and Bailey saw him flinch before giving the go-ahead.

She forced herself to sit straighter. "Overhaul? What does that mean?" Her mouth was dry, but her skin was damp with sweat as she fought another wave of nausea.

Ethan cleared his throat, and despite the August heat, he retrieved a blanket and draped it over her shoulders. "He means the teardown—we need to make sure there isn't any hidden fire in the walls or ceiling."

The loud crashing noises behind her made her jump, and discarding the blanket, she stood and moved closer to the garage. Ethan's hand on her arm prevented her from going too close.

"No farther," he said.

The front wall of the shop collapsed in front of her and her hand flew to her mouth. "They are destroying the place." She turned to Ethan. "Make them stop." The damage from the fire was more than enough mess to clean up.... If they kept tearing down the main structures, the entire garage would need to be rebuilt from the ground up.

"I can't, Bailey. This is protocol. It's a safety—"

"You know what? I'm sick to death of your safety measures. This is my shop, Ethan, it's my life, my livelihood—they can't just tear it down." Enraged, she blinked away the tears that stung her eyes.

"There could be more fire somewhere in there. We can't take the chance. I'm sorry." His voice was calm but she heard a note of anguish.

Desperate to argue but knowing it was no use, she watched the back ceiling give way, falling to the floor of the shop in a heap of rubble. Her shoulders slumped as she lowered herself down to the gravel parking lot, tucking her knees under her. "So that's it. They're just going to continue pulling down the entire building?" she said, more to herself than to him.

Ethan knelt beside her, wrapping an arm around her bare shoulders. "We won't leave until we're certain that we've put water on anything glowing."

CHAPTER FOUR

"So when you left last night at midnight, everything looked fine?"

The insurance adjuster from Newark, who'd introduced himself only as Phillips, had arrived early the next morning. The area around the garage had been roped off with caution tape to prevent anyone from going near the ruins of the building. The fire crew had instructed Bailey not to touch anything or attempt to clean up until the insurance adjuster had time to assess the full extent of the damage. She understood the reasoning, but driving away the night before from the shop that had been a major part of her life for ten years and was now lying in a heap of rubble had been difficult.

"Yes. I noticed the back door ajar when I drove past, so I stopped to close and lock it."

"An employee left a door open?" Phillips raised an eyebrow as he glanced up from his paperwork.

Bailey nodded, her jaw clenched. *Nick.*

"You know that your insurance wouldn't cover theft if the premises were left unsecured?"

"Yes…but this is Brookhollow. No one would ever think of stealing anything. Heck, I'm sure if someone in town had noticed the door open, they would have just locked up themselves." It was one of the things she loved most about her hometown—the neighborly comfort the residents enjoyed. Everyone looked out for one another.

"Maybe, but you can never be too sure," he said, stepping over the broken glass in the metal shell of the door frame to enter the shop. "Wow, quite a lot of damage." He studied the scene, flipping to a fresh page in his notebook.

Bailey found it difficult to look as she followed him inside, stepping over the large wooden ceiling beams that now lay on the ground.

"Yes. The fire from the vehicle spread very quickly, so the firefighters were forced to tear everything down." An image of the fire crew using their axes and hammers to bring down the walls and ceiling flashed in her mind and she cringed. She knew they had been doing their job, but they'd destroyed everything. All she had.

The man nodded. "Happens often," he said dismissively.

Not to her. What he casually shrugged off as just another insurance claim was one of the most stressful and heartbreaking events in her life. Bailey had worked in the shop since she'd moved out on her own at seventeen, and it had become a familiar and comfortable place. She knew what she was doing inside the shop, something she couldn't say for many other aspects of her life. Memories were buried within its walls and the building had stood in Brookhollow for over forty years. Noticing her calendar sticking out from under the charred desk, she bent to retrieve it. She dusted off the image of the St. Mark's, the August picture on the calendar of Italy that Ethan had given her for Christmas to keep her motivated to save for her trip. Rolling the calendar, she tucked it into her back jeans pocket.

Inspector Phillips continued to walk through the rubble, making several notes, until he stopped beside the charred Volkswagen Jetta. "This was the one that started the fire?"

"Yes." The one she never should have towed.

"Fire report says it had caught on fire on the highway the day before, as well."

It wasn't a question, so she remained silent. No doubt Ethan's report was detailed. Her palms sweat slightly.

"You were advised not to bring it here," he continued to read. "In Newark, a vehicle like this would have been impounded and deemed undriveable by the police."

This wasn't Newark. "We don't have an impound lot and I couldn't leave the man stranded." She fisted her hands at her sides. Maybe she should have called the police at the time, but it had been her first experience with this kind of thing. Unfortunately, her ignorance had cost her the shop. "The danger seemed to be past...."

"But the firefighter on the scene thought otherwise," he said, glancing at her, a look of disapproval behind his dark, thick-rimmed glasses.

"I made a judgment call," she said, knowing she sounded defensive.

"The wrong one, it seems," he said, then continued on before she could say anything else. Not that she had a great case. "Based on these fire inspection reports, it wasn't the first suggestion you ignored…. A sprinkler system was recommended on numerous occasions."

"The upgrades weren't exactly in the budget."

"I don't think I need to point out the irony there."

That was enough. "Did any part of your training teach you to have at least a little compassion for the business owners you are dealing with?"

He stopped, dropping his folder to his side. "Ms. Sheppard, I understand that this is the first time you've had to deal with this sort of thing, but try to see this from my tired perspective. Every day I see situations just like this one with people gaming the system. I'm not saying that is the case here, but let's go over the facts…." He paused and scanned what remained of her garage. "This place is at least forty years old. It needs upgrades. You just bought it from…" He skimmed his paperwork. "A Doug Sheppard—your father?"

"Uncle."

"You just bought the place from your uncle a month ago and you brought in a vehicle that you knew was a potential fire hazard?"

Put that way, it did look suspicious.

"Look, I'm not saying that I think you did this on purpose, but forgive me if I follow protocol on this one."

This was not good. "So my claim may be denied?"

"That's always a possibility, but I'll do my best to try to find something…anything to make this claim not look so much like a fraud."

FRAUD. THE WORD rang repeatedly in her head as Bailey parked her motorcycle outside of Joey's café on Main Street a short time later. In twelve hours, she'd lost her business, and was suspected of arson and fraud. Fantastic.

Right now Main Street was quiet, as most of the shops didn't open until nine o'clock. Bailey always loved the street at this time of day when the buildings blocked the sun's heat, casting a shadow over the brick-patterned sidewalk. Everything was calm. Within an hour, the merchants' displays would extend onto the walkway and the cafés would set up their outdoor seating areas and colorful umbrellas, ready for business. But today she couldn't enjoy the peace, desperate to get inside where her coffee waited.

Removing her helmet, she waved to Pearl

Richards, who was flipping the sign on the door of her flower shop, Pearl's Petals, to Open. The family-owned business was located in one of the oldest buildings in town on the corner of Main and Temple Streets. Pearl was the great-granddaughter of the original Pearl who'd owned the store eighty years before. She'd not only inherited the pretty name but the store as well, when the older woman had passed away. That's how things worked in Brookhollow. Businesses were kept in the family.

"Bailey." Pearl's greeting was terse as she hung several potted plants on an iron hook above the door before hurrying inside.

Weird. Bailey usually exchanged pleasantries with the woman on Sunday mornings before her weekly breakfast with her dad and brothers. It was just as well; she wasn't really in the mood to chat after the meeting with the insurance adjustor.

Entering the fifties-style diner, Bailey scanned the crowded room for her family. The Sunday-morning breakfast was a tradition they'd started when she and the boys had still lived at home.

"Hey, Bailey. Your dad's just in the kitchen, checking out a leaking pipe under the sink.

Your brothers are sitting at your usual booth near the window." Tina Miller set the tray of steaming coffee cups she carried onto the nearest table, then reached forward and enveloped Bailey in a tight hug.

The smell of the woman's lavender perfume made her eyes water.

"I'm so sorry about the garage…and we were all so relieved to hear no one was hurt."

"Thank you. It's been a tough morning," Bailey admitted, the tray of coffee tempting her to reach out and grab one. With literally no sleep at all the night before, it was a wonder her eyes were staying open.

Tina moved away and lowered her voice. "You know, it's okay if you did it. Heck, Joey and I talk about burning this place down all the time and taking the insurance money and moving to the Bahamas." She laughed, but the sincerity in her words surprised Bailey.

Tina actually believed she'd purposely burn down her own business? Who else thought that? Clearly it was a topic of discussion already. Small-town gossip made Brookhollow come alive. She hated to be the center of it.

"I didn't," she said, squaring her shoulders for the accusatory stares she expected to face on the way to the corner booth near the juke-box where her brothers sat.

The woman picked up her tray and saun-tered off with a wink. "Of course not. Your coffee's already on the table."

Joey, the diner's owner and cook, slid an order through the kitchen window. The French toast topped with whipped cream and strawberries made her stomach growl. "Morning, Bailey. I drove past the garage on my way in this morning. Terrible fire." He shook his head. "Glad to see you're okay."

"Thanks, Joey." Avoiding the stares and whispers from the tables as she passed, she slid into their usual booth. After tucking her motorcycle helmet on the seat next to her, she turned to her brothers. "Tell me what people are saying." Best to know what rumors were circulating before she was forced to confront them.

Jordan was on his cell phone but gave her a sympathetic smile. *Glad you're okay,* he mouthed.

Brandon swallowed a mouthful of coffee and leaned closer across the table. "Just what you would expect—that you burned down the shop in order to afford the repairs it desperately needs." He eyed her with suspicion. "Did you?"

"Brandon!" Her own brother? Come on. He should know her better than that.

"Had to ask." He shrugged.

Jordan disconnected his call and shot his older brother a look. "No, you didn't. Don't pay any attention to the talkers, Bailey. Remember what we went through after Grandpa died...."

Her brothers had opened their MMA club two weeks after the death of their last living grandparent several years before, and gossip had run wild with claims that the boys had had something to do with the ninety-four-year-old's death. People had gone so far as to surmise that the old man, who'd been living at the senior's complex, had had a small fortune that the boys inherited. Of course, none of it was true, and once the coroner's report declared cause of death to be a heart attack, the rumor mill had ceased. Unfortunately in Bailey's case, it was more than her reputation around town at stake.

"Anyway, that was Uncle Doug," Jordan said. "He feels terrible."

In the chaos of the night before and the headache-inducing inspection that morning,

Bailey had almost forgotten about the poor man. Her uncle would be feeling this disaster as much as she was. He'd opened the shop forty-five years ago. It had been his life. "I was going to stop by to see him this afternoon." After her dress fitting with Sheila Mason. It took all her strength and loyalty as a friend to Luke and Victoria not to use this turn of events to cancel that obligation.

"I think you should," Jordan continued. "At first he thought it was Nick's fault."

So had she. "Nope. All mine."

Her father slid into the booth next to her. "Hey, honey." Ben Sheppard leaned over to kiss her forehead. "I ordered our usual already, I was starving."

"Great, thanks." She bit her lip and toyed with the handle on her coffee cup.

"Rough night, huh?" He squeezed her hand on the table.

"Turns out the entire town thinks I'm capable of arson," she mumbled.

Ben gave a dismissive wave. "Joey and Tina are just annoyed that they didn't think of it first."

"You don't actually think I did it, do you?" She studied her father. At fifty-four, he was still handsome with just a few gray streaks in his dark brown hair and the first sign of wrinkles at the corners of his crystal-blue eyes. A plumber by trade, he kept himself in good shape, running five nights a week with the local running group at the YMCA. They had always been close, and his opinion mattered more than the rest.

"No. I know you loved that place."

Tina approached the booth with their orders, a slight sway in her curvy hips. She flashed a conspiratorial smile at Bailey as she leaned over Ben to refill the coffee cups. "Can I get anything else for you guys at the moment?"

"No, I think we're good. Thanks, Tina."

"Great, holler if you need anything."

Bailey sighed. "Ugh…this is a disaster."

"Look on the bright side," Jordan said, cutting into his breakfast steak. "The place really did need upgrades—now you can do them."

"Only if I get paid out by the insurance company." Bailey slumped against the seat, the hot coffee mug between her hands providing little comfort to her frazzled nerves.

"Why wouldn't you?" Ben asked, biting into a piece of toast and peanut butter.

"Apparently the people around here aren't

the only ones who think the fire may not have been an accident."

"The meeting with the insurance adjuster didn't go well?" Brandon asked, covering his omelet with ketchup.

She shook her head and sat straighter as Ethan approached in his soccer-coach uniform. She swallowed hard. The unexpected sight of his unshaven face and still-wet-from-the-shower hair made her pulse race, despite the annoyance she felt toward him for his part in this morning's inquisition from the insurance rep. Not to mention the grudge she held against him for tearing down the shop.

"Hey, Ethan. On your way to practice?" Brandon asked.

As well as his job at the fire hall, Ethan worked on the school board and coached all of the local junior boy's teams that his nephews played on—hockey, soccer and football. She didn't fail to notice that today his eyes looked as tired as hers felt.

"Yeah. Remind me again whose idea it was to hold practice at nine-thirty on a Sunday morning," he said grumpily, running a hand over his scruffy face. "Hey, Mr. Sheppard. Bailey, how are you?" he asked, reaching for her coffee.

She swiped his hand away, moving the cup out of reach.

"Okay, still mad at me." Ethan rocked back on his heels and shoved his hands into his shorts pockets.

Bailey sighed. "Because of your warning about the Jetta being a hazard and your countless inspection reports, my claim will probably be denied…and worse, I'm facing a fine for fraud."

Ethan frowned. "They think you started the fire on purpose? That's preposterous."

Despite her annoyance, she wanted to hug him for his immediate dismissal of the ridiculous suggestion. "Yeah, well, the facts point to otherwise. Did you really have to be so detailed in those inspection reports?" She knew she was mad at the wrong guy, but he was the closest person other than herself that she could blame for this mess.

"I was doing my job."

"I just wish you didn't do it so well." She took a sip of her coffee and rested her cheek on her hand.

"Want to join us for breakfast?" Ben invited.

"Love to, but I'm running late. I just called

in an order to go," he said, grabbing a strip of Bailey's bacon.

She reached for the hot sauce on the table and squirted a drop onto her plate.

Ethan dipped the bacon into it, folded it then popped the whole thing into his mouth.

"Ethan, order up!" Tina called from behind the counter.

"Gotta run." Ethan grabbed his sunglasses off the table and slid them over his disheveled dark hair. "Bailey, try not to worry too much. We'll figure this out, I promise."

"OKAY, GUYS, BRING it in. We're going to work on our tackle today." Ethan watched the group of six- to nine-year-old boys running laps around the hundred-yard field behind Brookhollow Junior High School. He pushed his Oakley sunglasses up over his New Jersey Devils baseball cap and flinched in the bright early-morning sun. Taking a final gulp of coffee, he set the cup aside and picked up a soccer ball.

The boys lined up in front of him and Mason Young raised his hand.

"Yes, Mason?"

"You said last week we weren't allowed to

tackle in soccer." The young boy wore a look of confusion.

"We're not tackling the way we would in football. This is a technique of stealing the ball, but with your feet," Ethan explained.

"I don't get it."

"Me, neither."

"Doesn't make any sense," the boys chorused.

"Guys, we just learned how to do this a few weeks ago."

Blank faces stared back at him.

"Okay, who remembers what I'm talking about?" He scanned the row of boys. "Any of you?" He placed his hands on his hips and let out a breath. "David knows what I'm talking about.... Hey, where's David Myers?" Both of his nephews were absent from practice. Odd, they never missed a week. Their mom, his sister, Melody, was adamant that if they committed to something, they followed through. The boys both possessed a natural talent well beyond their age level, something they'd inherited from their athletic father before he'd died in a car accident when the boys were four. Melody was raising them alone.

"They weren't at scouts on Friday.... I think they're sick," Michael Thompson supplied.

That made sense. When one of the twins got sick, the other one did, too. He would stop by to see them later in the week.

"Coach Bishop?" Evan Coles spoke up, raising a hand.

"Yeah?"

"Were you scared?" he asked, eyes wide.

All of the boys stared at him. Okay, he could see they wouldn't get through practice until he talked to them about the fire. He lowered himself to the grass, folding his legs. "Sit," he motioned.

The little boys moved closer and sat in a semicircle around him.

"Yes, I was scared," he said honestly. Fires were rare in the small town and the garage had many hidden dangers. Things could have gone much worse the night before. Though for Bailey, things were about as bad as they could be. He pushed away the rising guilt. He'd done what he had to do for everyone's safety. She'd realize that.

"But in an emergency situation, it's important to keep a clear head and work as a team," he continued. "Kind of the same way you guys are on the field. You work as a team so you can win games, right?" He hoped the young boys recognized the connection and understood the importance that teamwork played in all aspects of life.

"Were the flames big?"

"Did the windows explode?"

"Was the smoke hard to see through?"

The questions were fired at him and he held up a hand. "Yes, the flames were big and the smoke was thick, but we secured the premises first, so nothing exploded."

"I want to be a firefighter," Michael said with an excited nod.

"Me, too," the others chorused.

Ethan smiled for the first time that day. Kids had a way of putting things in perspective. "Great, the fire hall will be fully staffed for years," he said as he stood. "But first, my brave soccer players, you need to learn to tackle so we can win our first playoff game two weeks from now."

"I know how to tackle," Evan said, jumping to his feet with the others.

"Oh, yeah? Let's see."

All eight boys dived toward him, dogpiling him on the grass.

ETHAN CLIMBED THE stairs to the town council office in downtown Brookhollow later that day. The entire downtown consisted of five multistory buildings around Brookview Lake and served as the location for any government or formal business in the town. The mayor's office and the city's official archives were housed on the third floor of the Brookview Tower building.

"Ethan, what are you doing here?" The deep, familiar voice of Mayor Parsons, Emily's dad, resonated behind him. It was a voice he hadn't heard in months, since he'd been trying to avoid the Parsons family. Being around them was tough, a reminder that Emily was gone. Her free-spirited way had lit up the room and brought life to even the most boring family gatherings, and her absence now was obvious. He preferred to keep his distance from the family that he'd once planned to become part of someday. The lack of effort the Parsonses had made to keep in touch made him guess they felt the same. He'd only be a reminder to them of what they'd lost.

He turned and extended a hand. "Good afternoon, sir. Nice to see you." He hoped the words sounded convincing. "I'm just here to photocopy some documents."

Tom Parsons accepted the hand, pumped it once then released it. "Oh?"

"Yeah…I was hoping to find the original building specs for the garage."

"Doug's Motors?"

"Yes."

Tom nodded slowly and fell into step with Ethan as they entered the building through the revolving, glass door. The heels of the older man's dress shoes echoed off the spotless tiled floor of the lobby and he waved to the security guard at the front desk. "I heard about the fire last night. Glad no one was hurt, but I suspect that Bailey woman has a bit of a sticky situation on her hands."

Ethan tensed. "Sticky situation?"

"The whole town is talking about the possibility that this may not have been an accident." Tom lifted the sleeve of his tailor-made suit to check his Rolex.

Wow, taxpayer money did go a long way, Ethan mused. The cost of that watch alone could have paid for the upgrades needed in many of the older buildings in Brookhollow. Including the garage. "That's exactly all it is, sir—talk. Bailey would never destroy her own shop."

Tom paused near the elevators as Ethan stabbed the button. "You two have always been close."

Unsure whether it was a question or a statement, Ethan remained silent, watching the numbers illuminate above the elevator door. Even after so many years together, he'd never felt truly comfortable around Emily's father. Mayor Parsons had been constantly pushing him to look into the bigger fire halls in New Jersey and New York, claiming that Ethan was wasting his talents serving the small town's community. While Ethan appreciated the man's encouragement, he'd suspected it hadn't been entirely altruistic.

Emily had never hidden the fact that she found Brookhollow dull, and her desire to move away had been obvious to everyone. Mayor Parsons had higher political aspirations himself, and Ethan suspected his own wish to settle in the small town hadn't registered favorably with the family. Well, now it was no longer their concern.

"Sometimes I think that may have been part of the problem," the man said as the elevator doors opened and they stepped inside.

"Part of what problem?" Ethan scanned the directory. Archives, third floor.

Tom hit seven for himself and three for Ethan. "The one between you and Emily."

"You think my friendship with Bailey was

a problem in our relationship?" He frowned as he met the man's gaze. That was just ridiculous. Bailey was…Bailey. Emily had never said anything to him about the woman who'd always been just one of the boys. He'd sometimes sensed that she disliked Bailey…but he suspected the feeling was mutual. Emily and Bailey were so different. They'd never been exactly friendly.

"I'm just saying it couldn't have helped. I mean, men and women simply cannot be friends. Not without one or both getting the wrong idea…."

"Oh, no, sir. Bailey and I really are just friends, nothing more."

"Are you sure she sees it that way?"

The elevator opened onto the third floor and Ethan hesitated.

Tom held the door as it began to slide closed. "Marlene at the information desk will get you what you need."

Ethan stepped out into the hall. "Great, thanks," he mumbled as the elevator doors closed behind him.

A LITTLE PAST NOON, Bailey stared at her puffy, red-eyed reflection in the mirrored closet doors in Mrs. Mason's sewing room, upstairs in the family home on Albert Street. She barely recognized herself in the pale pink halter-style dress with the cinched waist and angular, calf-length train. The zipper had been a challenge and she struggled to take a deep breath, but otherwise the dress fit as if it had been made for her. It hung a little longer than it would have on Victoria's cousin, Adele, but the length covered the stone-angel tattoo on the upper half of her calf. While the tattoo, in memory of her mother, meant a lot to her, she didn't think Victoria would appreciate it appearing in her wedding photos. Bailey traced a hand along the shimmery satin, the pale contrast of the fabric making her dark, tanned skin glow.

"Bailey, do you need help with the zipper?" Sheila Mason asked from the hallway, before the sound of pacing resumed on the hardwood floor.

"Um...no, I've got it." Barely. Bailey opened the door and bit her lip, waiting for Sheila's assessment.

A look of relief spread across the woman's face as she clasped her hands together. "You look beautiful," she said, advancing toward her and turning her around to check the back. "How does it feel?"

"A little tight...." Bailey's voice was strained.

"Just don't eat the day of the wedding and it will be fine," Sheila said, then quickly shook her head at Bailey's wide-eyed expression. "Sorry dear, I didn't mean that. If you need me to let it out a little, I can." She picked up chalk to mark the fabric, then reached for her glasses where they hung around her neck, placing them over her tired-looking eyes.

Bailey empathized with her. Wedding preparations could be stressful for everyone involved. All she had to do was wear a dress and walk up an aisle, pose for some photos, sit at the head table during dinner.... Oh, God, she hoped she wouldn't have to make a speech or anything. Anxiety crept into her chest and she forced a calming breath. Remember, she told herself, as mother of the bride, Sheila had it much worse.

"No, you know, I think it will be fine, really." She'd rather buy one of those awful corsets that claimed to reduce a body by a dress size than give Sheila more to worry about.

"You're sure? It's no problem."

"I'm sure. Should I take it off now?" Please.

"Yes, thank you. That's one dress I can check off my list. Now, if only I could get that daughter of mine to commit to a pattern."

"I heard Vic was having a tough time deciding."

"It's so unlike her. My daughter spent twelve years in New York, climbing the corporate ladder, making business deals and important decisions...." She shook her head. "I'm just worried this is a sign of cold feet again."

"No, I'm sure that's not it. She loves Luke. Victoria's not going anywhere—she just wants to look perfect for him."

"After all this time and everything they've been through, she ought to know by now that Luke would marry her in anything. But she'd better decide soon, otherwise she'll be wearing your mother's wedding gown. That one is already made."

Bailey's eyes widened. "What? You have my mom's wedding dress?" She'd always wondered what had happened to the simple floor-length antique-white gown that had been uniquely her mom's style. Sheila had designed and made the dress years before and Bailey had just assumed her aunt Caroline had taken it for safekeeping after her mom's funeral.

"Yes. You mean your dad didn't tell you?"

"No." Sheila Mason had her mother's

dress—a dress she'd hoped to wear herself one day.

Sheila opened the closet doors. Moving aside various sewing projects, she pulled out a clear plastic garment bag.

That was it. Bailey recognized the lace overlay on the off-white gown. The last time she'd seen the dress was when her mother had shown it to her several months before she'd passed.

Sheila unzipped the bag and gently removed the dress. She handed it to Bailey. "This dress has always been my favorite creation. Your mother knew exactly what she wanted when she came here that day. The artist she was, she'd drafted the design herself. All I had to do was help with the fabric selection and put the pieces together. She looked beautiful in it on her wedding day."

Bailey allowed the lengths of the soft material to cascade toward the floor. She quickly gathered the ends before they hit the hardwood.

"Oh, don't worry. It's been stored away so long now, it will need to be professionally cleaned before you can wear it," Sheila said.

Bailey's head whipped toward her. "Before *I* can wear it?"

"Yes, sweet girl. That's why I have it here, safe and properly stored. Your dad had no idea how to care for it, and he knew when the day came, I would be doing the alterations on it. Or else I'd use the fabric to turn it into a completely different style—modern, whatever you chose."

A lump formed in the back of Bailey's throat. Her dad had kept the dress safe for her knowing she would want to wear it someday. Not trusting her voice, she just nodded, touching the delicate lace.

Sheila reached forward and, taking the dress, she held it in front of Bailey. Standing behind her, she pressed the fabric closer. "Although the style is still modern, its simplicity and elegance are timeless, and it really would suit your tiny frame."

"It's perfect," Bailey agreed. Turning, she hugged Sheila, always a dear family friend. Suddenly the idea of being in the Mason-Dawson wedding party didn't seem like such a chore. Brookhollow was like an extended family. "Thank you, Mrs. Mason."

"You're welcome. Why don't you take it with you?" she suggested.

After the night before, holding this piece

of her mom gave her comfort. "I'd like that. Thank you."

"Mom!" They heard Victoria's voice call up the stairs.

"Up here in the sewing room."

"Good news! I've decided on a…" Victoria's voice trailed off as her gaze fell to the gown in Bailey's hands. "Oh, my, that's beautiful. Your mother's?" she guessed, moving closer to examine the dress.

"Yes." Bailey nodded.

"You've decided on a design?" Sheila said, an eager note in her voice as she took the wedding-planning book from Victoria. She picked up the picture sitting on top. "Is this it?" she asked, her tone hopeful.

Victoria's attention was still glued to the dress Bailey held. "I thought it was, but now I'm not so sure…."

"I HAD A feeling I'd find you here."

Her uncle Doug turned as Bailey stepped through the open bay door on the side of the shop an hour later. The older man quickly wiped his cheek and sniffed, then shoved his hands into his coat pockets. "Even seeing it with my own eyes, I can't believe it."

"I know what you mean." Bailey looked

around them. Nothing had yet been touched, though she hoped to have a cleanup crew on-site within the week. Leaving the place in such a mess was disheartening. The faster she could have the debris taken away, the faster they could start a rebuild...if the insurance claim came through.

"I'm sorry," they said in unison.

Bailey frowned. "You're sorry? For what? This was entirely my fault. I should never have towed that car.... Ethan told me not to. I should have listened."

Doug removed his New York Giants base-ball hat, the one he didn't leave home without, and ran a hand over his balding head. "Non-sense. You did the right thing," he argued.

Bailey motioned to what was left of the garage around them. "The evidence begs to differ," she said.

Doug pointed to the painted words on the concrete wall above the charred bay doors. The black soot clouded some of the letters, making the words difficult to read, but Bailey knew the phrase by heart. *No car left behind. Driver...maybe.* The motto had been painted there on Doug's first day almost forty-six years before, and the John-Deere-green paint had prevailed. "You did the right thing," he repeated. Then, picking up an undamaged can of gear oil, he set it along the edge of the remaining wall in the back.

Funny, that can didn't seem so insignificant now. It was one of the only things to survive the disaster.

"Start with this and rebuild," Doug said. "Essentially, it was all I started with a million years ago."

"Thanks, Uncle Doug." His words and actions were somehow just what she needed to regain her confidence. Of course they would rebuild. With or without the insurance money. She'd find a way.

"I really should have installed that sprinkler system…."

"Don't," Bailey said. "We both thought it was unnecessary. Over forty years accident-free in this place…. We believed we were indestructible, I guess." She kicked the base of the vending machine. Its glass had exploded in the intense heat. Two cans of soda fell to the tray, and opening them, she handed one to her uncle. "Let's make a toast." She held up her can.

The older man looked at her as though she was crazy. "A toast? In the middle of all this?"

"Yes."

"Okay. To what?"

"To starting over…and making Doug's Motors even better than before," she said.

"You got one thing wrong," her uncle insisted. "It's not Doug's Motors anymore—it's Bailey's Place."

ETHAN KNOCKED ONCE on the front door of Bailey's bungalow-style home on Royal Oak Avenue, then reached for the door handle, knowing the door would be unlocked. In a town the size of Brookhollow, people rarely locked anything.

"Ethan?" she called from the bedroom. A few feet away at the end of the hall, the door was slightly ajar.

Her old gray cat, Harley, came sauntering out toward him and he bent to pet the animal. "What if I said no?" he chided, scanning the small two-bedroom home with its antique furniture. The place had been sold to Bailey fully furnished two years before when the previous owner had moved to Newark to live with her daughter. Mrs. Duncan had spent her entire life in Brookhollow, but rarely ventured far from the garden she'd planted on the acres of land behind the house. Ethan could understand the appeal of the "steal of a deal" that Bailey had gotten on the house and all the land. However, the old wood-burning fireplace in the corner of the main room was a troubling thought. He didn't trust the old thing. Bending, he peered through the chimney to make sure the ventilation system looked clear. He'd ask Chief Clarke to do an inspection on it before the fall, when he knew Bailey would use it to heat the house.

"Um...what are you doing here?" Her voice sounded strange—tired, strained and a little annoyed.

She was still upset with him about the report. Well, he hoped what he'd come to show her might change that. "I have some information that could help with your claim."

"Can you come back later...or tomorrow?"

"What are you doing? Can you come out, please?"

He heard her sigh loudly. "Just a minute."

As he passed the smoke detector in the hallway, he pressed the button to check the battery. It beeped twice. Battery low. "Bailey, I told you to change this battery two weeks ago," he said, going into the kitchen and opening the utility drawer near the fridge.

"You know I don't cook," she mumbled.

"That doesn't matter, a fire can start from other things…." He dug around until he found two double-A batteries and proceeded to change them himself. After the fire at the garage, it annoyed him that she would still be so nonchalant about these things.

Going back into the living room, he set the papers he'd gathered from the archives onto her coffee table and sat on her plush sofa. On the television screen *While You Were Sleeping,* the old Sandra Bullock movie from the nineties, was paused. It was her favorite, but she normally watched it every Thanksgiving, not in the middle of August. "What's with the movie?" he called, turning as he heard her bare feet on the hardwood floor in the hallway. His eyes widened and he gaped. "Is there something you forgot to mention?" he asked, recovering slightly, but unable to remove his gaze from the long antique-white lace wedding dress she wore.

Her shoulders slumped and she shifted her weight from one foot to the other. "It was my mother's."

"And you're wearing it because…?"

"I tried it on, and now the zipper is stuck." She folded her arms across her midsection.

"You tried on your mother's wedding dress?"

The sentimental gesture, the sappy movie—clearly she'd been wallowing in self-pity, which was something he'd never known her to do.

"Are you here for a reason?"

She was still annoyed with him. He could deal with that. Moving toward her, he took her shoulders and turned her around. "Lift your hair."

"I don't need your help," she mumbled, but she did as he asked.

The smell of her cinnamon shampoo reached his nose as her long dark hair almost whipped him in the face. He wiggled the stubborn zipper until it gave way and tugged it halfway down her back. "There, you should be able to get out now."

"I'll be back in a minute." She disappeared back down the hall, and he sat on the sofa. An open photo album caught his attention, sticking out from under the couch. Picking it up, he smiled at the pictures of Bailey as a young girl at the park with her family. Photos of her hanging from the monkey bars or sitting on a swing with her mom. She looked just like her mother, with her long dark hair and bright clear-blue eyes. They had the same full lips and wide smile. Candace Sheppard had been a beautiful woman, much like her daughter. Weird, he'd never paid much attention before.

Bailey reemerged a second later, wearing a pair of tan leggings and an oversize New Jersey Devils hockey jersey, her hair tied at the base of her neck. "So what were you saying about documents that might help?" She sat on the couch next to him.

Ethan picked up the folder of photocopied papers and moved closer to her. "I went to the town archives today and I was able to get photocopies of the original building permits for the garage, which prove that it was up to code. I also have inspection reports that date back five years and show that Doug also ignored our suggestions for improvements."

Bailey leafed through the documents. "You think these can help? To me, it just looks like we always ignored the warnings." She didn't look convinced.

"Exactly. Which proves that you didn't purposely start ignoring them just recently. See what I mean?"

"Not really."

"Look, it can't hurt to try." He reached into his coat pocket and handed her a folded piece of paper. "I also have this."

He watched as she read the letter he'd convinced Chief Clarke to write, stating that the garage's complete demolition was protocol only and that the fire caused by the vehicle had been localized.

She sighed as she refolded it. "Thank you," she said softly, turning to face him.

"You're welcome." He studied her tired eyes, red and puffy, a faded streak of dark mascara slightly visible on her right cheek. It hurt him to see her this stressed. She was usually so in control, so confident, so strong. This vulnerable side of her was new to him. He reached out to touch her cheek and she leaned her face into the palm of his hand. "It's going to be okay," he reassured, moving closer and wrapping an arm around her, pulling her back against him on the couch.

She rested her head against his shoulder and he felt her weight sink into him. He moved her hair away from her neck and kissed the top of her head. To his surprise, she pulled back and shifted to face him. Her gaze locked with his and in that moment her expression of sadness changed to something else. Something he couldn't be sure he was seeing, but it terrified him. She leaned closer, and her gaze fluttered to his lips, then back to his eyes as she lowered her full, pink lips to his.

Stunned, he remained still, unable to return the kiss, yet unwilling to push her away. Placing her hands on his shoulders, she moved closer to him and deepened the kiss. His breath caught as his mind reeled. What was she doing? Clearly she wasn't thinking straight. The stress of the past twenty-four hours was clouding her judgment. That had to be it.

Slowly, she moved away, searching his gaze.

"Bailey, I..." He what? What did he say to his best friend who had just kissed him? And why did part of him want her to do it again? That was the most disturbing thing of all.

"Look, I know you're still hung up on Emily, but I want to be the one to help you forget about her."

He blinked. She did? Since when? "Have you been drinking?"

"No. I'm just finally being honest. I realized today how short life can be and how important it is to take a chance." She ran a hand along his cheek, tracing a trail over his five-o'clock shadow. "Ethan, I've loved you for years," she whispered.

The confession shook him, and without thinking, he leaned forward and kissed her, hard, pulling her back toward him on the couch. Then just as quickly, he stopped. What the hell was he doing? "I'm sorry. I don't know where that came from." He stared at her pink, swollen lips, and couldn't resist sliding a finger along the bottom one. What was happening here? In a matter of seconds, things between them had gone from friendship to her confession of love? From simple to complicated. Who was this woman he was suddenly finding impossible to resist touching?

She closed her eyes and a small sigh escaped her lips, breaking his trance. Abruptly, he stood, letting her fall against the couch. He raked a hand through his hair and paced the living room, desperate to escape, but the hurt and confusion on her face made it impossible to head for the door.

"What's wrong?" she asked, standing and approaching him.

"Bailey, you have been through enough and I can only assume that this—whatever this is—is coming from a place of stress or desperation...or alcohol."

"I told you I wasn't drinking. I've been

wanting to tell you how I feel for a long time and I guess the fire helped me realize that things can happen so quickly.... You have to go after what you want in life." She touched his arm gently and a shiver ran down his spine.

She was serious. Oh, was she serious....

"Bailey, I am the last thing you need right now," he said, backing away from her. He was a mess. He couldn't go a day without thoughts of Emily haunting him at every turn. Heck, he'd been about to answer her call the night before. If the fire hadn't happened... It wouldn't be fair to start something with Bailey, not knowing how he really felt and not knowing if he was truly over Emily.

"I didn't say *need,* I said *want.* There is a big difference," she insisted. She moved closer and wrapped her arms around his neck, standing on her bare tiptoes to reach his lips and kiss him again.

"Stop." He unwrapped her arms from around his neck and held them to her sides. Her expression of hurt was too much. "Baby girl, don't think for a second that I don't want to take a chance on this. I just don't know if I can see this through, and that wouldn't be fair to you."

"Are you still in love with Emily?"

He let out a deep breath. "I'm not sure that I'm *not* still in love with her," he answered. But based on the emotions raging through him and his desire to take Bailey into his arms and kiss all her hurt away, he owed it to the both of them to figure it out, and fast.

CHAPTER FIVE

WITH A HEAVY heart and tired eyes hidden behind her sunglasses, Bailey pulled into the lot of the garage early the next morning. She'd been unable to sleep as worry over the shop competed with feelings of embarrassment over her play for Ethan. How could she have been so stupid to just throw herself at him the way she had? For years she'd been able to keep her feelings for him under wraps, but that was when Emily had been in the picture. Turns out, even thousands of miles away, she still was. Cutting the engine on the bike, she noticed Luke's new Ford parked out front and she could see him inside, walking amid the debris.

He turned and waved as she removed her helmet. Rushing over, he wrapped her in a big hug. "I was so relieved to hear you weren't working late the other night," he said, releasing her and raking a hand through his spiky, gelled hair.

A night owl by nature, she often did work late. If there had been other cars in the shop that evening, she just might have been there. She shuddered at the thought.

"Me, too. What are you doing here? I thought you were in Boston this week." Bailey noticed Bob and Darrell, Luke's crew, walking through the debris inside the shop. Luke had a crew here already? Amazing, wonderful Luke.

"Victoria texted me yesterday and I rushed back as soon as I could." He shuffled his feet on the ground, avoiding her eyes. "I need to apologize."

"For what, Luke? Rushing over here with your contractors doesn't exactly put you on the list of people I'm angry with right now," she said.

"I meant for constantly bringing that old truck here. I read in the fire report that it was that old clunker that caused the fire. That could have been *my* old clunker."

"Don't be crazy, Luke. That's what we fix around here. New vehicles rarely come through those bay doors. Besides, the shop has been open for forty-six years, and this was the first fire and no one got hurt. I'd say we've been lucky." She firmly believed that and took comfort in the knowledge that no one had been injured, but still, seeing the shop she loved in ruins was tough. "Thank you for getting here so quickly. How long do you think the renovations will take?" She bit her lip, still unsure how she was going to pay for them. She'd faxed the documents Ethan had given her to the insurance adjuster that morning, and she prayed he would have good news for her. After going over her finances the night before, she'd discovered her only other option would be to take a second mortgage out on her home and she hated to do that. But remembering her promise to her uncle the day before, she knew she would if she had to.

"Because the exterior frame survived the damage, it's just the interior that needs to be rebuilt, so…I'd say a couple of weeks at most and you should be up and running at least partially."

"Really? That fast?" He was amazing.

"My crews are the best in New Jersey," Luke said, turning as Bob and Darrell came through the broken front window, followed by Ethan.

Her eyes met his and the memory of his

lips on hers returned, making her uneasy. "What are you doing here?"

"Now that renovations are being done, I'm instating the new fire codes for this building."

"What does that mean?"

"A new sprinkler and ventilation system."

"Ethan, you know I can't afford that, especially if the claim gets denied." The cost of the renovations would sit on the books for a while.

Luke interrupted. "My guys have done their assessment. We'll draft up the final work orders, but for now here's the report and the breakdown of what's being done." He handed Bailey the slip.

She held her breath as she scanned it, looking for the total cost. The price balance sat at zero. "Um…Luke, it doesn't give a cost."

"Don't worry about it," he said with a wink. "I know the owner. Of course, this is just the framework to rebuild—the upgrade installs will be a separate contractor."

"Oh, no, Luke…" That was too generous of him.

Luke glanced at Ethan. "Why is it that all these beautiful ladies in Brookhollow try to refuse free labor and all my big-city clients haggle over the price of screws?" He turned to Bailey. "Don't worry about it. If the insurance claim goes through, you can pay me for the work, but in the meantime, I've worked out a deal with Nick."

"With Nick?" Nick was making trades on services?

"Yes. He's going to detail my work trucks with the new Dawson Architecture logo he's designing for me."

"Oh, that's great," Bailey said with forced enthusiasm as Luke waved and jumped into his truck. Nick could do that? Wouldn't it have been great if he'd told her?

As she watched Luke pull away from the shop, Bailey squirmed uncomfortably in the silence that fell between her and Ethan. Clearing her throat, she said, "I have a cleanup crew arriving soon, so…"

Ethan took a step closer and gently grabbed her arm. "About last night…"

The apologetic tone in his voice made her cringe. She pulled her arm away, and with a dismissive wave, she forced a light laugh. "You were right—it must have just been the stress of all of this." She took a step closer, and her gaze locked on his. "Don't worry, it won't happen again."

WON'T HAPPEN AGAIN.

Bailey's words echoed in his mind all afternoon, and he struggled to figure out why he didn't feel more relieved. Of course it couldn't happen again. They were friends. Great friends, but just friends. And he certainly wasn't in any position at the moment to get involved with someone. Sure, Emily had been gone for six months and his family and friends thought he needed to forget about her and move on, but so far he'd been unsuccessful.

For the sake of his future happiness and downright sanity, he wished that he didn't still see her face when he closed his eyes, and didn't have to fight every last instinct to answer his phone whenever she called. And until he was sure he was over his ex, how could he take a chance with someone else? Especially someone who meant as much to him as Bailey did. He refused to break her heart…any more than he probably already had. Yet her promise made his stomach knot, because admittedly a small part of him wanted that kiss to happen again, and the realization both shocked and scared him.

"CARE TO PLACE a bet on who pulled the alarm this time?" Jim asked as he turned the fire engine into the lot of the senior's complex, where they'd just recently had an emergency fire drill. More often than not, the alarm was set off by one of the elderly residents to create a bit of excitement or simply by accident. Today didn't look to be any different, but the fifty-three residents and ten nursing staff all stood in the designated section of the parking lot, waiting for permission to go back inside. They waved and cheered as the engine pulled up.

Ethan waved back. "I think I've lost enough money to you this week," he said to his brother.

"Okay, you take the west wing and I'll secure the east one."

Within ten minutes, they had secured the two-story, redbrick building and given the residents the go-ahead to return inside.

"Should we go see Grandma before we head back?" Ethan asked, checking his watch. Jim's shift had officially ended.

"Probably should," Jim said with a nod, leading the way to their grandmother Bishop's room in the west wing on the main floor of the complex.

Willa Bishop was on the phone as they entered. "Yes…you were right, they're both here. Thanks, son," she said, waving them inside. "Okay, you, too. Talk soon." She replaced the phone and smiled at the boys.

Ethan eyed her with suspicion. "Grandma, did you pull the fire alarm on purpose to get us here?"

Her thin shoulders shrugged in her oversize cable-knit sweater. "So what if I did," she said, sitting straighter in her armchair near the window. A long row of pill bottles lined the sill. That was new. The bottles hadn't been there last week. Her doctor had given her a clean bill of health at her last checkup.

"You know that's a criminal offense, Grandma," Jim said.

"Ha! Like your father would try to take his own mother to jail. Besides, it's the only way I can get my grandsons to visit. What judge would find an old lady guilty of that?" Her eyes widened in mock innocence.

"Grandma, Jill and I were here just last week."

"And I took you to bingo two weeks ago," Ethan said.

"I don't remember any of that." A deep frown wrinkled her forehead as she lowered her gaze. "It's the Alzheimer's."

"You don't have Alzheimer's." Jim sat on the bed and yawned.

"Sure I do. Why else would I be in here?"

"You moved in here to be with grandpa when he got sick."

She scoffed. "That doesn't sound like something I'd do. That man drove me crazy."

Ethan and Jim exchanged amused looks. Their grandparents had remained deeply in love until their grandfather's death from a stroke the year before. Their constant bickering had been part of the couple's charm. They pushed each other's buttons all the time, finding amusement in driving each other crazy. Ethan and his brother knew their grandmother was lost without him in the senior's complex and visited as often as they could.

"Anyway, the reason I wanted you both here is this. I want a great-granddaughter before the diabetes takes me out."

"Grandma, you don't have diabetes," Ethan said. "And these are serious diseases you keep claiming to have. It's not funny."

"Who's kidding? I used Gloria Kingston's diabetic test strips yesterday and my blood sugar was really high," she argued.

"Was that after the birthday celebration for Mr. Miller's ninetieth?" Jim asked, nodding toward the large half-eaten piece of black forest cake still on her nightstand.

"Yes…so?"

"You don't have diabetes."

"Well, I do have high blood pressure. Be a dear and grab me my pills, please." She pointed to the row of bottles.

"Okay, Grandma." Jim winked at Ethan as he opened the bottles and shook out several pills. Before handing them to her, he showed them to Ethan. Orange-flavored Tic Tacs.

They waited while she took them, then rested her head dramatically against the chair. "So about that great-granddaughter…"

"Don't look at me," Ethan said, grateful he could turn this one over to Jim.

"Believe me, I'm trying not to—you're a mess," Willa said. "You're looking thin and disheveled, and what's with the scruffy face?" She clucked her tongue disapprovingly at Ethan's two-day-old stubble.

"Ah, go easy on him, Grams. He's miserable," Jim said.

"Still?"

"I know, Grams. We keep telling him it's time to move on." Jim shrugged.

How did this conversation get redirected at him? Besides, for once his frazzled appearance had nothing to do with Emily. No, this new form of stress had Bailey and her perfect, soft lips all over it. Not that he could admit that to anyone.

"Sit down," his grandmother ordered.

Oh, great, here we go. Ethan sat on the edge of her bed next to Jim and punched his brother in the arm. "Thanks a lot, man."

"Hey, as long as we've moved away from the topic of a great-granddaughter, I'm good," Jim said.

"We're coming back to that," Willa said. "Anyway, Jim's right. It's been almost a year…."

"Six months," Ethan corrected.

"Don't interrupt," she said. "Six months, a year, doesn't matter. What matters is that she's gone, and honestly she was gone a long time ago. You just tried to hold on to something that wasn't there."

"Things weren't great." They had been drifting apart for a long time, but that just meant they had to work harder, didn't it? After more than a decade together, they'd just needed to find the spark again. Giving up on the relationship had never seemed like an option to him. Not when there had been so many good times, too…in the beginning. He and Emily had been crazy in love in high school—that had been real—and then they'd started to build a future together. Though he couldn't argue that their different life goals seemed to wedge them further and further apart. Especially in the past few years when their talks about marriage and children had only resulted in heated arguments. Children were not in Emily's future…and he'd had a hard time envisioning one without them. He'd hoped in time she'd have a change of heart.

"No, they weren't, and you deserve great. Why settle for anything less?" Willa was tough, but she had a point he couldn't argue. "Look at Jim and Jill—they are perfect together."

Jim sat up straighter. "Oh, really? What makes you so sure?"

"Because I've seen how crazy she makes you, and take it from someone who knows— it's not really love unless it makes you crazy."

THURSDAY EVENING, Bailey stretched on a padded workout mat on the hardwood gym floor of Extreme Athletics as several women strolled in for the self-defense class. Since deciding to offer the class earlier that summer, she'd been pleasantly surprised by the initial turnout, and the numbers increased each week. She was happy to see that the importance of knowing how to defend yourself against an attacker wasn't lost on the women in Brookhollow, despite living in a quiet, safe community. A false sense of security could be dangerous, and even she had fallen into that trap, as Ethan never failed to point out.

"Come on in, ladies. Grab a yoga mat from the wall and you can place your personal belongings in the lockers near the back," she directed. "Cell phones off, please. We will be getting started in just a few minutes." She glanced toward the front door for the millionth time, wondering if Ethan would show up and almost wishing he wouldn't.

But the next time the front door opened, he entered. "Hi," he said when he reached her.

"Hi." She met his gaze squarely, but her knees weakened slightly.

Several women in the front row stopped chatting to look at them with interest. Or more likely to size Ethan up. Well, they could have him...over her dead body, of course. She cleared her throat and turned her attention to her class. "Hi, everyone, welcome. First, I'd like to start off by saying that the best self-defense is always prevention. Attackers will usually strike against vulnerable or unsuspecting victims, so be smart—walk in well-lit areas at night, keep your keys, or pepper spray if you have it, in your hand. If you are approached, give the attacker what they want if it's a material thing they're after. Your wallet, purse, watch—yes, ladies, even your wedding rings can be replaced, but *you* can't. Hand them over. I can't stress that enough."

A series of nods confirmed the women understood, so turning to Ethan, Bailey moved on. She spread her legs shoulder width apart, one in front of the other. "Okay, if the attacker is getting physical or looks like he is about to, there are many ways to defend yourself to get the maximum benefit for your size and ability." Hesitantly, she waved Ethan closer. Next week, she would have to find a different attacker. "First of all, always shout, 'Back off!' It shows the attacker that you will not be a silent victim."

She took a step closer to Ethan, desperate to avoid the unusual expression in his dark eyes. Why was he looking at her as though he'd never seen her before? She forced herself to focus, but her train of thought was lost. "Um…where was I?" she asked herself as she stared at the floor.

"The weak spots," Ethan supplied.

Right. He was hers. End of story. And he didn't want her. "Yes, thank you. Always go for the weak points on the body first—the eyes..." Like those beautiful deep soulful ones staring at her.

She shook her head. *Get hold of yourself. These people are paying customers.* "The nose, ears, neck, groin and knee." Forcing her attention to remain on the class, Bailey demonstrated several moves to illustrate her point that attacking the most vulnerable points on the body could buy necessary time to escape. "Everyone got those?" she asked.

"Yes," the room chorused.

Great. Now on to the grab attacks. Where Ethan would have to touch her.

She paused, studying the man in front of her. Hesitated. No. Brookhollow was a safe place. No one was going to get grabbed from behind....

"Bailey, should I get in rear-attack position?" Ethan asked, looking as nervous as she felt.

Bailey swallowed hard, fighting every instinct in her body that was telling her to skip the technique. What if someone was attacked next week and she could have helped them by demonstrating the effective moves for a counter attack? She sighed as she said, "Yes."

Ethan moved into position directly behind

her. "I'm sorry about what happened," he whispered.

A shiver danced down her spine, but she ignored him. "So if your attacker comes at you from behind like this—" Her breath caught in her throat as Ethan's muscular arms wrapped around her chest and waist in a hold position.

Oh, this was not good. She was certain he could feel her heart pound against the palm of his big, strong hand placed against her chest. All thought of how to defend against the attack went right out the window. She didn't want to thrust his arms away from her body and elbow him in the face and stomp on his foot as she had in previous weeks. She just wanted to close her eyes, lean back into him and stay there.

"Bailey, I think it would be crazy for us to…you know…" he continued as her hands gripped his wrists. "I just don't want you to end up getting hurt…."

That was it. Bending and turning in one rapid motion, she flipped him over her shoulder. Ethan's body crashed against the mat below. Quickly Bailey moved away, freeing herself. Leaning down to look at his shocked expression, she asked above the chorus of applause from the class, "What were you saying about getting hurt?"

"Okay, so Ethan and Mark are team captains this week," Jim said, pointing to him and Mark and gesturing for them to take their respective positions on the football field behind the high school on Friday afternoon. Jim tossed the oblong ball from one hand to the other. "The game is tag football—no tackling, no illegal hits. I want a clean, fair game."

"Same rules every week, Jim," Ethan said, taking a quarter from the pocket of his loose-fitting sweatpants. "Call it," he said to Mark, tossing the coin into the air.

"Heads."

The coin landed in Ethan's left hand and he flipped it onto the back of his right one. "Heads it is."

Mark immediately pointed to Bailey. "I've got Bailey. We need to separate you two this week," he said by way of explanation for picking one of the only two women on the field.

Ethan's gaze met Bailey's and she shrugged. He couldn't blame Mark for the calculated move. He would have done the same thing. Together, he and Bailey were unstoppable. On the field, she anticipated his every move. If he threw her the ball, he could be confident she would catch it, even if it meant diving for it or snatching it out of the air away from another player. He was amazed that, at five nothing, she could hold her own against men twice and three times her size.

He couldn't help but compare her to Emily, who hated the mere thought of physical sports. She didn't like to run and hated to work up any kind of sweat, preferring to sit on the sidelines and watch, desperate to leave as soon as the game was over. Not Bailey. She'd often be the one insisting on a second game, her enthusiasm for the sport backed by her competitive nature.

"Okay, my first pick is Jim." Next to Bailey, Jim was his most compatible team member, having played side by side with Ethan since they were kids. Jim high-fived him.

"I'll take Derek," Mark said.

"Noah," Ethan said. The newest volunteer firefighter may not be the fastest, but what he lacked in speed, he made up for in intimidating size at six foot five and two hundred and fifty pounds. He'd recently moved to Brookhollow from Beach Haven to train at Extreme Athletics with Bailey's brothers, hoping to pursue a career in MMA. Bailey had introduced him to the group.

"Kyle," Mark said.

"D.J." The high school senior often played

with them for extra practice. Thanks to Ethan's coaching, he'd gotten accepted to Penn State University on a football scholarship. Ethan studied the remaining choices—Kayla Dawson and Mike Hayes. He wasn't sure which would hurt their team more—the young girl who avoided the ball at all costs or the man who didn't possess an athletic bone in his body but tried his hardest, usually getting in the way with his fumbling. Kayla only faked an interest in playing for Derek's sake, and Mike desperately wanted to fit in with the jocks at the high school and felt this would be a good way to learn how. Either way, it was Mark's choice.

Across the field, Mark whispered with his team, then nodded. "Mike, you're with us."

Great, Ethan thought. They were stuck with Kayla and no Bailey. Oh, well, they did have a star quarterback on their side. He waved Kayla toward them.

"Okay, bring it in," he said, wrapping his arms around Jim and Kayla's shoulders for a huddle to discuss strategy. "Mark is the biggest guy over there, so, Noah, I'm going to need you on him. Don't let him pass you."

"I'm on it," Noah said with a nod.

"Jim, you take Derek, and I'll cover Bailey." He stole a quick glance to the other team's huddle circle. Bailey's back was to him and his mouth went dry as he took in her tight yoga capris and blue mesh Dallas Cowboys jersey, her long hair tied in a braid hanging down her back beneath the New Jersey Devils baseball cap he'd given her for her birthday. He'd attempted to make amends and move on from their awkward situation by texting her throughout the day, but her responses had been brief or not at all. Clearly, she was still peeved. He wished he could make her see that he was holding back for her sake. The last thing he wanted was to use someone as amazing as Bailey for a rebound fling.

"What about me?" Kayla asked.

"Um…" Where could she do the least amount of damage? "I need you in the offensive zone. If the ball happens to come near you and it's not too much trouble, maybe just catch it, okay?"

"No promises," she said.

Wow. "Okay, well, just try to remember which team you're on this week and don't throw it to Derek."

"That was one time," Kayla said, rolling her eyes as the other team broke up their huddle with a cheer.

The captains flipped the coin for first ball and Ethan's team won the toss. Getting into position, he counted down and hiked the ball to Jim, who took off toward the offence zone in a hurry.

Mark approached as he passed the ten-yard point zone and tagged him, his team gaining control of the ball.

Ethan shot a glance toward Noah. "What was that?"

"Sorry, man. Unless I can knock him to the ground, I'm not really sure how to stop him from passing me," Noah said with a shrug.

Back in position, Ethan squared off against Bailey, who was bent and ready to hike the ball behind her to Mark. "Don't think I'm going to go easy on you," he said.

"I would be disappointed if you did." The look in her clear blue eyes told him she meant business, and he remembered how she'd dropped him to the floor the night before.

"And by the way," she said, "don't think I didn't notice you checking me out a few minutes ago. But you can just forget it—that offer the other night was a onetime thing."

Her words, issued from those perfectly shaped lips, made him lose focus, and as she hiked the ball and dashed toward their end zone, Ethan stumbled backward, off-balance. Mark tossed her the ball and she was able to gain twenty yards before Ethan could tag her. Tossing him the football, she flashed a wide smile. "Looks like someone is off his game today." Jogging toward Mark, she accepted his high five.

"No mercy on your former teammate. I love it." Mark shot a look toward Ethan.

Struggling to compose himself, Ethan said, "Yeah, she's brutal, all right." Removing his baseball cap, he ran a hand through his disheveled dark hair as he rejoined his team. He had to take control of his emotions. Bailey Sheppard was not an option. At all. Ever. And this game she was playing had to stop. Friends were not supposed to evoke these feelings of confusion and frustration he was experiencing this week. And what annoyed him most of all was the fact that he didn't know what bothered him most—Bailey kissing him or her refusing to do it again.

"What's with you?" Jim grumbled. "She's only a hundred pounds and she almost took you off your feet."

"Just a rough start. Don't worry—I've got this," Ethan said with determination as they began the next play.

But despite his best efforts, he couldn't pull it together. He fumbled and dropped the ball, missed easy passes and even accidentally threw the ball to Mike, who of course made the play of his life with an unexpected touchdown.

Jim called a timeout when Mark's team only needed another two points to win. "Ethan, we're down by six points. Kayla's even playing better than you. It's not in your nature to let them win, so what's going on?"

Ethan shook his head. He wished he knew. His eyes were glued to Bailey, yet his footing was off and he was unable to block her. "I don't know—off day I guess."

"Well, I hate to say it, but I think we're in trouble."

You're telling me.

CHAPTER SIX

EVERY WEEK AFTER their Friday afternoon football game, the players took turns hosting a barbecue at one of their homes. This week it was Jim's turn, and his girlfriend, Jill, took it as an opportunity for a board-game night.

"Okay, guys, the next game of the night is…drumroll please…" Jill glanced at Jim for the sound effect as she reached behind her seat toward the pile of games.

Ethan sat back in his chair and took a swallow of his beer, desperate to look anywhere, but across the table where Mark had his arm draped over the back of Bailey's chair. Could he get any closer to her? Bailey didn't seem to mind, though, and he wasn't sure which bothered him more. Mark was the town's biggest player—Bailey couldn't possibly be enjoying his attention. She'd barely glanced his way all evening and something felt off. Before the fire they'd been so close. He knew she was still upset with him because his inspection reports had had a negative impact on her claim, but he wasn't dumb enough not to recognize that the main source of her new frigidness had everything to do with the kiss they'd shared. She felt rejected by him. He understood how she could feel that way, but how did he make her understand that he was just trying to protect her from his own confused emotions?

"Taboo!" Jill announced.

"Great, how do we play?" Jim asked, reaching for a handful of veggie straws. He grimaced as he crunched the healthy alternative snack food.

Jill, a personal trainer at the local YMCA, refused to have junk food in the house, even when she played hostess. "We partner up, then we take turns describing a word or phrase on a drawn card to our partners without using the five additional words or phrases on the card. We set the timer and the team gets a point for each word or phrase they guess correctly," she explained.

"Okay, how should we do teams?" Jill's sister, Marla, asked, looking around the table.

"Boy-girl?" Jill suggested. "We're all kind of paired up where we sit."

"Sounds great to me. Ready to win, Bailey?" Mark asked, grinning from ear to ear as he leaned even closer to her.

Ethan's eyes narrowed as he watched the record-breaking heartbreaker. Why was he even still here? Ethan checked his watch. Eight o'clock. Normally, Mark would have ducked out by now, having prior commitments—usually a blonde with long legs, but never the same one two nights in a row. The other guys at the fire hall had bought him a calendar for his locker so he could keep track of his sometimes conflicting social calendar. It had been meant as a joke, but Mark actually used it. Ethan had never imagined Bailey's name would appear on it. But she was looking at Mark with unconcealed interest…less than a week after she'd confessed her feelings for him. Taking a swig of his beer, he looked away. What did he care? Hadn't he told her he wasn't an option?

"Okay, you two should start," Jill said, handing them the cards and positioning the timer in front of her. "I'll flip the timer once you're ready."

"Do you want to guess or give clues?" Bailey asked Mark, tossing her hair from her shoulder.

The amber highlights of the dark, thick

strands caught the glow of the dining room light and Ethan just stared. He'd never noticed the shimmering locks before, or how long and graceful her neck was.

"I'll guess," Mark answered, rotating his broad shoulders. "Game face on." He plastered a serious expression on his face.

Oh, come on, it was a board game. Had Mark always annoyed him this much? Rubbing his forehead, Ethan tried not to let the scene in front of him bother him, hating that it did. If he didn't have feelings for Bailey, why did the memory of her kiss haunt his every thought? They were friends, and friends were not supposed to evoke these insane feelings of jealousy in each other.

"Okay, ready, guys?" Jill asked.

"Let's do it," Mark said.

"Go!" Jill flipped the timer.

Bailey turned the first card. "Okay...um...a place I've always wanted to visit."

"New York" was Mark's guess.

New York? Seriously? She'd been there a dozen times. The answer was Venice. She talked about it all the time and had a calendar hung in the shop. Or at least she used to. She'd been planning a trip for the following year. He wondered if that would still be possible with the garage rebuild? Certainly, it would be a challenge if the insurance claim was denied.

"No…. Overseas…. I had a picture of it hanging on my wall at the shop…." Bailey prompted.

"Paris?"

Bailey shook her head. "Great food…."

"Greece."

"No…um…"

"Skip it, try another card," Jill suggested.

"You can do that?" Mark asked.

"Yeah, but hurry. Time is running out."

Bailey hurried to flip a different card. She cocked her head to the side. "You should know this one. The thing I forgot on the May long-weekend camping trip this year," she said quickly.

Her pillow.

"Your toothbrush?" Mark guessed.

"Um…no…Ethan loaned me his." Her voice was soft as she glanced in his direction. Their eyes met and held. In actuality, they'd *shared* his. An image of the early-summer camping trip forced its way into his mind and he remembered how comfortable it had been to lie there in her tent, listening to the calming sounds of the river and the wind blowing through the trees. Then she'd fallen asleep and her head had slipped from the pillow onto his chest. At the time, his mind had been so preoccupied with thoughts of Emily, he hadn't noticed the intimacy of the situation or how nice it was to be close to her, but now...

"Ethan loaned you his toothbrush?" Mark glanced between the two.

"No..."

"Time!" Jill yelled, a little too emphatically, startling everyone.

"Honey, it's just a game," Jim reminded her, placing a hand on hers.

"Sorry, right, got carried away," Jill said. "Okay, Ethan and Marla, you're up."

Ethan drained the contents of his beer and reached for the cards. "Guessing or giving clues?"

"I'll guess," Marla said.

"Okay, ready." Ethan told Jill. As she flipped the timer, he turned the first card. North Pole. That was an easy one. "Santa Claus."

"Elves," Marla guessed.

Ethan shook his head. "Desolate."

"North Pole!" Marla almost jumped from her chair. The excitement over board games ran in the Vanderwolf family.

"Yeah, good." He flipped the next card. Red Bull. "Bailey's favorite drink."

Marla shot him a quizzical look. "How am I supposed to know that?" She turned to Bailey, "No offense."

Bailey's cheeks flushed as she shrugged.

Where had that clue come from? Of course Marla wouldn't have known. "Sorry, um… You shouldn't drink it at night…."

"Coffee," Marla said.

"Time!"

Ethan shrugged. "Well, at least we got one."

Jim and Jill followed, and by the end of the game, Bailey and Mark had yet to guess even one card right. Ethan and Marla trailed behind the host team by two.

"Another game?" Jill asked, looking hopeful.

Ethan suppressed a laugh, amazed at how much Jill enjoyed board games and how much Jim did not.

"Actually, Jill, I think I'm going to sit this one out," Jim said, checking his watch. "The football game is on."

"I'll join you," Mark said as he stood.

He was sticking around? Something was up, and Ethan wasn't sure he liked it.

JENNIFER SNOW   149

Jill turned to Ethan and Bailey. "And I bet you two are just dying to take off into the living room, as well," she said knowingly.

"Would you mind? Dallas is playing," Bailey jumped up from her chair and disappeared into the kitchen with her wineglass.

"Go," Jill said, folding her arms in mock annoyance. "You all suck. Next time, there may not be any board games." The words were meant as a threat.

"You shouldn't make promises like that. You'll get Jim's hopes up," Ethan teased, kissing the top of his future sister-in-law's head as he passed her on his way to the kitchen with his empty beer bottle.

He tossed the bottle into the blue recycle bin near the door. At the counter, Bailey was pouring sangria into her glass. Coming to stand behind her, he rested one hand on either side of her. "It was your pillow," he whispered.

"Don't you just know everything?" Bailey's voice trembled slightly as she turned within his arms and stared defiantly into his eyes.

He noticed how her hand shook on her glass. "Not everything," he said, lowering his gaze, then slowly glancing up to meet her eyes once more. "What I don't know is why I'm suddenly remembering that night under the stars a whole lot differently."

THE NEXT DAY at the shop, Bailey sorted through the service area, collecting salvageable parts and supplies in a box. The cleanup crew had done a remarkable job removing the rubble, and the interior wall rebuild had begun.

"Hello," she heard a familiar male voice say from the front of the shop.

Setting the box aside and wiping her hands on the legs of her coveralls, she headed toward the front. Dwayne Adams, Mark's brother, stood near the remaining counter, studying the damage inside. "Hi, Dwayne."

"Wow, I can't believe this place...." He shook his head.

"Tell me about it. I watched it burn down and I still can't believe it."

"You know what people around town are saying, don't you?"

Bailey sighed. "Which version did you hear? That I purposely set it on fire when I came back here to lock up? Or that the Jetta was a setup? Or that I paid Nick to do it, knowing his inexperience would make it look more accidental?"

Dwayne laughed. "Sorry, it's not funny what people are coming up with, it's just hilarious that anyone could actually believe it." He stepped forward and wrapped her in a hug. "Anyway, talk will die down. Have you heard from the insurance adjuster yet?" he asked, bending to pick up several bottles of gear oil and put them on the exposed window ledge.

"Not yet…soon."

"Great because I'm going to need you back up and running…and fast," he said, gesturing outside. "*She* is going to need work."

Bailey shielded her eyes from the glare of the sunlight as she glanced toward the parking lot. A cherry-red and lime-green stock car sat parked on the gravel. "You're racing?"

"Yeah. Always wanted to try, so I thought why not? It's late in the season, but a guy in Newark was selling her for next to nothing, so I couldn't resist." He shrugged, leading the way outside.

"She's beautiful," Bailey said, touching the car.

"That she is. I just put a new engine in…."

"What kind?" She was genuinely curious

and a little annoyed that he hadn't brought it to her to install. Specialty, souped-up engines were something she didn't get to work on often.

"A Chevy 396 Stage 3 Race Engine."

"Impressive."

"Thanks. I'm hoping to win the modifier challenge tonight in Bridgeport. And that's why I'm here."

"Oh?"

"Yeah. If I have any chance of winning, I need you on my pit crew."

LATER THAT EVENING, Bailey climbed the concrete stairs in the covered grandstand of the dirt racetrack to get a better view of the course. If she was going to help Dwayne, she needed to know the conditions of the track—which areas to avoid and which turns were the most challenging. The layout had changed a lot since the last time she'd attended with her dad and brothers years before. The five-eighths mile, high-banked, dirt oval track was bordered by sponsor signage, and the two-tiered guardrail along the outside had been upgraded for the safety of the viewers as well as the drivers. The roomy corners, wide enough to take three or four cars, were also reinforced with concrete walls for additional safety. The premier division cars, the modifiers, often raced at speeds of up to a hundred miles per hour.

Bailey turned as Dwayne and his brother, Mark, approached. Dressed in racing coveralls plastered with sponsorship logos, Dwayne looked like a professional racer already.

"Hey, Bailey. Thanks for coming," he greeted, taking a seat on the other side of her.

"Great thinking, man," Mark said, "bringing the best mechanic we know. I doubt anyone on the pit crew can throw on a new tire faster than Bailey."

"It took very little convincing," Bailey said.

"Come on." Dwayne waved a hand to motion them up. "Let's go take a final look at her before the races start."

Bailey followed them to the pit where the colorful Chevy Impala, covered in logos from Joey's Diner to Play Hard Sports, was awaiting inspection from the race officials. Hood up, it displayed the souped-up engine proudly.

Bailey approached and gingerly touched the frame of the refabricated vehicle. "Looks great." She bent beneath the hood to examine the engine. "This thing is going to fly down the track."

"It better." Dwayne laughed. "I'm going to need to win an awful lot of races to pay for it."

"Well, I've sized up the track and the only thing I'd recommend is watching your back right tire along the third corner if you're driving on the inside—it's sharper than the rest," she cautioned.

"Great, thanks. I appreciate the advice."

"I'm going to go grab a bottle of water. Want anything?" she asked as she exited the pit.

"Nah, I'm too nervous."

Rounding the corner near the concession stand, she saw Ethan walking toward her.

"Dwayne put you to work?" he asked.

What was he doing here? "May as well be doing something. With the garage shut down, I'm not sure what to do with myself," she said, feeling her cheeks warm under his intense gaze as his eyes traveled the length of her body. Suddenly her shorts seemed a little too short and her tank top a little too tight.

He moved closer to her and, lowering his voice, said, "You know, I've been thinking about that kiss...."

Good. That was the point. "Look, Ethan... you were right. You and I would be a terrible idea." *Call my bluff, please.*

"But, I…"

Swallowing hard, she had to call on all her strength to push on. "No buts. You're still hung up on Emily and I'm not prepared to get involved with that." The lie rolled much more easily off her tongue than she'd expected. She was so ready to get involved with repairing the damage to his heart…but first she had to know he wanted her to.

He raised his chin. "Actually, Bailey, this is the first day since she left that I haven't thought about Emily—until now."

Pushing up on her tiptoes, she fought to calm her quickened pulse as she let her hands graze his muscular arms, arms she longed to be in. She kissed his cheek with the quickest of pecks and said, "Yeah? Well, let me know when you don't think about her all day *and* you don't realize you haven't."

"I STILL CAN'T believe they put her to work," Jim said from his seat next to Ethan in the stands.

Bailey was in the pit crew several yards away, a new tire at her feet as she unscrewed the back right one on Dwayne's car.

"She's the only reason Dwayne has a shot at winning this race." Already Bailey had changed the left tire and had fiddled under the hood of the old stock car.

"Look how fast she got that new tire on the rim," Jim said, glancing at his watch. "What was that? Thirty seconds?"

"Not even." A small smile played on Ethan's lips as he watched her stand and wipe her dirty hands across her forehead, leaving a streak of dirt. She could be covered in dirt and still be beautiful, he realized, and the thought unnerved him. Could there be more between them than friendship? The kiss had certainly held passion...but love? He wasn't sure if he could or would take a chance on that again...at least not for a very long time.

Jim turned to Jill. "Why can't you change a tire that quick?"

Jill glanced up from her iPhone, where she was reading a fitness article, obviously unimpressed with the races. "I think the correct wording is *at all*. I don't need to know how. That's what I have you for." She raised an eyebrow. "I could learn, but that would make you obsolete."

Jim wrapped an arm around her. "Oh, come on. I must be good for a few other things...."

Jill pretended to think. "Well, I guess you are handy when it comes to opening jars or reaching things on high shelves."

"So squeeze bottles and a step stool could eliminate the need for you," Ethan chimed in, happy that the teasing was turned on his brother for a change.

"Remember you said that," Jim told Jill grumpily.

She placed a kiss on his unshaven cheek, snuggling closer to him as the race started again.

Ethan watched the playful interaction. He wanted that. The bond his brother shared with his girlfriend, the understanding they had with one another and the commitment they shared. At one time, he'd had that with Emily. Would he ever find it again? His gaze locked on Bailey, and unable to resist, he reached into his pocket and took out his cell phone. *Impressive, baby girl,* he texted.

He watched as Bailey retrieved her phone from her tight jean shorts' pocket and read. Turning in the pit, she met his eyes, her face lighting up in a wide smile as she shrugged and waved.

Oh, man, she's perfect, Ethan realized. Things just got more complicated.

CHAPTER SEVEN

"I CAN'T BELIEVE you actually agreed to participate in this event," Bailey's aunt Jeanette said as she scanned the list of challenges in the local Fire Fit Challenge competition on Sunday afternoon.

Brookhollow was home to one of the best fire training academies in the U.S., with an emergency training center for hands-on practical instruction as well as teambuilding skills. The focal point of the center was the seven-story fire tower, a big reinforced concrete structure with mock windows and doors, an elevator prop on a fixed platform and a six-story rescue wall with multiple anchor points.

This year the fire department had decided to hold their annual fund-raiser at the training center, giving the community members a more intimate look at the challenges firefighters faced on a daily basis by holding a competition for civilians. Each firefighter had teamed up with a willing community member to compete the timed obstacle course. Earlier that summer, Bailey had agreed to compete with Ethan, and despite the game of cat and mouse they appeared to be playing lately, she was determined to see the challenge through.

She stretched her legs on the red-and-white checked blanket in the shade of an oak tree and pushed her sunglasses up onto her head, checking her arms and legs for any sign of a sunburn. She reached for the sunblock in her backpack. The blazing August rays shining through the thin cloud cover couldn't be trusted.

"Yeah, well, the money it raises each year for the fire hall is certainly needed. Besides, I think it will be a lot of fun."

"I heard the guys had a hard time recruiting civilian volunteers," her uncle Doug said, opening one eye. He'd fallen asleep the moment they'd arrived and his forehead showed a distinct white band where his arm had rested over his now-red face. "Bailey's braver than most, especially after witnessing that fire at the garage last week."

"Actually, Uncle Doug, after seeing the guys in action that night and the potential danger they faced, I'm even more determined to get through this course. They were amazing." She glanced across the field to where Ethan stood near a parked fire truck, lifting young children inside to take a closer look. Among so many other qualities, she admired his love of children. She knew he enjoyed spending time with his nephews and coaching the local sports teams. He'd make a wonderful father someday.

"Any word from the insurance adjuster?" Doug asked.

"No." It had been less than a week since she'd submitted the claim, and the insurance adjuster had said it could take a while. She tried not to worry about it, but she was desperate to receive an answer soon.

"Well, I admire you for going ahead with the rebuild," her aunt said. "We drove past the shop on the way here today and it looks so much better already."

Bailey nodded. The cleanup crew had done an amazing job in no time at all, and Luke's construction crews had been working nonstop, rebuilding the external structure of the garage. The main exterior walls were up, and two of the three bay doors had been operable when she'd checked on the progress herself that morning. The sprinkler installer was scheduled for the following day, though she still worried about that additional cost. "It's going to look great. Luke's crews are fantastic."

"Do you want to tell her or will I?" Jeanette nudged Doug.

"Go ahead," he said.

"Tell me what?"

"We're paying for the sprinkler installation."

"What? No, I can't let you two do that." It was a nice gesture, but her uncle had sold her the garage last month. He was free and clear of any responsibility. This was her concern now.

"It's not open for debate," her uncle said. "In fact, it's already paid for. We spoke to Automatic Sprinklers this morning."

"But…"

"Bailey, I should never have sold you that place not up to code. Consider it part of the purchase price."

There was no point arguing, so she accepted the gift of peace of mind with a hug. "Thank you."

ETHAN STOOD IN the center of the kiddie water park they'd set up on the training grounds for the family events, enjoying the cool, refreshing spray in the humid heat. His firefighter gear lay on the ground a few feet away and he cringed at the idea of putting it on. In the distance he saw Bailey sitting with her family under the shade of a big oak tree.

He was going out of his mind thinking about her. And it made no sense at all. They'd been friends since grade school, growing up in Brookhollow together. They'd always been close, but could there be more to their relationship than friendship? With Emily, his attraction had been immediate, strong…maybe immature and undeveloped? After all, he hadn't really known her well when they'd gotten together before prom. Bailey, on the other hand… He knew her stubborn, independent nature, her love of sports, her connection to her hometown and her desire for a family one day. And he loved everything about her.

The kiss had shown him yet another side of Bailey. Her passion and attraction to him had caught him completely off guard. How could he not have seen it coming? How could she never have said anything? Well, the message in that kiss was perfectly clear. Maybe it was time to take a closer look at his best friend.

AN HOUR LATER, Bailey struggled to run under the weight of the firefighter gear as she dashed around the plastic hydrants, placed two feet apart on the course. Ethan was ahead of her by several feet and she was desperate not to slow him down. Being the only female competitor made her even more determined to get through the training course with a good time.

At the end of the hydrants, a one-hundred-and-fifteen-pound "Rescue Randy" dummy, plus coveralls and boots, lay waiting to be dragged backward a distance of a hundred feet. She glanced at the large clock on the tower. They were making good time, both having cleared the hydrants in less than forty-five seconds. She grabbed the dummy under the arms and lifted. Groaned aloud. This thing weighed almost as much as she did. She marveled how in the event of a real emergency, the guys were expected to carry someone twice this size to safety. She struggled to drag the limp, lifeless dummy, her legs heavy, her pace slow. This for sure would cost them a bit of time on the scoreboard.

"Come on, Bailey, you've got this," Ethan called from the end of that challenge. He waited until she'd dropped "Randy" on the other side of the one-hundred-foot line and smiled. "Great job," he said, leading the way to the water hose event.

Unable to catch her breath to speak, she just nodded. Panting, she joined him at the hoses and the two set off, dragging the long, heavy equipment toward the target seventy-five feet away. The training bull's-eye was ablaze with a small, contained fire, and despite the distance, the heat made her cheeks flush. It was so intense, and this display was on a much smaller scale compared to what the fire crews faced in a real emergency. She couldn't imagine how hot it would be in a building filled with flames and smoke.

Naturally, Ethan got there first and sprayed his hose, hitting the bull's-eye with expertise.

Only seconds behind, she fumbled with the angle of the water spray, finally landing it in the center of the target, eliminating the flames and raising the flag. All clear. Following Ethan across the field, Bailey stopped just short of the open hole in the grassy field. She watched Ethan climb down the hole, then turn around and start his descent on the metal rungs attached to the concrete walls of the vertical tunnel.

"Where are we going?"

He paused and looked up at her. "To the underground tunnel. This is the confined-space part of the challenge."

"Confined space?" She hadn't signed on for that. A wave of terror rose up in her and she turned toward the crowd of spectators behind the safety fence watching and cheering them on. Fire she could handle, feeling safe in the flame-retardant suit and helmet, but enclosed dark spaces were a different story.

"Yes. It's nothing. Ten feet at most, then up the other side," Ethan said. "Come on. You go first." He climbed back up the ladder.

Bailey shook her head quickly. "No freaking way. I'll follow you," she said with a sigh, forcing her heart rate to slow. Ten feet underground, in a dark tunnel no problem. She could do this. *Think of it as being under a car in the bay at the shop.*

Hardly the same thing.

"Ready?" Ethan asked, halfway down the ladder again.

"Not really," Bailey mumbled, but she turned backward and descended the eight or so metal rungs into the hole.

The space grew darker the lower she went,

but as she reached the bottom, a bright beam of light lit up the passageway in front of her.

"Click the button on your helmet," Ethan said.

Turning on the flashlight, she was relieved to see that the corridor wasn't as small as she'd expected. Bending low, she followed Ethan through the concrete structure, stepping over the dummy props they used in their regular rescue training. Thankfully she didn't have to get one of them out of this trench. Again, she marveled at the courage and strength of the local firefighters. She could never perform these challenges for real. This training course taught them the skills they needed in an emergency situation, but it took a special person to be able to risk their own life for others. Reaching the other end, she climbed the ladder through the exit hole after Ethan.

At the top, he turned and reached for her hand, helping her up the last rung. The large crowd cheered as they resurfaced. "That was great. You're amazing."

"I was just thinking the same thing about you," Bailey said.

TAKING BAILEY'S HAND, Ethan led the way to their final challenge. He was impressed.

Actually, impressed was an understatement. While she'd been hesitant at first, Bailey had conquered that confined-space area like a pro. In his training, he'd seen many firefighters freeze in fear in the four-foot-high and three-foot-wide tunnel. It was one of the primary reasons for the training—anxiety in an emergency situation could only lead to disaster.

Bailey had sailed through it effortlessly. But as they approached the fire tower, he glanced back at her, unsure how she would react to the seven-story concrete building. He'd never known her to be afraid of heights, but there was always the possibility once she looked down with only a harness and rappel cable. Pausing at the base of the ladder, he was relieved to see her smiling as she approached.

"What are you waiting for? Let's go. We're making great time." She moved ahead of him to climb the ladder first.

Shaking his head, he followed. How could he not be attracted to her? Courage was definitely an appealing feature in a woman and Bailey had plenty of it. At the top of the wall, he reached for their harnesses. Tugging on them to make sure they were secured, he motioned her closer.

"Step through the holes," he said.

She did and he fastened the waist belt tightly. "How does that feel? Any pain or discomfort in your legs or groin?"

"No, I'm fine. Hurry," she urged.

Ethan slipped into his own harness and turned to her. "Ready?"

"Yes, let's go," she said, stepping back onto the edge of the wall and lowering her body over the side.

The woman was amazing. Approaching the edge himself, Ethan felt his head swim, and his vision blurred. He was thrown slightly off-balance as he peered down. His chest tightened and his palms sweat. Moving away from the ledge, he forced a breath. What was that?

"What are you doing?" Bailey called up. "Let's go. I can't cross the finish line without you." She lowered herself another few inches. All that remained visible over the wall was her head and shoulders.

"I don't know. I don't feel great," Ethan said, approaching the edge again. His knees buckled as he drew closer to the drop off and his stomach lurched. Fear kept his feet frozen to the spot. How was this possible? He'd done this course before. Once at nineteen.... Though he'd never been this high since.

"Are you okay? You look really pale." A frown formed on Bailey's forehead beneath her helmet as she studied him with concern.

"I'm not sure I can do this," he admitted.

"What do you mean?"

"Every time I get close to the edge, I feel like I'm going to pass out." This was embarrassing. A firefighter afraid of heights? Come on.

"You're afraid of heights?" Bailey asked in disbelief. "But you've done this before in training."

"Only once, and a long time ago." The size of their fire hall and the types of calls they answered really didn't require an annual refresher on the course. While he often trained new recruits, he hadn't been up here himself for quite a long time. "I can't breathe."

"Close your eyes and I'll guide you to the edge."

Closing his eyes and approaching a drop-off didn't sound like the best idea he'd ever heard. "Are you crazy?"

"Trust me, if you can't see the height, you can't be afraid of it. I'll wait here for you and we'll go together."

"Okay." Ethan closed his eyes, terror making his arms numb as he tightened his fingers on the rope.

"Great, now sit back slowly," Bailey said.

Sitting back, he immediately shuffled his feet to secure them to the side of the wall.

"That's great," she encouraged. "The hardest part is over. Open your eyes and let go of the rope little by little."

Relieved to see she hadn't moved even an inch lower, keeping her promise to wait for him. Ethan let out a little of the rope. The sudden jolt and speed of the short descent made his pulse race. There was no way he could do this. Gripping the rope, terrified, he moved his body closer to the wall, looking for security. Instead, his feet lost contact and he was dangling by the harness.

"Oh, no."

"Don't panic. The harness has you secured," Bailey said, swinging closer to him.

"I'm terrified." Frozen in fear, he couldn't move. How was this happening? He couldn't be afraid of heights. His job depended on him being able to do this.

"Ooh," Bailey said, a note of anxiety in her own voice.

Ethan opened his eyes and turned to look down at her. "What? Are you okay?"

"Not really. I'm starting to lose circulation in my legs.... I don't think that's a good thing."

Ethan swallowed hard. Great, she couldn't hang there long without circulation in her legs. He had to pull it together and reach the bottom of the wall. "It's getting worse," she said, a note of desperation in her voice. "Ethan, I need your help."

Releasing the rope quickly, he fell a full story, springing back toward the wall next to her. Swinging his body as close to her as he could, he reached for the harness, but her rope let out and she dropped several feet. He dropped lower...so did she.

"Bailey, quit moving so I can check your harness," he said. What was she doing?

Looking up toward him, she released the rope once more, dangling just inches from the ground. Shooting downward to meet her, he cocked his head to the side. "You think that was funny." She'd tricked him.

"It worked," she said. "I knew once you thought someone else was in danger, you'd forget your own fear." Her voice softened. "That's what makes you so good at what you do."

Reaching across to touch her cheek beneath her helmet, he said, "What if it was just because it was you?" He moved closer and un-latched her helmet, dropping it to the ground, then raised his hand to brush the windblown, messy strands of dark hair from her flushed cheeks.

"What are you doing?" She backed away a step, but grabbing her harness belt, he pulled her to him, closer this time until their bodies met. "Ethan, seriously, everyone in town's staring at us." Nervously, she glanced toward the crowd of people lining the field.

"Good. Maybe this way you'll have to kiss me. You don't want people thinking you're an arsonist *and* a heartbreaker, do you?"

"Ethan…"

His lips landed on hers, muffling her protests, and he wrapped his arms around her as he deepened the kiss, just barely aware of the applause and cheers from the spectators.

AN HOUR LATER, after waiting to hear the final announcement that Mark and his cousin Ed had won the challenge and were awarded the Fire Fit trophy, Ethan pulled into Luke's driveway. The old home had belonged to the Kingston family until Mrs. Kingston sold the house to Luke a couple of years before when she decided to move into the senior's complex in town.

Grabbing the new building-code paperwork from the passenger seat, Ethan jumped down from the Jeep and jogged through the unexpected sun shower toward the front door. Knocking, he heard Madi, Luke's husky, barking on the other side.

Finally, as he was about to turn away, the door swung open.

"Ethan, hi," Victoria said.

Ethan took in the disheveled bride-to-be, her blond, wavy hair coming free from her ponytail. White flour dusted her cheeks and forehead and she was wearing an apron. "What are you doing, Vic?"

"Honestly, I wish I knew.... Come on inside." She moved aside to let him in.

The smell of burning baked goods and the haze of a light smoke drifted into the large, open foyer of the magnificent old home. He coughed. "Do you have something in the oven?"

Her eyes widened. "Shoot, I did it again." She took off in a rush toward the kitchen.

He followed, scanning the house for a fire extinguisher just in case. He spotted one in the kitchen as she opened the oven door and a blast of smoke poured out. Within seconds the smoke detector sounded and he rushed to it, standing on the edge of a chair in the hallway to hit the reset button. Then, rushing back into the kitchen, he opened the kitchen door and window.

"Thanks," Victoria said grimly as she tossed the tray of charcoal cookies onto the stove. "I don't know what I keep doing wrong. I'm not leaving them in any longer than the recipe calls for." She glanced at the premade cookie-dough wrapper and frowned.

"Um, that's not a recipe, that's baking directions."

"What's the difference?"

"Not a thing." Homemade was overrated anyway. He glanced at the oven. "Do you have it turned to the convection setting?" he asked.

Victoria looked confused. "English, please."

He approached the oven and studied the dials. "See here—regular oven and convection. You have it set to convection."

"Yeah, but I still have no idea what that means." Victoria placed her hands on her hips and studied the oven dials.

"Convection distributes the heat evenly, so you can usually reduce your baking time by twenty-five percent," Ethan explained.

"How is it that you know that and I don't?" Victoria sounded annoyed as she scraped the round chunks of hardened dough into the trash can under the sink.

"My mom had two boys and Melody, who was always too busy with her music to bake. Between Jim and me, I drew the shorter straw I guess and got stuck baking with her on Sundays." He shrugged. He'd actually liked learning to bake as a kid, not that he'd ever admit it out loud.

"Oh," she said, taking another tray from the oven drawer and placing lumps of the cookie dough on the sheet.

"Um, Vic. Shouldn't you grease the pan first?"

She looked confused. "Huh?"

"Here, I'll show you." He opened the fridge door and took out a container of margarine. "Plastic baggies?"

She pointed to the second drawer near the fridge and folded her arms, watching him.

He slid his hand into the baggie and scooped out a lump of margarine, smearing it across

the pan and into the four corners. "Like this.
It keeps the cookies from sticking."

"Oh," she said, handing him the cookie
dough and allowing him to spoon it onto the
pan and slide it into the oven. He set the timer
for eight minutes. "I didn't even know that
feature existed."

"Can I ask why you're baking?" Victoria Mason was about as far from being "do-
mestic" as one could get. A career-minded
businesswoman, she'd busied herself with
turning the Brookhollow Inn into a place
tourists would be happy to stay, but he knew
the food preparation for the Inn was taken
care of by Ginger Snaps on Main Street, with
fresh baked goods delivered daily at 6:00 a.m.

"Luke loves his cookies, muffins and
cakes." Victoria looked really distraught.

"Victoria, you and Luke have known each
other for years. He knows you can't bake. He
doesn't expect you to. He loves you despite
your inability to boil water," Ethan teased.

"I'm not that bad…."

Ethan struggled to look serious. "He told
me about the hot dogs."

"He did what?" she asked, mortified.

"He thought it was the cutest thing ever,"
Ethan reassured her. "And trust me, he doesn't

expect you to change just because you're getting married."

Victoria slumped into a kitchen chair. "I hope not…." she said as her cell phone rang on the table next to her. She silenced the call.

"If you have to answer that…"

She shook her head. "No way. It's Mrs. Dawson. She's making the wedding cake this weekend and she's calling to see if I've decided on a topper yet."

"Have you?" It seemed like a reasonable question to ask, but Victoria narrowed her eyes.

"No, I haven't."

Ethan cringed, taking a step back. "Sorry, none of my business."

Victoria's shoulders relaxed and she shook her head. "No, I'm sorry. You know, before, in New York, my friend Heather and I would watch those crazy wedding reality shows and make fun of the stressed-out brides and their lavish wedding plans, but I'm telling you, karma is kicking my butt right now. I'd totally forgotten since the last time we did this how stressful planning a wedding can be. I'm seriously turning into one of those bridezillas." She rubbed her forehead as the home phone rang.

"Should you get that?" Ethan asked.

"Probably," Victoria answered, letting it ring.

"Are you going to?"

"Nope. Anyway, you must have stopped by for something other than putting my fire out...unless your training gives you a sixth sense about when a house is about to burn down?"

"There was something, actually." He handed her the fire safety codes for the new garage. "I stopped by to give these to Luke for Bailey's garage."

Victoria scanned the paperwork. "A new sprinkler system, ventilation system.... Not taking any chances, huh?"

Actually, he was about to take the biggest chance of all where Bailey was concerned. "Nope," he said instead, answering her question.

The oven chimed and she scanned the kitchen. "What was that?"

"The timer. The cookies are done," Ethan said, grabbing the oven mitts. "I may as well just finish the job, huh?" he teased, taking out the perfectly golden chocolate-chip cookies.

"They...they actually look edible." Victoria eyed the cookies in shock. "I did it...."

"Well…"

"Shh, I'm totally taking credit for these," Victoria said with a laugh.

CHAPTER EIGHT

BAILEY RUSHED INTO Klip and Dye, the hair salon on Main Street, several hours after the competition. She'd been neglecting her highlights and if she was posing for wedding photos in a few weeks, they needed to be done. Admittedly, she had been tempted to skip the appointment or reschedule, reluctant to leave Ethan after their passionate, public display on the field. A wide smile crept across her face. He hadn't wanted to rush off either, but he'd been satisfied with her promise to go out with him that evening. Where he was taking her, he was keeping to himself. A surprise date... with Ethan. If she was dreaming, she'd kill the person who woke her.

"Hi, Alice, I'm here for my appointment with Amanda."

Alice had owned the salon for as long as Bailey could remember, but she'd retired from doing hair the year before, claiming the arthritis in her hands couldn't be trusted not to give someone a mullet. She nodded as she consulted the computer screen and glanced at the clock. "Sure. She's just running a few minutes late with Lindsay, but have a seat. I'll let her know you are here."

She hobbled into the back cutting area, divided by sliding doors to keep the salon private from the main retail and waiting area. With a big window looking out on one of the busiest streets in Brookhollow, Alice claimed her clients didn't want the town to see them with silver foils in their hair.

Bailey sat and sighed. Lindsay Harper was here. She'd noticed her on the field earlier that day and she suspected the other woman wouldn't be leaving the salon without gathering more information to spread throughout town. Lindsay was one of the best nurses on staff at the medical center, but she was also the town expert at making sure gossip spread as quickly as possible, and she prided herself on being the source.

Bailey's cell phone chimed with Ethan's familiar tone and all thoughts of Lindsay vanished. Can't wait to see you tonight. Hugging the phone to her chest, she enjoyed the wave of euphoria. Finally, after all this time loving him and wanting to be with him, did she dare hope it was finally happening?

"Bailey!" Lindsay's high-pitched squeal shattered her fantastic thoughts.

"Hi, Lindsay," Bailey said, tucking her phone into her denim purse. "Your hair looks great."

Lindsay wouldn't be put off course. "So what does it mean?"

"What does what mean?" Stalling for time was probably a futile effort, but she did it anyway.

"That kiss with Ethan!"

Bailey cringed as Lindsay's voice rang through the shop, capturing the attention of several women Bailey recognized from the bank on the corner. Intrigue flashed in their eyes before they turned their attention back to their product selection. Bailey suspected they were keeping an ear tuned to the conversation, so she said, "Oh, you know Ethan, always goofing around." She hoped the lie sounded nonchalant.

Lindsay raised one perfectly shaped eyebrow. "Goofing around? Bailey, I dream of a kiss like that. If that was goofing around… Hmm." Her face took on a look of contemplation and she was silent—a true rarity—for a long moment.

"Lindsay? You still with me?"

"Yeah, I was just thinking maybe I should make a play for him."

"No!"

Lindsay grinned and Bailey realized she'd been set up.

"Just goofing around, huh?"

Her heart bursting at the seams with happiness, Bailey didn't care if Lindsay told everyone in Brookhollow about them. After all, Ethan hadn't been concerned when he'd kissed her.

"Fine. I'm in love with him," she said, her first time admitting it to anyone but Ethan. Who would believe she'd be telling Lindsay Harper?

Her cell phone rang in her purse, the generic ringtone, not the specific ones she'd assigned to family and friends. She thought about not answering as Amanda walked through the doors with a wave, but on the third ring, she unzipped her purse and answered the private number.

"Hello."

"Bailey Sheppard?" a man's voice asked.

"Yes."

"This is insurance adjuster Phillips."

Her mouth went dry. *Please have good news.* "Hi, Mr. Phillips, I hadn't expected your call so soon or on a Sunday." Was a fast response from the company a good thing or a bad thing?

"Yeah, well, I didn't want to keep you waiting any longer," he said, then paused.

Bailey listened to silence. *Well, come on then—don't make me wait any longer.*

Lindsay shot her a questioning look and she shrugged in response. "Insurance adjuster," she mouthed. Lindsay crossed her fingers. She really wasn't as bad as everyone thought.

"Mr. Phillips?"

"Yes, sorry…. Didn't mean to be dramatic. A coworker just caught my attention for a second. We had a lot of claims lately, so we are working the weekend to catch up…." He cleared his throat loudly. "So I have good news."

Oh, thank God.

"Your claim went through."

"Thank you, Mr. Phillips. That's great news."

"We will need to get some paperwork signed…. Can you meet at the garage tomorrow morning?"

"Yes. Um…can I ask, after all the questionable circumstances, why was the claim approved?"

"Actually, believe it or not, it had a lot to do with the letters I received from the residents over there in Brookhollow."

"Letters?"

Lindsay's smile was wide.

"You didn't know? I must have received fifteen letters from different people, sent in an email from a Lindsay Harper? All validated your character. I mean, it wasn't the deciding factor by any means, but it didn't hurt. You've got some great friends, Ms. Sheppard. See you tomorrow."

Bailey remained speechless as she disconnected the call. Lindsay had organized that support? Standing, she wrapped the other woman in a tight hug. "Thank you."

Lindsay struggled. "Don't ruin my hair."

ETHAN TURNED BAILEY'S motorcycle onto the gravel driveway, leaving the small freeway that ran through the center of town. She'd insisted on taking her motorcycle and he'd insisted on driving to keep the surprise of their location a little longer. Bailey had no problem sitting behind him, arms wrapped tightly around his waist. He could drive anytime. The Theatre under the Stars sign blinked as they drove past the rusting marquee announcing that evening's movie lineup.

Ah, the drive-in. Perfect, she loved this place. Two movies for three dollars and fifty cents. Couldn't beat that price. Brookhollow was full of hidden gems like this old drive-in, but few people took advantage of the low-cost, nostalgic entertainment often enough.

"Bailey, Ethan, hi!" Ginger Norris's granddaughter, Leigh, smiled as she pushed back the window at the ticket booth. Leigh had just opened a day care next door to the Brookhollow Inn, but she was a committed movie lover and still worked the entrance booth at the drive-in on weekends.

"Hi, Leigh," Bailey said, reaching into her pocket.

Ethan pushed her cash aside and handed Leigh his money instead. "It may have been a while since I was on a date, but I'm pretty sure beautiful women don't pay for anything."

Bailey blushed at the compliment and Leigh said, "You guys know the rules—lights off, no honking the horn except during the intermission cartoons, concession stand is open before the movie and during intermission only. And tune your portable radio to 88.6 FM."

"Got it, thanks, Leigh," Bailey said, as they continued through the gate onto the large, grassy field where cars were already lined up in front of the large screen.

Removing his helmet, Ethan turned to face her. "Do you want to park closer to the screen or farther back?"

"Back on the hill might be best."

Driving slowly, he parked the bike on the hill as she'd suggested. Multicolored outbuildings bordered the field behind them, and the concession stand was to their right. Families, teenagers and older couples formed a long line to buy popcorn, hot dogs and sodas. The smell of the warm buttered popcorn made Bailey's stomach growl.

"Why don't you lay out the blanket and tune the radio while I grab some snacks?" Ethan said.

"Would it do any good to argue?"

"Nope."

"Fine. Just a hot dog with—"

"Mustard and a diet soda. Yeah, I got it."

"Wow, am I that predictable?" Bailey asked with a laugh. He knew her too well.

"You're not. Just your food choices," he

said, walking backward down the hill toward the concession stand.

Bailey opened his backpack and tossed the blanket onto the ground. After tuning the small portable radio to the appropriate station, she kicked off her flat canvas shoes and sat, taking in the scene before her. A few other couples stretched out on blankets nearby and a group of teenage boys tossed a football back and forth in the light of the pole lamp while they waited for the movie to start. Surrounded by the sounds of laughter and fun, she relaxed, removing her jacket and laying it over the seat of the bike behind her.

Ethan returned moments later, arms full of popcorn, hot dogs and drinks. Reaching up, Bailey took the drinks from him and set them on the level patch of grass next to the edge of the blanket, before accepting her hot dog. Ethan removed his running shoes and sat next to her.

"I hope this surprise location for our date is okay," he said, before tossing a handful of popcorn into his mouth.

"Are you kidding me? It's perfect. I love this place." She smiled as a memory returned. "On Friday nights when we were kids, Mom and I would get a picnic ready and some blankets and load up the car. Then the boys and I would put on our pj's, and as soon as Dad got home from work, we'd head out. Have dinner under the open sky and watch the movies. Back then, they always featured a kid-friendly movie first, then the adult one. We'd fall asleep before the end of the first one." Those special family moments were etched in her mind.

"That sounds like fun," Ethan said, moving closer and leaning back on his hands.

His genuine, easy smile encouraged her to continue. "I remember one night, I woke up at the end of the adult movie, and when I opened my eyes, I could see my parents dancing to the credit music next to the car." Her voice took on a dreamlike quality. "I remember thinking that it was the most romantic thing I'd ever seen." She was quiet for a long moment, thinking about her parents and their love and passion for one another.

Ethan remained silent, and when she glanced at him, he was studying her, a serious look in his handsome, dark eyes.

"That's why you came out here that night," he said, surprising her. "The night you ran away when you found out your mom was sick.

We couldn't find you anywhere. You had the whole town scared stupid."

Bailey nodded slowly. She hadn't really connected the two until now. "Yeah, I guess so. You know, you never did explain to me how you convinced your dad to let you ride along with him that night."

"I didn't. I just snuck out and hid in the back of the squad car when I heard him tell Mom you were missing. I was supposed to have been in bed. Don't you remember the Spider-Man pajamas I was wearing?"

Bailey laughed. "No." All she remembered about that night was feeling confused and alone and scared, and then Ethan's reassuring hand on hers in the back of the squad car all the way to her house. Did he remember that?

He slid his hand across the blanket and brought her palm to his lips. Then, reaching for her waist, he lifted her from the blanket and set her between his knees, drawing her back against his chest as the screen lit up and a cartoon clock counted down the remaining thirty seconds until the first movie started.

Setting her cup aside, she lay back and rested her head on Ethan's chest, tilting her face toward his. She kissed the stubble along the side of his chin until he lowered his head, burying it in the curve of her neck. "Bailey," he whispered, before leaving a trail of kisses along her neck and exposed collar bone.

She closed her eyes, enjoying the moment. One she'd waited a long time for. One she thought she'd never experience. "Yes, Ethan?"

"I think I may be falling in love with you."

The words caused a ripple of delight to course through her and a small sigh escaped her lips as she hugged his arms tighter around her body. "Well, let me know when you're sure."

THE SUN WAS bright and high in the sky as Bailey pulled into the lot of the garage early the next morning. The heat rising from the concrete promised a scorcher, but the mild breeze countered its effect, creating a perfect August day. The forecast had called for rain, but the dark clouds looked to be drifting away from town. It didn't matter—rain could pour out of the heavens and it still wouldn't destroy her sunny mood. The night before had been magical. Everything she'd been waiting for, hoping for, was within her grasp. There was no doubting the love and affection in Ethan's eyes the night before. No more games or mixed signals or holding back—just love.

As she removed her helmet, she saw Mr. Henderson, owner of Decals and Designs, the local sign and promotion shop, leaving by the newly installed front door. "Good morning, Mr. Henderson," she greeted.

"Oh, hey, Bailey. What are you doing here?" he asked, looking a little frazzled as he approached, heading toward his bicycle parked in the lot.

"I own the place, remember? What are you doing here?" That was the better question. Mr. Henderson had never owned a car in his life. As far as Bailey knew, he didn't even have a driver's license. His photo ID for the town council, where he was treasurer, was his supper club membership card.

"Oh, well… You know…" he stammered. He wiped a bead of sweat from his forehead that she suspected had nothing to do with the blistering heat so much as nervousness.

"Mr. Henderson, are you okay?"

"Fine. I've gotta go," he said, jumping onto his bicycle and pedaling away.

What a strange little man, Bailey thought, letting herself in through the side entrance. She was amazed by the amount of work Luke's crews had accomplished in such a short period of time. The old, burned bay doors had been replaced and now a new wall sat ready to be plastered and painted where the old wall had been torn down.

No wonder Luke's business did so well, Bailey thought. In the back of the shop area, two men were perched on extended ladders, installing the new mandatory sprinkler system on the metal ceiling. Despite her earlier protests, having the extra safety measure in place was a great idea, and now that the insurance claim was approved, she no longer felt the stress over the additional upgrade costs. She just hoped they never had to set the sprinklers off.

"Bailey? What are you doing here?" Nick's voice behind her made her jump.

"I'm meeting the insurance adjuster here. What are you doing here?" Technically the shop was still closed, so there were no vehicles to be worked on.

"I came in to work on Dwayne's stock car." A wide smile spread across his face.

"He brought it in? When?" Bailey's eyes widened, and setting her helmet down on the counter, she rushed toward the last bay where Dwayne's car was parked…looking incredible. The base color was perfectly matched and the details were crisp and clean. She swung around to face Nick, who'd followed her. "You did this?"

He shrugged. "Yeah."

Bailey moved closer to the car, running a hand over the metal, inspecting the work. Up close, it looked even better. His line work was perfect and the shadowing detail he'd added gave the lettering dimension and depth.

"Does it look okay?" Nick asked, his smile fading in her prolonged silence.

Bailey swallowed hard. In truth, it was better than okay. Nick had a real talent with an airbrush. "It's great, Nick."

He let out a sigh of relief. "I know how much you hate to do cosmetic work, so I thought I'd do it for you…to make up for my messing up…well, everything else."

"So you were the one who did those other paint jobs last week?"

"Yeah. Those were easy," he said with a nod. "So about Mr. Henderson… I was hoping to surprise you, but I guess you already saw the new sign?" He looked disappointed.

"I came in through the side door. What new sign?"

"You haven't seen it yet?" His face lit up.

"No."

"Come with me." He headed toward the

front and she followed. She hadn't yet ordered a new sign. Everyone knew the shop as Doug's Motors, and she hadn't been in a rush to change that, partly out of respect for her uncle's legacy and also because of lack of funds. Walking across the gravel lot, she held her breath as she turned, not sure how she felt about Nick going around her to order something as important as this.

Shading her eyes from the sun, she glanced toward the front of the shop. And did a double take. On the sign, Bailey's Place was scribbled across the side of a bright red fifties Corvette on a black background, edged in a metallic silver paint.

Nick came to stand beside her on the gravel parking lot. "Mr. Henderson said that if you don't like it—"

Bailey turned and quickly wrapped her cousin in a hug, eyes brimming with tears. "Thank you," she whispered.

"So you like it?" He sounded relieved.

She liked that it was her name on it more than anything, but she loved the design. "How could I not? You put my favorite car on there," she said, turning to look at the sign again. She let out a deep breath. All the worry and frustration of the past week melted away. At that moment, life was perfect.

The insurance adjuster's Toyota Tercel pulled into the lot. "Hey, I have to go into this meeting, but could you do something for me?" she asked Nick.

"Sure."

"I need you to make another sign for the bay side entrance," she said, an idea forming in her mind.

"Okay. What do you want it to say?"

"Nick's Detail Shop."

Her cousin's mouth fell open and his eyes bulged. "For real?"

"Yeah."

"Are you sure? I mean, I still have so much to learn about the shop."

"And trust me, you will. You'll have to if we're going to be partners."

"THAT WAS QUITE the display yesterday," Melody said, coming to stand next to Ethan on the coaching field. David and Joshua were already practicing with the rest of the soccer team. The season was coming to an end, and this would be their final regular season game before playoffs started.

He turned to face her, surprised. Melody

worked two jobs and barely had time to attend community events. "You were there?" He didn't remember seeing her.

"No, but the rest of the town was, including your impressionable nephews," she chastised playfully, slapping him on the arm. "All I've heard since yesterday is 'Uncle Ethan kissed Bailey for like ten minutes.'" She rolled her eyes.

Ethan couldn't keep the grin from his face. "It wasn't ten minutes." Though that didn't sound like a bad idea. "Maybe seven…or eight."

"Well, I'm happy for you, but I gotta say I'm a little annoyed to be left in the club all by myself."

"What club?"

"The 'brokenhearted, never falling in love again' club. It was just me…then you joined six months ago…and now it's only me again."

"Sorry, sis. Didn't mean to leave you there alone. You know, it's been over two years since Pat died…." He broached the subject carefully. Rarely did they talk about Melody's late husband or the tragic accident that had happened the day he'd signed a record deal with a recording studio in New York. Despite Melody's own vocal talents and musical am-

bitions, raising the boys and her two jobs—
at Play Hard Sports and behind the bar at the
pool hall—kept her far too busy to pursue her
childhood dreams.

"Maybe you're right. I'll look into schedul-
ing a date on my next day off…which should
be in 2024 when the boys move out." She
checked her watch. "You have to get this
game started. I told the boys I'd stay for the
first half, but then I need to get to the bar.
You'll drop them off at home to the babysitter around six?"

"No problem," he said, picking up a soccer
ball and advancing toward his team. "Okay
guys, bring it in."

"HEY BAILEY," MELODY greeted as she stood
and collected her sweater and purse from the
wooden bleachers.

Bailey glanced at the scoreboard above the
field. The game was tied at two with five
minutes left in the first half. "Heading off
to work?" she guessed. She'd always liked
Ethan's sister and she sympathized with her
situation. Melody worked around the clock
and was raising twin boys alone. Bailey didn't
know how she did it, but she admired her
strength.

"Yes. I'm guessing you're not here because you're a fan of junior league soccer?"

"You caught me. I came to stare at your brother."

"Gross," Melody said.

Bailey laughed. "Actually, after the game we were going to grab dinner." She'd been looking forward to it all day.

"Oh, sorry, Bailey, I just asked him to drive the boys home to the babysitter after practice. I didn't know you two had plans."

"No worries. We'll take the boys for pizza."

"Are you sure? I can ask someone else."

"No, really. No problem at all. We were probably just going to go to Joey's anyway," Bailey said, taking a seat on the bleacher. Ethan glanced toward them and she waved. His face lit up and he didn't notice a stray soccer ball fly past him, barely missing the side of his head.

"Okay, thanks, Bailey." Melody jumped down from the stands and waved at her boys as she rushed off to her minivan parked in the school parking lot.

Bailey couldn't keep her eyes off Ethan for the rest of the game. He was a wonderful coach and the boys loved him. He was a terrific uncle to David and Joshua and Bailey knew how much the boys looked up to both their uncles now that their father was gone. She didn't doubt for a second that Ethan would make a great father himself one day. One thing at a time. It had only taken twenty years for him to realize she could be more than just a friend—a baby and marriage could be a long time coming.

She didn't care. She wasn't in a rush. She wanted those things in time and definitely with him, but she was happy living in the moment, enjoying their newfound love for one another.

When the game ended, she slowly made her way to the field, where Ethan was collecting the soccer balls from the boys and putting them in the oversize equipment bag. David and Joshua sat on the grass nearby, changing out of their cleats and into their regular running shoes. "Hey, Aunt Bailey," Joshua said, and the two collapsed into a fit of giggles.

Bailey hid a smile, shooting an expectant, teasing look at Ethan.

"Whoa, slow down there, boys. One thing at a time," he said, tossing their cleats into the bag, then approaching Bailey. "Though that's not a half-bad idea," he whispered, kissing her cheek.

Did he mean that? Only moments before she'd had to stop herself from getting too far ahead. Composing her features, she decided to see who would cave first. "Well, I do already have a dress."

He hesitated just a beat before saying, "And I know a wedding singer."

She struggled to find a quick comeback but the serious look in his dark eyes stole all her best retorts. Suddenly, she realized she'd be okay with it if he was serious. Thrilled, in fact. "I'm starving. You guys ready for pizza?" she asked, turning her attention to the boys.

"Yay!" they said in unison, each grabbing one of her hands as they made their way across the field.

"Hey, what about me?" Ethan called after them.

"Sure, you can come, too—you're paying." Bailey tossed the words back over one shoulder as she raced the boys to Ethan's Jeep.

ETHAN HELD HER hand tightly in his as he pulled into the lot of Bailey's shop much later that evening. After pizza, they'd taken the boys to the new Disney movie playing at the Cineplex. The babysitter had a pretty easy evening, as the boys had immediately fallen asleep in the back of the Jeep after the late showing and Ethan had carried them into the house and put them to bed.

"Are you sure you have to go?" he asked now.

Bailey suppressed a yawn. "I don't want to, but…"

"No buts…just say you'll stay," Ethan said through a big yawn of his own.

"You're exhausted, too."

"Sleep is overrated. Besides, the moment my head hits the pillow, I'll be wide-awake thinking about you anyway. We may as well be together."

"While it's hard to argue that logic, you need to work tomorrow morning…. Actually, in four hours."

He leaned closer and pulled her into his chest. "What about you? Don't you have to work?"

Bailey snuggled closer and closed her eyes. "Nah, I own the place. Didn't you see the sign? It says Bailey's Place."

"I did see the sign…. It looks great. Who knew Nick had that talent, huh?" Ethan's words were slightly muffled as he burrowed his face in her hair.

"Yeah, who knew?"

He kissed the top of her head. "Why didn't you tell me before? About how you felt?"

"I couldn't. You had Emily." She wrapped her hand around his on her waist and drew tiny circles along his palm.

"But all along you knew this…this fantastic connection between us was possible?"

"I knew how I felt and I knew I could make you happy given a chance."

He turned her in his arms, staring into her eyes. The only light illuminating the dark between them was the glow of the full moon through the windshield. "You are so beautiful. I'm so sorry we wasted all this time." He kissed her lips gently.

"Time with you was never wasted. I wouldn't have traded our friendship for anything," she whispered, snuggling closer to him.

"Except maybe this?" he teased.

"Except maybe this," she agreed.

ETHAN SPILLED HIS coffee as he abruptly pulled his Jeep into his driveway behind the fire hall the next morning, fifteen minutes late for his shift. Who knew he could sleep sitting up in his car, with Bailey slumped against him.

Not only had he slept, it had been one of the best night's sleeps he'd had in a long time. He jumped down from the Jeep and entered the hall through the side door, heading straight for the locker room to shower and get into uniform.

"You're late."

His brother's voice made him stop.

"First time in over a decade," Ethan said. "I think we can let it slide." He took a gulp of his coffee under Jim's scrutinizing gaze. Of all the days for his brother to actually be on time for a shift. He hated the fact it was Jim catching him sneaking in late.

"Hmm… Soccer uniform, your Jeep wasn't parked in its stall last night…. If I were a betting man, I'd say you were with our pretty little mechanic all night."

"We fell asleep in the shop parking lot." Ethan hated to admit as much to his brother, knowing he was bound to take a ribbing, but it was better than any other rumor flying around.

"Couldn't say good-night, huh?" To Ethan's surprise, Jim didn't tease. In fact, he looked a little envious. "I remember those days."

"That's all you have to say?"

"Yeah, man. Believe it or not, I'm really happy for you two."

"I can't believe I didn't see how perfect Bailey is before." Ethan headed into the locker room.

"Emily always did cast a pretty big shadow… and she knew how to get what she wanted."

"Well, those days are over." He was sure of it now. What he had shared with Emily had been great in the beginning, but over time, with separate life goals, they'd drifted apart. He'd been desperately clinging to something that didn't exist anymore. With Bailey, things were different. They already had a foundation of friendship, trust and common aspirations to build upon. And now this unexpected passion and attraction he couldn't deny, and didn't want to, was turning a wonderful life-long friendship into something more. He was excited to see where they were heading.

"You sure about that?"

"Absolutely."

ETHAN STOOD ON the deck of the Sheppards' family cabin on Wednesday evening, over-looking the sandy artificial beach that served as the backyard. A half hour outside of town, the cabin was the perfect summer getaway.

Family and friends were enjoying the boat and Sea-Doos on the still lake, and around the fire pit near the water the kids roasted marshmallows and hot dogs over the flames under Nick's supervision.

Several feet away, Bailey and her brother Jordan played the final round of the family's annual horseshoe tournament and Ethan couldn't tear his eyes away from her smiling face.

Brandon joined him on the deck and handed him an open beer bottle. "She took me out of the tournament the first round," he said.

Ethan accepted the beer and took a swig. "Thanks."

Bailey tossed her last horseshoe, landing herself a ringer and once again the Sheppards' homemade trophy, which had sat on her mantel all year. She threw her arms up in the air and her tanned bare feet did a victory dance on the sand.

"That girl is good at everything," Brandon said with a shake of his head. "Drives me absolutely crazy."

Ethan studied the bottle in his hands. "I love that about her." It was true. He loved that Bailey was a challenge and played to win. If it hadn't been for her going after what she wanted, he may never have realized how great they were together. In a little over a week, his feelings for her had changed so drastically he had a hard time remembering they hadn't always been together like this.

"Listen, Ethan, you're a great guy," Brandon started.

Here it was. The concerned-brother speech he'd been expecting. He owed Jim twenty bucks, though—he'd totally bet that Jordan would have been the first to approach him with the "hurt my sister and I'll snap you in two" speech.

"But Bailey has had enough to deal with lately with the garage and the insurance claim, and I know that wedding is stressing her out more than she's letting on."

"I think so, too," Ethan agreed.

"We just don't want to see her get hurt, you know."

"That's the last thing I want." Ethan took another gulp of his beer. Hurting Bailey was what he'd been worried about, the reason he'd held back as long as he had after that first kiss. But now he knew for sure what he wanted, and it was her. "Brandon, I promise you, you and your family have nothing to worry about."

"Good to hear." Brandon pattcd him on the back as Bailey approached on the deck.

"Did you see that?" Her smile was wide as she displayed the family's homemade trophy—a golden horseshoe on a wooden plaque. "They even had my name preengraved this year."

"Yes, we did see. Some people couldn't tear their eyes away," Brandon said. "See you two later." He disappeared inside just as the dark storm clouds that had threatened all day gave way to a full downpour of rain.

Grabbing her hand, Ethan pulled Bailey under the shelter of the overhang, but the big raindrops continued to soak them. Removing his plaid shirt, he wrapped it around her bare wet shoulders. "Want to get out of here?"

"Yes."

CHAPTER NINE

FROM HER WINDOW seat in the fourth aisle of the crowded plane from Miami, Florida, to Newark, New Jersey, Emily Parsons watched as a young woman made her way down the aisle toward the two vacant seats next to her. A baby was strapped to her chest in a Snugli and she clutched the hand of a young toddler. Emily moved closer to the window and picked up her copy of *Elle* magazine from the middle seat as the woman dropped her carry-on bag onto the end seat and guided the child into the row. She offered a quick, sympathetic smile in greeting as she secured the young boy's seat belt.

"Looks like you're the lucky one who gets to experience these two on their first flight. I apologize in advance."

The little boy eyed Emily with interest as he kicked his feet free of his tiny flip-flop sandals. They actually made shoes that small? Incredible. She shook her head, bending to tuck them under the seat in front of him. The simple gesture took more out of her than she'd expected and she rested her head against the seat.

"It's perfectly fine. No worries at all," she assured the woman. She watched as the mother unhooked the Snugli from around her neck with one hand while securing the sleeping baby to her with the other. Emily looked down the aisle as the flight attendant closed the doors. "You're flying with the two of them alone?"

Brave woman. Emily hated to fly alone. The stress of arriving on time for the flight, passing through the security checkpoint and the possibility of missing connecting flights made traveling less than ideal for her. On the way to Miami, she'd at least been with Greg. The mere thought of him made her eyes water and she forced away a feeling of emptiness.

"I do everything alone with them," the woman answered, opening her oversize purse—or maybe it was a diaper bag—to remove a package of chocolate-chip cookies for the boy, who was flipping through the stations of the entertainment system.

"Oh." Emily turned her attention to the magazine on her lap, which she'd already read cover to cover, having arrived two hours early for the flight.

"My husband is overseas. He's a marine," the woman continued.

"That must be tough. How long is he gone?" She'd always marveled at military couples. Their relationships went through such struggles of distance and uncertainty. It wasn't a lifestyle she could ever handle. Ethan's job as a firefighter in sleepy Brookhollow had caused her stress enough. For years she'd begged him to consider a different career, but he'd insisted that firefighting was the only thing he was passionate about. Would he reconsider now?

The woman interrupted her thoughts with the answer to the question she'd forgotten she'd asked. "Usually six months at a time. Though he promises that this is the last one. Then he's getting a desk job that I know he will hate." A concerned frown wrinkled her forehead.

"I'm sure it will be worth it to be closer to his family."

"That's what he says." The baby stirred and yawned in her sleep before tucking her tiny fists under her chin and cuddling closer to her mother.

Emily stared at the precious child. So tiny, so beautiful, so…terrifying. Her hand almost unconsciously flew to her stomach and she shifted in the seat as the plane began to taxi away from the gate. She hated this part. Once they were in the air she was fine, until they had to land. Then her nerves shattered again. She wished it hadn't come to this, but if Ethan refused to acknowledge her attempts to contact him, she didn't see that she had a choice. He couldn't ignore what was standing right in front of him.

The woman smiled. "So how far along are you?" she asked, nodding toward Emily's stomach.

Emily's eyes widened. "You can tell?" She'd hoped her oversize blouse and leggings would hide her slowly developing baby bump. No one in the office at Play Hard Sports had noticed yet. At least, if they had, they hadn't said anything.

"Barely." She pointed to the open bag of soda crackers in the compartment behind the seat in front of Emily. "Those were a dead giveaway. I lived on them for the full nine months…with both of the kids."

The soda crackers. Her lifeline. She couldn't get through the never-ending waves of nausea without them. "I'm six months." She wasn't sure why she'd said it. This woman didn't know any of her family or friends. Telling her the truth, that she was a little over five months, would have been okay.

"Wow, you're still very tiny. First baby, right?"

Emily nodded. Hopefully the one and only. She wasn't even sure how she'd allowed this pregnancy to happen. A career-minded woman, always waiting for her opportunity to leave Brookhollow, she'd assumed she'd never have children of her own. And they certainly hadn't been in Greg's life plans.

"Well, if you get sick of crackers, Cheerios help with the nausea, as well."

"Thanks for the tip," Emily said. The plane began to pick up speed along the runway and she gripped the arms of the seat, just as the little boy reached for the one between them, as well. "Sorry," she mumbled, instead clasping her hands together on her lap. As the plane left the ground, she closed her eyes and prayed for a smooth ride even as her stomach began to twist and turn more than normal.

In two hours she'd be back in Brookhollow. The thought made her palms sweat. No one knew she was coming and no one was going to believe why. Five months into her pregnancy, she still didn't quite believe it. Finding out that she was going to have a baby had turned her life upside down. She hadn't told Greg. After all, he was hardly father material. He'd repeated time and again that his career demanded a lot of his time and commitment, and trying to raise a family wouldn't be the right decision for him. He'd said it was one of the reasons they were perfect together. *Had been* perfect together.

And now here she was, having a baby by herself. Countless times she'd picked up the phone to call her parents, but she just couldn't bring herself to tell them that way. But time was growing short and decisions had to be made about her future and the future of the baby. She needed a safety net and she knew where to find one. Ethan was a good man. She could count on him to take care of things.

"WE ARE NEVER going to get through this movie if you keep pausing it," Bailey said in mock annoyance as Ethan turned to face her on the couch in his loft apartment.

He leaned toward her and stopped, his lips just inches from hers. "Are you even watching it?" His eyes teased her as he traced a finger along her lower lip.

"Yes," she lied.

He sat back an inch. "Okay, I'll leave you alone and let you watch the movie if you can tell me what the main character's name is."

Shoot. She tried to remember. John? Jack? "Jake?" she guessed.

"Wrong," he said, closing the gap between them and kissing her.

She shut her eyes and allowed herself to melt toward him. She still couldn't believe they were here together like this, the way she'd always wanted. The way she'd always fantasized. Cuddled on his couch, too wrapped up in each other to even care about anything happening around them. She moved closer and slid her arms around his neck.

He rested his forehead against hers. "This feels so good."

"Kissing me?"

"Yes," he said with an easy laugh. "But also just being with you, holding you, opening my mind to the possibility of us."

"So can I tell you 'I told you so' now?"

"Yes, baby girl, you can."

Bailey snuggled closer to his chest, loving the way his big arms made her feel so safe and secure. She could sense the pounding of his heart against her own and she shivered as he placed a trail of kisses along the base of her neck. "Still interested in the movie?" he teased.

"What movie?"

"Ethan!" Jim's voice called from the fire hall below.

"He's not home," Ethan called through the open front door, where a warm night breeze blew into the apartment.

"Sorry to interrupt your evening," he said, appearing in the doorway, "but I need you to sign off on the weekly inspection reports. They are due tomorrow morning."

Ethan groaned as he lifted Bailey's legs from his lap and stood. "And this is why you shouldn't live where you work," he said. "Be right back."

"Sorry, Bailey," Jim said.

"It's no problem. Maybe now I'll actually get to watch some of this movie," she teased.

She hit the play button and settled back against the cushions on the sofa, pulling her long hair out from under her and letting it drape over the side. The apartment didn't have air-conditioning and the heat they were creating inside the small space was intense.

"I'm so sorry." A familiar voice behind her made her jump.

Bailey sprang to her feet. "Emily?" She blinked, refusing to believe the sight in front of her. What was Emily doing here?

Emily's expression of surprise turned to relief as she entered the apartment. "Oh, thank heavens, it's just you. For a second, I thought Ethan was with someone."

He was with someone. Her. She hesitated, unsure of what to say, grateful for the appearance of Ethan in the doorway.

"What are you doing here, Em?" he asked, his voice void of emotion.

"Ethan, hi. I tried to call…." When he remained silent, Emily glanced fleetingly from one to the other.

"I noticed. What are you doing here?" he repeated.

"I needed to talk to you and you weren't answering my calls, so—"

"You flew here?" Bailey interjected. This couldn't be happening. How was it even possible that one of the best moments in her life could be interrupted this way, right now?

"It was important," Emily said, moving into the room.

Clearly. Bailey turned to face Ethan, who

seemed frozen to the spot, staring blankly at his ex. His lack of expression made his feelings hard to read and her heart fell to the floor.

"Can we talk?" Emily asked after an excruciatingly long silence that was actually just seconds.

Ethan folded his arms across his chest and the color came back to his cheeks. "Go ahead." Entering the apartment, he took the television remote and turned off the movie.

Emily glanced at Bailey. "I was hoping you'd be alone."

Of course she was. No doubt she'd been hoping to find him alone, depressed and still in love with her. Well, he wasn't alone or depressed...and dammit, she wished she could say he wasn't still in love with Emily, but the tension filling the air between them was excruciatingly obvious.

"I'll go," Bailey said. What choice did she have? She wanted to tell Emily to leave. That she was too late, but it wasn't her place.

"No, Bailey, you don't have to.... Whatever Emily has to say, she can say in front of you."

Bailey cringed. While her mind was more at ease after Ethan's insistence that she stay, she wasn't sure she was ready to witness whatever was about to happen.

"Ethan..." Emily crossed the room and reached toward him.

Bailey looked away, but she heard the sound of the armchair slide against the wooden floor as Ethan backed into it and away from Emily. "You know what, Emily, whatever it is can wait. Please leave."

"Ethan, I'm pregnant."

FROM THE CORNER of his eye, Ethan saw Bailey head toward the front door. Where was she going? And what exactly had Emily just said? He wanted to race after Bailey, tell her not to go, but his feet were frozen in place as he stared blankly at Emily. What was she saying?

"Say something."

Ethan shook his head. "I don't understand. Why are you here? Why are you telling me this?" He glanced at her stomach. She'd definitely gained weight. Her abdomen stretched against the thin fabric of her lacy white tank top, making a tiny bulge above her loose-fitting jeans. But she couldn't be that far along. He did the math back to the last time....

"The baby is yours," she said, a desperate look in her pale blue eyes.

He blinked twice and a pool of sweat gathered on his back under his T-shirt. The baby was his? How could… How was that… He needed to sit. Slowly, he lowered himself into the chair behind him and rested his head in his hands.

"Ethan…"

"Shh… Please, just don't talk." He needed a minute to digest what she'd just said. Pregnant. His baby. Bailey gone.

Emily moved closer and sat at his feet on the floor. She touched his knee and he flinched. Jumping up out of the chair, he paced the living room floor. "How far along are you?"

"Six months," she said, raising her knees to her chest and wrapping her arms around them.

"You don't even look pregnant."

"They say for a first baby, I probably won't get very big until the last trimester."

"They?"

"The doctors in Miami at the women's pre-natal ward."

"So you've been to a doctor…." He remembered his sister's pregnancy with the boys.

At six months, Melody had already heard the babies' heartbeat. He stopped. "You've heard...its heartbeat?" Before she could answer, he swung around, searching the room. "Where's Bailey?" His mind reeled and he couldn't think straight.

Emily struggled to push herself up off the floor and slowly approached him. "She left. And yes, I've heard the heartbeat."

"But I... How did this happen?"

"Don't you remember? A week before..."

He put a hand up to stop her. Of course he remembered. It had been one of the memories he'd clung to in those first few months after she'd left. "But that was..."

"Six months ago."

A realization struck him. "What about Greg Harrison?"

Her gaze fell to the floor. "That ended a few months ago."

About the time she'd started placing calls to him, he suspected. "When he found out about the baby...and me?"

Emily nodded.

Ethan grew angry. His pacing resumed. The man was a piece of work. He came to town and made a play for Ethan's girlfriend and then left her after she revealed she was pregnant. Of all the low, slimy moves.

Emily stepped forward and placed a hand on his arm. "Please stop pacing. You're making me dizzy."

He was making *her* dizzy? Did she hear herself? She'd come into his home and turned his entire world upside down in a matter of minutes and he was making *her* dizzy. When he turned to face her, he frowned. She did look pale and her hand was resting on her belly. His baby was inside there. The thought nearly set him on his behind.

"Are you okay?"

"This nausea is killing me…. Do you have any soda crackers?"

"No, I don't…"

"Cheerios?"

"Yes," he said, disappearing into the kitchen. Taking a bowl from the cupboard, he opened the pantry and pulled out the cereal. His hand shook and the little round Os littered his counter as he filled the bowl. "Milk?" he called, still trying to grasp the reality of the situation. His ex-girlfriend was in his apartment pregnant with his baby and eating Cheerios. He opened the fridge. And he was out of milk…. Of all times…

"No, just dry is fine," she answered.

Returning to the living room, he found her lying on the couch, her back resting against the pillow Bailey had just been leaning on. Bailey. He longed to go find her, but he had to deal with this first. He handed her the bowl. "Do you need anything else?"

"No, thank you." She ate several Cheerios slowly, then she sat up and patted the couch next to her. "Please, sit."

Ethan folded his arms across his chest. "I'm okay here," he said, locked in place across the room from her. He didn't want to get too close. He had no idea what to say or how to act. He wanted to be furious with her. Tell her to leave. That it was too late to just waltz back in and claim what she obviously thought was still hers. But one look at her tired, frightened expression and he softened. She was having a baby. His baby. And she was alone.

"I'm sorry. I did try to tell you sooner."

He nodded. "So what happens now?" He hoped she had the answers, because he sure didn't.

"I was hoping you would consider giving us another chance," she whispered.

Another chance. The one thing he'd been longing for…craving for so long. And now here it was. Too late and too complicated. He nodded slowly. "And you're moving back home?" It wasn't really a question. Of course she would move back to Brookhollow....

But she was shaking her head. "Um...no. I'm going back to Miami. I took a two-week leave to come back. It was the only way I could get you to talk to me."

"You're leaving again? But I thought you just said you wanted to give us another chance."

"I do."

She did, but she expected him to move to Miami. "You want me to move?"

"I have a great job in Miami, Ethan. They know about the baby and they are offering a paid three-month maternity leave. And my apartment is a two bedroom...with room for a nursery." She paused and scanned his loft apartment. "We couldn't have a baby here."

"There are other homes in Brookhollow, Emily." He couldn't believe this. She really wasn't moving home. She'd made up her mind...and *his* apparently. "You have family here. Won't your parents want to be near their grandchild?" He knew his would. His chest hurt and he struggled to fill his lungs with air. Was he really even having this conversation with her?

"They will understand. We'll visit. They can visit. My life is in Miami now."

Her life may be. But his life was here in Brookhollow. How many times had they had this conversation in the past? But now she had an edge. If he wanted to be part of his child's life, it had to be in Miami.

Setting the Cheerios aside, she stood and crossed the room toward him. Forcing his arms away from his chest, she wedged herself closer to him, then taking his hand, placed it on her stomach. "We can make this work," she whispered.

A lump formed in his throat as he thought about what she was asking. She expected him to give up his apartment, his job, his family, Bailey. Oh, God, Bailey. He couldn't breathe as he thought about having to tell her. After so many years of being blind to the possibility of the two of them together, he'd finally discovered a real love...only to have it disappear in seconds.

CHAPTER TEN

FOUR SETS OF unblinking eyes stared at him in his grandmother's ten-by-ten room in the senior's complex. The members of his immediate family sat, openmouthed, expressions of disbelief plastered over their faces. Maybe telling them all together like this had been a mistake. The only one who wasn't there was his sister. Melody had had to work, missing the big announcement he'd just laid on the rest of his family. It figured that the one person he knew he could count on to support his decision, despite her dislike of his ex, couldn't be there. He cleared his throat, but waited, knowing his family was processing. In a few seconds, he'd be wishing for the silence.

His mother, June, spoke first, but it wasn't to him. "Are you okay, Willa?" she asked the older lady, who was perched on the edge of her rocking chair.

Willa nodded, then surprised everyone by saying, "I think this may be my fault."

"Mom, that's ridiculous. How on earth could you have had anything to do with this?" Ethan's father turned from staring at Ethan to look at his mother.

"I wanted a great-granddaughter."

"Grandma, that's not why this happened," Ethan reassured her. "Emily is already six months pregnant."

The woman nodded emphatically. "Yes, it was about six months ago when it happened."

"What happened?" Jim asked, finally joining the conversation.

"Claudette Jansen and I saw a fortune teller in Somerville with her daughter Jude. I wished for this…." The older woman looked pale.

Ethan moved forward and touched his grandmother's shoulder. "Grams, that's not why this happened, I can assure you."

"I feel dizzy," Willa said, closing her eyes.

Willa might be a hypochondriac, but even he could see this had shaken her. He'd hoped she'd be happy to hear the news. He hadn't meant to unnerve her.

"Boys, why don't you go get your grandmother a drink from the nurse's station down the hall?" June suggested, helping Willa out of her chair and into her bed.

Jim and Ethan left the room, and the moment the door closed behind them, Jim punched his shoulder. Hard.

"What was that for?" Ethan asked, rubbing the tender spot.

"For upsetting Grams," he said, then hit him again.

"Ow, stop. What's wrong with you?"

"How could you have let this happen?"

"It wasn't exactly planned, Jim," Ethan mumbled.

"And you're sure…"

"Jim, don't even go there." His voice was hard when he turned to his brother. Of course the thought had crossed his mind ever so briefly the evening before, but he hadn't asked. If Emily said he was the father, he believed her.

"I don't understand what took her so long to tell you," he said as they made their way down the hall of the west wing of the building.

"She tried."

"Not hard enough."

"Look, Jim, I know how you feel about her, but what I need from you right now is support." He stopped and faced his brother. "Can you do that?"

Jim hesitated. "I don't know. I need more information first."

"That's fair." If the roles were reversed, Ethan would probably feel the same. He folded his arms across his chest and prepared to answer Jim's questions the best he knew how.

"You're sure she won't consider moving home?"

"Her job in Miami is offering paid maternity and the company has its own day care center for employees. She says she's not interested in being a stay-at-home mom. If I want to be involved, I have to move to Miami." Ethan took a glass from the desk and filled it with water from the dispenser in the hallway.

"What about your job at the fire hall?"

"Adams is next in line for the promotion to captain. I guess that's the way it would go."

"And you're okay with that? Walking away from the job you love? The home you love... Your family."

"Jim, put yourself in my shoes. If the roles were reversed, what would you do?" He knew the answer and so did Jim.

Jim sighed. "Fine. I guess you really don't have many options this time."

"Thank you."

"Okay, but now for my toughest question—what about Bailey?"

What about Bailey? What could he do about hurting the woman he was falling in love with? The choice he was being forced to make meant that someone was going to get hurt. "I'll let you know as soon as I have an answer myself."

LATER THAT EVENING, Ethan knocked on the front door of his sister's bungalow-style home. Melody's Chevrolet minivan sat in the driveway of the quiet cul-de-sac neighborhood and the sound of the boys playing in the living room came through the open windows. The television blared in the background and the telephone was ringing. He tried the door handle, but it was locked. That didn't surprise him. As the only daughter of the town's police chief, Melody knew to always keep her family safe. He waited, then knocked again.

His sister answered a second later. She was wearing her Play Hard Sports smock from her day job, her cordless home phone resting between her shoulder and ear while she mixed what looked like mashed potatoes in a large salad bowl. She gave him a wary look, but nodded with her head, gesturing him inside. "What do you mean something came up? You're thirteen.... A date?" She spoke into the phone, rolling her eyes at Ethan.

He shut the front door behind him and removed his running shoes before entering the living room.

"Uncle Ethan!" David rushed to him.

Josh waved from the sofa where he was glued to a Nintendo video game. Controller in hand, he navigated a race car down a dirt track on the family's television.

"Hey, guys," Ethan greeted.

"What are you doing here?" David asked.

"I was just in the neighborhood, so I thought I'd stop by," he said, ruffling David's hair.

"Fine, I'll figure something out," Melody said, as she set the phone back in the cradle in the hallway. She rubbed her forehead and stared at the ceiling for a long moment before turning to him. "You look about as worn out and exhausted as I feel. Coffee?"

"Do you have anything a little stronger?"

"No, but I have an emergency stash of rocky road ice cream...and while normally I wouldn't share that with anyone, I'll make an exception this time."

"Honestly, sis, it would just be wasted on

me." Not even an emergency stash of ice cream could make his most recent problems disappear. "Coffee's good enough."

Melody turned to the boys. "Guys, why don't you play in the yard until dinner's ready, okay?"

"But I'm almost finished this level…." Josh argued.

Melody looked more than a little defeated.

Ethan jumped in where he wouldn't normally, but he needed to talk to his sister. "Hey, guys, why don't you both go outside and practice for a bit, then I'll come play for a while," he suggested, picking up their soccer ball near the door and tossing it to David.

Josh immediately dropped the gaming remote and, grabbing the ball from his brother, ran outside into the large fenced yard.

"Wow, you made that look easy." Melody's voice held a mixture of gratitude and envy.

"Yeah, well, kids always listen better to other people than they do their parents." He shrugged. "Rough day?" he asked, following her into the kitchen.

"Rough two years, eight months and twenty-three days." She picked up several toys in the hallway and tossed them into the boys' bedroom at the end of the hall, shut-

ting the door on the mess of toys and un-
made beds.

"Want to talk about it?" His news could
wait.

Melody sighed. "I wouldn't even know
where to start. Just when it seems things are
going smoothly..." She lowered her voice
and glanced toward the backyard, shutting
the kitchen door. "Josh's goldfish died this
morning, then my shifts at Play Hard got
cut and on the way home I get a message
from the optometrist in the city cancelling
David's appointment that we've been waiting two months for...and the thing is I'm relieved because I know that kid needs glasses,
but I have no idea where that money's coming from. Then of course I feel guilty." She
paused. "Heard enough yet?" she asked,
opening her clothes dryer and tossing the
clean, dry towels into a basket.

Taking it from her, Ethan carried the laundry to the living room and set it down next to
the sofa. "Sorry, Mel," was all he could think
of to say. He picked up a towel and started
to fold.

"Drop that towel," she said pointedly. "The
day I need my brother to help keep my house
clean is the day I'll give up. But thank you,"

she added, remembering her manners. "Besides, I'll have plenty of time to fold them tonight, since the babysitter just cancelled an hour before my shift at the bar that was supposed to start at seven...."

Ethan checked his watch. 6:50 p.m. He glanced at the clock on the kitchen wall—5:50 p.m. The microwave read the same. Only the tiny red lights on the stove revealed the correct hour.

"Um, Mel...I don't mean to make things worse, but your clocks are an hour slow."

Her eyes widened and she jumped up from the chair. "Great, he did it again." She looked frantic as she slid the mashed potato–topped casserole into the oven and set the timer.

"Who did what?"

"David keeps changing the clocks. Putting them back an hour."

"Why?" Ethan asked.

Melody's shoulders slumped and her eyes misted with tears. The emotional display shocked him. Tears were something very few people witnessed with this tough-as-nails single mom, including her family members. "He says he never sees me. That I work too much. It breaks my heart, but what am I supposed to do? I need to work."

She looked at Ethan, but he held no answers for her.

"Sorry, Mel."

"It will be fine." She picked up the phone again. "I'll just have to call in." She dialed the number to the pool hall, biting her lower lip. "This is the second time this week." A worried frown wrinkled her forehead.

Ethan stood and gently took the phone from her. Talking to her about Emily would have to wait. She had enough on her plate to deal with.

"What are you doing?"

"I'll watch the boys so you can go to work," he offered, disconnecting the call and setting the phone back on the charger on the counter.

"Really?"

"Sure. Why not?" After all, he was going to need all the practice he could get if he was going to be a dad. *Dad.* No matter how many times he repeated the word in his mind, the concept just didn't register.

Her eyes filled with fresh tears as she hugged him tightly. "You're a lifesaver, Ethan. No pun intended." She hesitated. "It will be late, though. It's inventory night at the bar."

He waved a hand. "No problem. I've got it."

"Okay, if you're sure?"

"Go."

"Thank you. Bedtime is at eight-thirty and the casserole should be ready in an hour."

"Mel, I'm a bachelor impromptu babysitter so don't kid yourself. The boys will be up until midnight and I'm ordering a pizza as soon as you leave."

"Psst, babysitters are not supposed to fall asleep."

Ethan jumped at the sound of Melody's voice waking him from a light sleep. Tossing the homemade quilt back on the couch, he sat up wide-eyed. "I'm awake."

Melody raised an eyebrow.

Ethan slumped back against the couch. "Okay, you caught me. Wow, those boys can really tire you out." While they'd waited for the pizza, they played soccer, then after dinner they played basketball in the driveway and street hockey with the neighborhood kids in the cul-de-sac. He was beat.

"I see they made it to bed on time," she said, shooting him a look and nodding across the living room.

David and Joshua snored at opposite ends of the tiny love seat, sleeping soundly, limbs dangling over the side. Melody bent to kiss both of them before turning her attention back to him. "So you're going to be a dad?"

He should have known she'd find out quickly. He suspected Emily had gone to Play Hard Sports already to see her old co-workers and share her news. Good news? He wasn't quite sure how she actually felt about the pregnancy. They'd had little time to talk and her reaction to it was hard to read. Kind of like his sister's.

"That's what I've been told," he said.

"How do you feel about it?" She lowered herself down to the carpet next to the sleeping boys and studied him.

She was the first one to ask, and he actually wasn't sure.

"Happy…angry…confused…terrified…"

His emotions had roller coastered from one extreme to the other in the past twenty-four hours. The news that he was going to be a father had taken his breath away and he still didn't think the realization had quite sunk in yet, and while he was obviously excited about the prospect of having a child, his thoughts constantly returned to his growing feelings for Bailey and what this meant for them. Ultimately, it meant there couldn't be a them, and the thought left him numb.

"The girls at work say she's six months?" She looked at him for confirmation.

"Yes."

"You've missed a lot," she pointed out.

That had been one of the major sources of hurt he'd experienced after the initial shock. Emily had seen the positive pregnancy test, heard the heartbeat, felt the baby move. All the things that he'd thought he would be part of if they'd ever had children. Instead, he'd been robbed of those experiences because she'd been scared to tell him? "I'm hoping to make up for that."

Melody gave a sad smile. "I'm sure you will. Can I ask how Bailey is handling the news?"

Ethan closed his eyes and leaned his head back against the couch cushions. He wished he knew for sure, but she was avoiding him. Three unanswered voice mails, six text messages and no answer at her home were starting to make him feel like a stalker, but he was desperate to talk to her. Right now, all he could do was speculate how hurt and disappointed she must be feeling. If it was anything like he felt... "She's ignoring me."

"So she's stepping aside?"

"What choice does she have?" What choice

did either of them have? He was the father of Emily's child. Nothing could change that, and while things were complicated and confusing and impossible to figure out, he had to do the right thing. Even if the right thing meant putting his own happiness on hold for the sake of this baby.

Melody shook her head. "None, I guess. Not if you are determined to stand by Emily."

"I have to, Mel."

"Do you still love her?"

He let out a deep breath. Such a complicated question. Did he love her? He suspected part of him always would, but he wasn't in love with her. His time with Bailey had shown him the difference between caring and affection for someone and passionate, life-altering love. "I love her enough."

"Enough to give up everything here—your job, your friends, the woman you love—to follow her back to Miami?"

He swallowed hard and nodded.

"And you're sure you can't convince her to stay here? I mean, her family's here…."

"I tried. She has a great job in Miami and the place she is leasing has two bedrooms…." He raked a hand through his hair. The idea of moving to Miami and giving everything up made his chest hurt. But as Jim had pointed out, if he was going to break Bailey's heart by being with Emily, it would be kinder if he did it in another city where she wouldn't have to face him every day. He just dreaded the moment he had to tell her he was leaving. He prayed she hadn't heard it from someone else already. She deserved to hear it from him.

"I'm sorry things didn't work out the way you deserved, little brother," she said through a yawn.

Ethan studied his sister with a wry smile. Melody's life was far from a fairy tale. In his opinion, she had things a lot harder than he did. "Who exactly do things work out for?"

Their gazes met and simultaneously they said, "Jim."

Ethan stretched as he stood. "I'll carry the boys to bed for you before I go," he offered as Melody stifled another yawn. The clock on the wall above the electric fireplace, with the corrected time, revealed it was after two o'clock. She hadn't been kidding about a late night.

"You may as well put them in my room. That's where they'll end up soon anyway."

Ethan carried the two boys down the hall and placed them under the comforter on the king-size, four-poster bed. Tucking the blankets around them, he didn't fail to notice that both sides of the bed had been turned down, and the picture of her late husband, Patrick, stood on the bedside table next to the two alarm clocks. Patrick's wedding ring lay next to Melody's in front of the family photo on her tall dresser in the corner of the room. He hated that the boys were growing up without their dad. He couldn't let the same thing happen to his own child.

CHAPTER ELEVEN

"TOMORROW NIGHT AT six at the Fireside Grill, okay.... Yeah, I'll let her know." Nick ended the call on his cell phone the next day.

"Nick, I need that quarter wrench," Bailey called from under the Nissan Pathfinder she was working on in their nearly reconstructed garage. Luke hadn't been kidding when he said they would be back in business within a few weeks. Thankfully at least at work Bailey could keep her overactive mind partly occupied with something other than Emily's announcement and the rumors she'd heard circulating around town already that morning.

"Here it is." He handed her a fifth wrench and she resisted the urge to scream. Instead, she sailed out from under the vehicle and reached into the tool kit herself, blindly feeling for the right tool. "So that was my mom," Nick said, sitting on the floor next to her.

"She said she's finally talked Dad into

going out to dinner to celebrate his retirement. She's made reservations for seven of us at the Fireside Grill for tomorrow night."

Great. The last thing she felt like doing was celebrating anything, but she knew she had to attend. For over a month, they'd been trying to convince Doug to allow them to take him out. "Okay."

The shop phone rang and Nick rushed to answer it. "Nick's Detail Shop."

"Nick!"

"Sorry, Bailey's Place," he corrected. "Yes, she is…. Just a minute. I'll get her."

Bailey's pulse quickened. Ethan? She'd been ignoring him, not knowing what to say, too angry and hurt not to say things she knew she would regret. Avoiding him was best.

"Bailey, phone's for you," he said.

She slid out from under the car. "Who is it?"

"Some lady," Nick answered with a shrug.

Not Ethan. Good enough for her. Removing her work gloves and setting them on the counter, she picked up the phone. "Hello?"

"Bailey. Hi, darling." Her aunt Caroline. Bailey's shoulders sagged in relief.

Pulling out the stool from behind the counter, she sat. "Hi, Aunt Caroline. How are you?" They spoke about once a month and Bailey tried to visit her aunt's family in Beach Haven at least once a year, usually during the summer. But with everything happening in the past few weeks, the trip had been neglected.

"I'm great. I'm just calling to see if you were still planning to come down this year. I know you've had a lot going on."

"Yes, it has been busy." She'd given up on the idea of making the trip that year, but maybe now might be the perfect time to get away for a few days, at least. She hesitated, scanning the shop. Only one other vehicle sat in the farthest bay. She could repair the damaged bumper that evening, and unless they had a sudden rush of work, she could head off to her aunt's the day after her uncle's dinner. She could spend two or three days at Beach Haven and still return in time for Victoria and Luke's wedding. "But, you know, I think I can still make it. How about two days from now? I won't be able to stay long, though."

"That sounds perfect. We would love to see you, even for just a few days."

The sound of her uncle's voice in the background caught her attention.

"Oh, that's right. Your uncle is wondering

if maybe while you're here, you could help him winterize his new boat."

"Sure, no problem. It's actually quite simple."

"Bailey, dear, I think you're forgetting which side of your family you're speaking to."

"I STILL CAN'T believe you're actually leaving." Mark said, leaning against the weight bench in the fire hall workout room.

The day before, after handing his official resignation letter to Chief Clarke and apologizing for the lack of notice, Ethan had called a staff meeting at the hall to let the men know he would be leaving by the end of the following week. Jim had already known, but the others had been shocked.

Ethan replaced the weight bar on the bench and slowly curled up to a seated position. He reached for his towel and wiped sweat from his forehead before switching places with Mark. "Hey, look on the bright side. It means you get my job."

He forced his tone to be light, but the words were difficult to say. He'd never envisioned himself leaving the fire hall. He had planned to retire there. It was what he loved to do—protect his family and friends. Now he was moving away. Mark had been next in line for the promotion and he deserved it.

Mark took his position beneath the bar on the bench, struggling under the weight. "Did you add more weight to this?"

"No, you're just weak," Ethan said, taking the shaky bar from his friend's hands and setting it back in the rack.

Mark finished his set and sat up. "So there's something else I need to ask you."

"Shoot," Ethan said, kicking off his running shoes and heading toward the showers. This was most likely his last workout at the fire hall. He planned to clean out his personal items from his locker that afternoon. He had decided to approach this whole thing like pulling off a Band-Aid—quick.

"I was wondering what was happening with your apartment?"

Ethan paused. He should have known that was coming. The furnished apartment above the fire hall customarily belonged to the captain until he decided to start a family or move on to other opportunities. Of course Mark should have it now. "It's yours."

"I'm sorry, man. I know this was terrible timing…."

"Nah, it's fine. We needed to have this

conversation at some point. I'll start packing up my personal belongings this week." He planned to have his belongings shipped to Miami the following week. He didn't own many big pieces of furniture, so at least that part of the move would be easy.

ETHAN PULLED INTO the garage lot just as the setting sun created a bright yellow and orange glow over the horizon. Two days without a word from Bailey was more than enough. He needed to talk to her, was desperate to see her. Jumping down from the Jeep, he approached the door just as she shut off the open sign in the front window.

A bell chimed as he opened the door. Her back was turned to him where she stood behind the counter, packing up her tool kit. She'd already changed out of her coveralls and his breath caught at the sight of her in her jeans and pale blue T-shirt.

"Sorry, we're closed," she said, turning. "Ethan?"

"Yeah, remember me?" he chided gently with a nervous laugh. Her serious expression was a mix of annoyance and hurt.

She lowered her gaze to the floor. "Yeah, sorry, I got your messages. I've just been…"

She threw her hands up. "You know why I haven't answered." She grabbed her motorcycle helmet from under the counter and flicked off the lights in the back of the shop. Only the emergency lights lit the bays in the back.

"I was hoping we could talk." He needed to talk. There was so much he had to tell her, so many apologies he knew she deserved, and he longed for her to lie to him and say the choice he was making was okay.

"Is there anything you could possibly say that doesn't end with 'I choose Emily'?"

His shoulders sagged. Is that what she thought he was doing? Choosing? He sure didn't feel like he'd been given any say in the direction his future was now heading. But he could understand that her hurt and frustration would make her think in those terms.

"No," he said finally.

"Then I guess we're done here."

"How can we possibly be done? Don't you have anything at all to say to me?"

She picked up an empty box and turned away from him. "Nothing I say will make a difference."

Moving toward her, he took the box from her and covered her hands with his. His grip tightened when she tried to pull away. "Bailey, for the first time in my life, I'm feeling something real, something exciting. I haven't been able to sleep or eat. My stomach turned at the mere notion of you with Adams...or anyone else for that matter."

He paused. "Look at me, please." His voice was gentle as he lifted her chin. He rested his forehead against hers. "I'm falling for you, Bailey, and my biggest regret is not having realized how perfect, how beautiful, how strong and compassionate you are before now...when it's too late."

Pushing him away, Bailey backed up until her back hit the wooden shelf. She shook her head, avoiding his eyes. "No, Ethan, I'm sorry. I don't know what you think was happening between us...."

"Stop. You're a terrible liar." What was she saying? That she didn't have feelings for him? That was crap and they both knew it.

Touching her cheek, he wiped a tear away, but another fell in its place. "I'm sorry." The words were so empty, so meaningless. But they were all he had.

Her smile looked forced when her pained eyes met his. "You get her back. It was what you wanted."

"You think this is what I wanted?" She couldn't be more wrong.

"Please go now," she whispered, moving past him.

"Bailey, what do we do now?"

"The same thing we've always done."

"Can you do that?" he choked out.

"Maybe not today...or tomorrow, but eventually. Like you, I have no other choice. Bye, Ethan."

"I'D LIKE TO propose a toast to my much older brother here," Ben said with a wink as he raised his wineglass across the table at the Fireside Grill. "Congratulations on your well-deserved retirement."

"Congratulations, Doug," everyone chorused as their glasses clanked together.

Bailey took a sip of her merlot as her father continued. "I also want to take a second— not to intrude on Doug's night too much— and offer another congratulations, this one to Bailey. I'm proud of you."

"I'll drink to that," Doug said. "I couldn't be leaving the shop in better hands."

"Thanks, Uncle Doug," Bailey said, before picking up her menu. Not that she had an appetite. For three days, the mere thought of food had made her stomach hurt and she'd barely slept. The few hours of sleep she had gotten had been plagued by nightmares of Ethan and Emily together.

She scanned the items and a familiar laugh caught her attention outside on the restaurant's covered patio. Turning, she noticed Emily and her family take their seats at the reserved table in the corner.

Oh, you've got to be kidding me. Of all nights. Grateful for the large wooden pillars between the tables, creating a more intimate dining experience, she peered over her menu to see if anyone else was with the Parsonses. No Ethan. The relief she experienced was overwhelming. She couldn't handle seeing him tonight.

Then his familiar voice at the restaurant entrance made her hands shake. He was here. With his entire family. She shouldn't be surprised. It made sense that the Parsonses and the Bishops would spend time together, discussing the baby. Still, witnessing Emily and Ethan together would tear a hole in her already battered heart.

Thankfully, the waitress led them around the other side of the restaurant toward the patio and they didn't notice Bailey's group.

Bailey, however, couldn't tear her eyes away. Dressed in a dark blue suit and light blue shirt, his dark hair gelled in a spiky mess and his jawline smooth, Ethan looked amazing. He'd obviously gone to a lot of effort for this dinner with the Parsons family, for Emily. She found it hard to breathe.

"Bailey," Nick said to her right, waving a hand in front of her.

She blinked. "Yeah?"

"Looks like you're going to have to choose something else."

"What?"

He pointed to the menu. "The waitress just said they're out of the salmon. That's what you said you wanted. You'll have to choose something else." Then he noticed the Parsonses' table and lowered his voice, giving her a sad smile. "Story of your life, huh?"

THE FIRESIDE GRILL, situated in a heritage home at the edge of the town park, overlooking the lake, bustled with patrons. Ethan scanned the inside dining room for the Parsonses' table.

"We don't have to stay long, do we?" his father muttered, yanking on the tie his wife insisted he wear to the upscale restaurant.

As chief of police, Frank Bishop didn't always see eye to eye with Mayor Parsons, despite their common goal of doing what was right for the community. Often, their ideas of just what that was seemed to differ. In the ten years that Ethan had dated Emily, family get-togethers such as this one had happened rarely.

"Shh," his mother said. "We're doing this for Ethan."

"But what am I going to eat? You know I don't like all this fancy stuff."

"Don't worry, Dad, I'll take you to Joey's for a burger after I drive Jill home," Jim whispered.

The hostess, a teenage girl he didn't recognize, approached with a smile and a stack of menus under one arm. "Are you folks meeting someone or do you have a reservation?" she asked.

"Mayor Parsons and his family," Ethan said, straightening his tie. He hated wearing one, but the big-city chain restaurant had a dress code and enforced it even in the small town.

"Sure, please follow me," she said, leading the way past the mahogany bar and the tables adorned in white linen, small candles flickering in the center. She led them to the outdoor patio, where four large tables were grouped for a more private setting. "Here you are. Enjoy your meal."

"Thank you," Ethan said, forcing a smile as he waved a greeting to Emily's family at the far table.

Emily waved from her seat, gesturing to the chair she'd saved next to her. Dressed in a white strapless sundress, her long blond hair tied in a low ponytail over one shoulder, she beamed at him. Her small baby bump was hardly visible in the flowing fabric.

"You're sure she's pregnant?" Jim asked, earning him a slap on the shoulder from Jill. "What? She looks the same to me," he said with a shrug.

"Everyone just get through this one night, okay?" Ethan pleaded in a hushed tone. Family meetings had been easy to avoid before, but with a baby on the way, he suspected the two families had better get used to spending time together, whether they enjoyed it or not. At least he'd be in Miami most of the time. Funny, he'd never expected to see a bright side to the move.

"Don't worry, sweetheart. I'll keep everyone in line," his mother said, sending the other men warning looks.

"Thanks, Mom." Ethan was grateful for her. She was the one he'd been most worried to tell about the baby. They were close, and the idea of disappointing her bothered him. But she'd been encouraging and supportive of his decision, saying she only wished that this wonderful life experience wasn't coming at such a personal cost. He shouldn't have been surprised by her support. She'd always been there for Jim, Melody and him.

"Hi, everyone," he greeted, pulling out the seat next to Emily.

"Hey, Ethan, Jim, Jill, June and Frank. Great to see all of you." Mayor Parsons stood and extended a hand.

"You, too, sir," Jim said.

Jill waved at everyone before taking a seat near Kim.

His father mumbled a hello and sat.

"Emily, you look beautiful," his mother said. "We were just commenting on how tiny you still look for six months."

"The doctor says it's normal for a first baby." The note of defensiveness in her voice made everyone pause for a beat.

His mother sailed through the awkwardness with ease. "Oh, I'm sure it is, dear. Lillian, I haven't seen you since your annual Fourth of July party at your cabin...." She turned her attention to Emily's mother.

The other woman, elegantly dressed in a white business suit, her slightly graying hair tied at the base of her neck in a style similar to Emily's, offered a tight, polite smile. "We refer to it as the cottage."

Cottage, cabin—it didn't matter what they called it. The showy, rarely used summer home that the Parsonses owned an hour outside of Brookhollow was more like a mansion with antique furnishings and real fireplaces in every room. With six bedrooms and two full kitchens, the cottage was bigger than their extravagant four-bedroom, four-thousand-square-foot home here in Brookhollow. Ethan had always hated the place. It was pretentious, unwelcoming and not at all fun. Unlike Bailey's family cabin in Beach Haven, a tiny two-room shack with lots of beachfront property where they could set up tents and sleep out under the stars. The realization that camping trips like that were probably not in his future anymore hit him.

"Speaking of the cottage, I thought we

could hold the celebration after the baby's christening there," Emily said.

"What a wonderful idea," Lillian agreed. "I'll email our party planner next week."

"Party planner?" June said. "I'm sure that's not necessary. We could put something together at our place…something small and intimate—family only."

"This baby is the mayor's grandchild… first grandchild," Lillian said. "I'm afraid there will be nothing small and intimate about the event. Besides, we wouldn't want to put you out."

"Well, either way, I think it's a little early to be discussing it," Ethan said. "The baby is not even due for another three months."

"There's a lot to do in three months," Emily told him. "We don't have that much time."

He bit his cheek. They would have had plenty of time had she not kept this whole pregnancy thing to herself until now.

The waitress arrived to take their order and a collective sigh of relief could be heard across the table.

When she left, Mayor Parsons said, "Great performance on this year's Fire Fit Challenge, Ethan."

"Let me guess—you and Bailey took home the win?" Emily asked, turning to face him. The note of jealousy didn't escape him. Odd how he'd never noticed any sign of that before.

He broached the subject of that day with caution, noticing the silent looks the others exchanged. Emily had yet to learn about his quickly developing relationship with Bailey, and he hoped she wouldn't find out. It would just complicate things even further.

"Um, no, we came in last."

"Yeah, they were doing great, but they had some trouble on the rappel wall," Mayor Parsons said. "I couldn't really tell from the podium, but it looked like Bailey froze. A little fear of heights?"

Jill shook her head. "No, Bailey's not afraid of heights. She rock climbs at the YMCA all the time."

Ethan cleared his throat. "No, Bailey isn't. I am."

"You are? I never knew that." Emily looked at him in disbelief.

"Neither did I until I got to the top of the wall." There were a lot of things he'd discovered for the first time that day. Not that any of it mattered now.

BAILEY KICKED HER feet free of her strappy, two-inch sandals and carefully made her way down the bank toward the lake's edge. Their dinner over, she'd refused the offers of drives home, deciding to stay for a while, enjoying one of the last few mild evenings of summer. Soon the leaves on the park's large maple trees would turn vibrant shades of red and yellow, and one violent wind storm in early October would loosen them all from their branches, littering the ground. She wished there was some way she could hold on to summer a little longer, but it was yet another thing beyond her control. She sat on the grass and brought her knees to her chest, wrapping the edge of her flowing skirt around her legs as she stared out across the calm, glass-like lake.

"I thought you left." Ethan's voice behind her made her heart pound. She hadn't thought he'd noticed her in the restaurant.

She turned and shielded her eyes against the setting sun as she glanced up at him. "We did. I just thought I'd sit out here awhile before heading home."

"Sorry I didn't come over to say hi."

"No, don't be. It was totally understandable."

He sighed, loosening the tie at his neck and shoving his hands into his dress pants pockets. "I've really made a mess of things, haven't I?

"Yeah." His saddened expression softened her a little. "But you had a lot of help in messing things up."

"I don't know what I'm doing, Bailey," he said, lowering himself next to her on the grass. Having him so close was too much, so she shifted slightly away as he continued. "I feel as though I'm making the worst decision of my life, yet I don't even feel as though it's mine to make."

"The baby changes things…for everyone." *Baby*. His *baby*. The word still stuck on her tongue and sounded foreign to her ears.

"I just wish doing the right thing didn't have to be so hard."

In the past, she'd always been there for him. She'd been his best friend, sitting on the sidelines for years, hoping one day he would realize how perfect they could be together. She'd been his shoulder to cry on when Emily left and the kick in the butt he'd needed to pull himself together. And now she desperately wanted to be that woman again. His friend, his confidant, his savior. But she couldn't.

Too much had happened and things were different now. She wanted more and she couldn't have it. Well, this time neither could he. She stood and collected her shoes. "Good night, Ethan."

"Tell me it's okay, Bailey," he pleaded, anguish in his voice. "You are my best friend. I need to hear it from you."

"I stopped being your best friend two weeks ago. Now I'm just someone who's finally realized she can't win this one."

THE SMELL OF the salty ocean air on the warm breeze helped to ease her tension as Bailey drove slowly down Beach Avenue toward the boardwalk the next day. Families and couples lay about on blankets and lawn chairs, enjoying the two-mile stretch of beach along the Atlantic Ocean, basking in the last hot days of summer. Kids teased the lapping waves and local performers played guitars and saxophones near the pier. The smells coming from a hot dog stand to her right tempted her to stop and the sound of the ice-cream truck's familiar melody playing in the distance brought back childhood memories of days spent building sand castles along the water's edge with her brothers.

Parking her motorcycle in an angled parking spot a few doors down from her aunt's shop, Bailey swung her leg over the bike and stretched. The two-hour midmorning drive had been almost traffic-free, and she'd been able to allow her mind to wander as she drove. Unfortunately, despite the back-and-forth game she'd played in her mind, the facts remained the same. Emily was pregnant and that was the end of whatever had been happening between her and Ethan.

She removed her helmet and grabbed her backpack. She refused to think about Ethan anymore on this trip. Okay, that was a stretch. She refused to think about him for at least the next hour.

A bell chimed as she entered Caroline's Closet, and she forced a smile when her aunt waved her in, the shop phone cradled against her shoulder. "Yes, actually she just walked in." *Your dad,* she mouthed.

Bailey nodded, setting her bag down near the door and checking her cell phone. Three missed calls from her father, one from her aunt Jeanette but nothing from the person she refused to think about. As she glanced around the shop, a sense of familiarity washed over her. Except for the stock, nothing had changed. Her aunt's homemade wind chimes made out of beach shells and hand-crafted metal charms still hung in the front window, and potted plants lined the shelves on the walls. Racks of clothing were positioned in the main showroom of the store and a single wall of shoes was displayed toward the back near the counter.

"Yes, I'll ask her to call once she gets settled...Okay, you, too. Bye, Ben," her aunt said, disconnecting the call. Setting the receiver back into the cradle of the old-fashioned rotary phone, she joined Bailey on the other side of the counter. "Bailey!"

Caroline wrapped her in a tight hug and then pulled away, studying her. "If I hadn't known you were coming, I would have sworn I was seeing the ghost of your mom walking in. You look more and more like her all the time." Caroline's eyes misted. "You're not even here thirty seconds and I'm a mess," she said with a laugh.

"Hi, Aunt Caroline," Bailey said.

"Your dad was starting to worry. Said he tried calling your cell a few times."

"I turned off the ringer while I drove. I didn't want to be distracted," she mumbled.

It was partly true. She also didn't want to be haunted by the silence of a nonringing phone.

"That makes sense," her aunt said, then hugged her again. "I heard about the shop. I'm so glad you're okay and that the rebuild went smoothly."

"Yeah, it was awful to watch it being destroyed, but it really does look fantastic now with all the new upgrades."

"I wouldn't let that insurance adjuster hear you say that," her aunt teased.

"Heard the rumors all the way out here, huh?"

Caroline nodded. "People are crazy," she said, studying her for a long moment.

"What?" The keen, piercing gaze made Bailey uncomfortable. It was the same look her aunt would give them as kids when they were trying to hide the shenanigans they'd gotten up to during the day while she worked.

"I'm just waiting to see if you're going to tell me about him or if I'm going to have to ask?"

"Him who?" Bailey toyed with the zipper on her leather jacket. Unlike her father's side of the family, where the men were mostly oblivious to personal issues until they hit them in the forehead, her mother's family had always been intuitive to each other's feelings. And unlike her father's family, they wanted to talk about it.

"The guy you drove two hours to get away from."

"What makes you think I'm hiding from a guy?" Bailey stalled, removing her jacket. "I just thought it would be a good time to visit, before the weather changes and I have to put the bike in storage." That part was true, at least.

Her aunt placed a box of stock onto the counter and leaned against it, moving closer to her. "Darling, you're not the first person to come to Beach Haven with a broken heart reflected in her eyes. How do you think I ended up here?" she asked softly.

Bailey's eyes widened. "I thought you moved out here to be with Uncle Dan?"

Her aunt's smile was faraway as she said, "That happened later."

"Oh. I had no idea." Bailey's curiosity was overwhelming, but she waited. Her Sheppard DNA prevented her from asking any questions.

Caroline opened the box of fall sweaters and sighed. "This is the one thing I hate about working in the clothing industry. The summer sun hasn't even cooled yet and I have to start putting out the warmer clothing." She reached into the box and pulled out a teal-green cashmere V-neck, folded it neatly and reached for another.

Bailey shifted on the stool behind the counter and pulled out a sweater, as well. One thing she'd learned from the rainy summer days stuck inside the shop on family visits was how to fold.

"Would it help if I told you about him?" Caroline asked after a long, excruciating silence.

"Only if you want to," Bailey said, not wanting to pry but desperate to hear a story that might make her feel better...or worse. After all, her aunt had obviously not ended up with the man she was about to tell her about. Bailey bit her lip as she waited.

Caroline reached under the counter for a box of saltwater taffy, opened it and offered it to Bailey.

Taking a pink one, her favorite, she popped it into her mouth.

"Okay, but please keep in mind that this was a long time ago," Caroline said. "The feelings I had back then have been long gone for quite some time."

Bailey nodded, eager to hear about the mystery man in her aunt's past. Family secrets were rare in towns the size of Brookhollow and Beach Haven, so she could appreciate how much trouble her aunt must have gone to to keep this one.

"Okay, well, the truth is…before your mom and dad got together, I dated Ben first." Caroline paused and waited.

Bailey's mouth fell open and she quickly closed it. Swallowing the taffy, she said, "My dad broke your heart?"

"Yes. I was eighteen and completely in love. We were in the same grade in school and I purposely selected all of the same classes. Your mom was a junior that year. On our third date when he picked me up, he noticed your mom drawing on the porch—she was an amazing artist even then—and that was it. The connection between the two of them was instant. They had so much in common and they even shared the same silly sense of humor. You know those jokes your father tells that no one else gets? Your mom did. Even I could see they were perfect together."

"What did you do?"

"I broke up with him. It broke my heart to do it, but I couldn't stand being in their company and seeing the looks they shared, obviously denying their true feelings for my sake." She shook her head.

"And they just got together…just like that?" It was hard for Bailey to believe that her parents could be so callous to her aunt's feelings.

"Oh, no," Caroline insisted. "It took months of prompting and encouraging on my part for your mom to say yes to Ben's requests."

"You pushed them together? That's admirable. Most people would have been happy to keep them apart." Bailey was seeing her aunt in a whole new light. She knew her mother's older sister had always looked out for her, but this took a lot of strength.

"I couldn't," she said, her voice not holding the slightest trace of sadness. "What the movie producers of every love story may fail to remind us is that for every happily ever after, there are a dozen broken hearts, but in my case my disappointment in love led me here to Beach Haven and your Uncle Dan." Her smile was wide.

"Wow," Bailey whispered.

Caroline reached forward and touched her hand. "No, sweet girl, the wow was what happened next—finding your uncle and having the boys. It turned out that was my happy ever after, I just didn't know it."

"So what you're saying is, this guy is not the one and something even more amazing is waiting around the corner...or in a different town?" she asked with a gulp. She seriously doubted there was anyone better than Ethan. As angry and hurt as she was over their situation, deep down she just admired and respected him even more for his decision.

"What I'm saying is you have to figure out if Ethan is really Emily's happy ever after or if he's yours."

"How did you know it was Ethan?"

"It's always been Ethan, hasn't it?" Caroline asked with a knowing smile.

Bailey nodded and thought for a long moment, touching the soft cashmere on her lap. "But what if my heart and my head are telling me two different things?"

"IT WAS GREAT seeing you again, Bailey. You shouldn't wait so long to visit next time." Her cousin Troy hugged her tight with one arm as he carried a baby's car seat in the other. The sleeping bundle of joy was oblivious to the noise of the farewells around her.

"I promise to visit more often, especially now that I've met Ella," Bailey said, bending to place a gentle kiss on the baby's forehead. Ella smiled in her sleep and a strange sense of longing stirred within her. Then the reminder hit. Ethan would have a baby soon.

"Good night, Caroline," Troy's wife, Bridget, said. "Great meeting you, Bailey. Sorry to rush off, but this little princess needs to be in bed."

Bailey covered her own yawn with her hand. "Looks like Ella isn't the only one." The terrible night before with little sleep and the early-morning road trip were catching up to her and she'd struggled to keep her eyes open during her aunt's salted-cod-and-potato casserole. She'd forced her troubles away for her family's sake, but she hadn't been able to shake the nagging loneliness as she'd watched the loving affection between Troy, Bridget and baby Ella. She wanted all of that. With a man she couldn't have.

"Bye, you guys. Drive safe." Caroline blew several kisses before closing the door behind them.

Bailey scanned the messy kitchen and dining room. Her aunt didn't believe in cleaning as she cooked. Nor did she allow her guests to help tidy up. Countless plates, cups and pots and pans littered the counters. At least an hour of cleanup awaited Bailey before she could be reunited with the down-filled pillows she remembered from the guest room upstairs. Tying her hair back from her face, she filled the sink with soapy hot water.

"Oh, no, you don't have to clean up," her aunt said, entering the kitchen and taking her hands from the sink.

"It's no problem," Bailey said through another yawn.

"Look at you. You're dead on your feet." Tossing Bailey a dish towel to dry her hands, Caroline opened the fridge. She grabbed a bottle of Reisling and two glasses. "Come on, let's have a drink before I kick you off to bed. It will help you sleep."

"Oh, I doubt I'll have any trouble...." Bailey could barely force her eyes to remain open.

"You will once the quiet hits and you're once again alone with your conflicted heart and troubled thoughts."

"Wow, you really have been through this before." She accepted the wineglass, suddenly not so eager to retire to the solitude awaiting her in the room upstairs. Her aunt was right. As tired as she was, unanswered questions would keep her awake most of the night.

"Let's go sit on the porch. It's beautiful out there as the sun sets."

"Okay," Bailey said, following her aunt outside and taking a seat on the wooden porch swing on the white wraparound patio of the two-story beach house. The view from the front porch was a familiar one as her mother had painted a picture of it on a family vacation to Beach Haven the summer before she got sick. The painting hung above her fireplace at home—a reminder of those family vacations.

Her aunt lay back in the hammock on the deck several feet away.

The warm breeze drifting off the water and the sound of the gentle waves lapping against the beach rocks were enough to lull Bailey to sleep right there on the gently swaying, creaking swing. Kicking off her shoes, she leaned her head back and relaxed her tense shoulders, desperate to find the sense of calm that eluded her despite the serenity of her surroundings. "Maybe I should just move out here."

"Uh-uh," her aunt said, her eyes glued to the setting sun as she swayed in the hammock.

"Why not? It worked out well for you. You have a wonderful life out here—beachfront property, a great shop and a fantastic family."

"That's all very true, but it was because my prince charming was waiting for me here. Believe me, yours is elsewhere. There are only three single men in this town under the age of fifty and let's just put it this way—they are not Ethan. Besides, you made a promise to your mom."

"To look after Dad and the boys. I remember."

"In her final days, your mom asked everyone she knew to be a source of support for your dad, but to let him figure things out in his own way, on his own time. She made all of us promise not to help too much in raising you three or with the housework. Technically I guess Tina Miller from the diner broke hers by bringing food, but you kids needed to eat, and Lord knows Ben was so lost without Candy those first few weeks that food would never have crossed his mind. Anyway, Candy knew Ben needed to learn how to cope as a way to heal. He had to prove to himself that he could take care of things the way she did and raise you three the way they would have together. Keeping Ben busy was the only way she knew to help bring him back to life after hers was over."

"I know." A memory struck Bailey with a soft blow. "The mailbox," she said with a nod.

"What about the mailbox?"

Bailey swallowed the lump in her throat. "I remember coming home from school to find a post office slip stuck to the front door saying that no more mail would be delivered until Dad cleaned out our mailbox across the street. He looked at me and all I wanted to do was go get the mail for him, but I heard Mom's voice and I realized this was what she'd meant. Dad had to figure out these day-to-day things on his own, so I handed him the mailbox key and went inside." She paused, taking a sip of her wine.

Her aunt's eyes misted. "That was exactly the kind of stuff your mom wanted—no, needed—your dad to learn how to do on his own. In nine years of marriage, he'd never once checked the mail or bought the groceries or paid bills, but it was something he would need to do going forward."

"I watched him from the window," Bailey

said, "trying that key in every slot. Mentally I was screaming, 'It's the second row of boxes, number twelve,' but I stayed silent. When he finally found the box and opened it, the mail just flew out, scattering across the ground. His shoulders slumped and shook for just a second, but when he turned, he was smiling and he held up the mail as a sort of victory." Bailey laughed through the lone tear streaming down one cheek. "I'd totally forgotten about that until now. Thanks, Aunt Caroline."

"Your mother had been right, as usual. Your dad needed the confidence that accomplishing even the smallest tasks would give him, the confidence that he could survive without her and needed to for his sake and yours and the boys." Caroline drained the contents of her wineglass and swung her legs over the side of the hammock. "I'm going to go clean up, leave you to your thoughts." She stared out at the ocean. "This place always has a way of helping me figure things out. Hopefully, it will have the same effect on you." She kissed Bailey's forehead and disappeared inside.

Bailey reached for her phone and tossed it between her hands. There were several frantic voice mails from Victoria wondering if Bailey planned to be back in time for the wedding, but no messages or calls from Ethan. Disappointed, she put the phone down. Although she wasn't sure what she wanted or expected from herself or Ethan.

CHAPTER TWELVE

ETHAN PULLED INTO the parking lot behind
Brookhollow High School, on the opposite
side of the soccer and football field. Drain-
ing the contents of his Red Bull, he grabbed
the duffel bag of soccer balls and slid his
baseball cap over his head. A sense of relief
washed over him as he noticed the Myerses'
van parked several spots away. His star players were here for his last game as coach. He
hoped Melody planned to stay. He could use
her support in the stands that evening.

The game against the Camden Crushers
started in an hour, but he wanted to talk to the
boys first. In truth, he didn't want any more
time than necessary alone with his thoughts.
Or rather, one consistent thought—Bailey.
When he was working or coaching, he had
little time to think about her…or at least she
wasn't the only thought driving him to the
brink of insanity. Four days without her and
he already felt lost. He had so much to tell her

and he longed to make her listen, but more than that, he missed his best friend. Without being able to see her or hear her voice whenever he wanted, he realized just how big a part of his life she really was. How was he going to live in Miami and not see her every day?

Readjusting the bag on his shoulder, he made his way around the side of the high school. As he rounded the corner, the large crowd gathered on the soccer field began to cheer and clap. Squinting in the early-evening sunlight, he read the banner hung across several cars parked in front of the field. "We will miss you, Coach Bishop" was handwritten across the paper. The gesture had caught him completely off guard and he smiled, momentarily forgetting the troubles that had plagued him all day.

Balloons were tied to the fence and bleachers, and a table was set up under a small white tent with cookies, cupcakes and refreshments. His nephews were the first to approach him with a large construction-paper card, the rest of the junior boys team following. The parents waved from the sidelines and Melody smiled at him from her spot behind the food table.

"Hey, guys. What's all this?" Ethan asked, setting the duffel bag down on the grass and bending to accept the card from the boys.

"We all just wanted to say goodbye…before you left," David said.

Ethan opened the card and smiled at the boys' signatures and their heartfelt messages. Setting the card aside, he hugged the boys, swallowing a lump in his throat, thankful for his dark sunglasses. Kids had a way of reducing even the toughest man to a softie. "Thanks, guys."

"Come on. We have cake," Josh said.

Ethan let him lead the way. "Hi, Mel."

"Hey, Coach, can I interest you in a cupcake?" Melody extended a cupcake with a candy soccer ball on top.

Ethan eyed the chocolate treat suspiciously, remembering her casserole. "Did you bake these?"

Melody raised an eyebrow. "We wanted to say goodbye, not poison you. They're compliments of Ginger Snaps."

"In that case, I'd love one." He'd barely eaten in days and his stomach growled.

"I also have something for you," she said, retrieving several folded papers from her pocket. "I had a lot to say and I'm not great with words. I wrote it down." She hesitated before handing him the pages.

Biting into his cupcake, Ethan opened the letter to see her loopy handwriting and began to read.

Melody reached out and took the papers back. "That's just embarrassing, and it's too long and you probably can't decipher my handwriting anyway." She paused, then folded the pages and put them back in her pocket. "What it basically says, in a nutshell, is this—you will make a terrific father and Emily and the baby are lucky to have you. The boys are really going to miss you, so keep in touch. Okay?"

"You got it. Thanks, Mel."

Melody's eyes grew shiny and she waved him away as she cleared her throat. "Don't you have to go coach that team one last time?"

"Yes, ma'am."

CHAPTER THIRTEEN

"WHY EXACTLY ARE we here again?" Kayla Dawson asked, examining a perfectly manicured hand where she sat next to Bailey on the love seat in the main sitting room at the Brookhollow Inn. Also present were Luke's other sister, Alisha, and Rachel's sister-in-law Lindsay.

"I'm not sure," Bailey said. "Rachel didn't say. She just texted everyone that it was important for all of us to show up later than seven, once Vic had left for the day. It must be some wedding surprise." When she'd gotten the text, she'd rushed back from Beach Haven a day earlier than she'd planned.

"Hi, everyone," Rachel said. "Thank you all for showing up on short notice. I had to wait till the last minute to call this meeting to be sure Victoria didn't find out about it. Some of you have trouble keeping things to yourselves." she added with a pointed look to Lindsay.

Lindsay rolled her eyes. "I can keep a secret."

"Really? Who told me my husband was going to propose a week before he planned to do it?"

"I thought maybe you needed a warning," Lindsay said with a look of innocence.

"And you told everyone I was pregnant with the boys before I had a chance—"

"Okay, look, I guess I just have a different idea about what constitutes a secret than you do. Everyone was going to find out eventually. What was the big deal?"

Rachel placed her hands on her hips and shook her head, then turned her attention back to the group. "Anyway, I promise this won't take long."

Take all the time in the world, Bailey thought. She wasn't in a rush to leave. She still hadn't decided whether or not she would attend the going-away party Melody had organized for Ethan at the Green Gator, the karaoke bar in town, that evening. After years of friendship, she should be there to say goodbye, but she wasn't sure she could do it.

"What won't take long? What are we doing here?" Alisha asked, still in her work apron. The Dawson family owned the only pharmacy and convenience store on Main Street and Alisha had followed in her father's footsteps, becoming a pharmacist after school.

"Operation Bridewatch," Rachel said.

"Huh?" Lindsay glanced at Bailey, who just shrugged. She didn't pretend to understand any of this wedding stuff. And if she was honest, she was only half listening.

Kayla Dawson nodded enthusiastically. "See, Alisha, I told you this would be a great idea." She looked annoyed that she'd failed to execute the plan, whatever it was, before Rachel.

"I think you two are crazy," Alisha scoffed. "Victoria's not running this time."

Though Luke's older sister had had her reservations about Victoria's intentions when she'd first returned to Brookhollow, the two had rekindled a sisterlike bond.

"Well, I think we still need to be safe…for Luke's sake," Kayla said. "Go ahead, Rachel."

"Okay, here's the deal. The closer the wedding gets, the crazier Vic is acting. Her inability to make decisions until the last minute is unlike her and, frankly, a little unnerving. So for the next two days, I want us all to volunteer shifts to make sure she's alone as little as possible. She's here with me every day, so days are easy, but Luke's out of town until late Saturday, so it's the evenings we're concerned about."

"Does Luke know about this?" Bailey asked.

"No, I didn't want to put any ideas into his head or freak him out. So, volunteers?"

"I'm going to Ethan's going-away party at the Green Gator tonight," Kayla said. "Victoria's welcome to come along."

Rachel shook her head. "Thanks, Kayla, but you'll never drag her there."

"I'm working at the bingo hall tonight—she could come," Alisha offered.

"Again, not really her thing, but thank you. Anyone else?"

Bailey hesitated. This provided her with the perfect opportunity to miss the going-away party. "I'll invite her to a movie tonight."

Rachel looked surprised. "Really? I thought you would be going to the Green Gator, as well," she said softly.

"No," Bailey said. If she tried to give an excuse or elaborate on her decision, she would just turn into a bumbling idiot. Best to not say anything more.

"You're sure?"

Bailey nodded.

"Okay, so that just leaves the overnights. That's where you come in." Rachel turned to Lindsay.

"Why me?"

"You live next door to the old Kingston house. Victoria's been staying there, moving things in and organizing while Luke's been away. You are the logical choice."

"And what am I supposed to do?" Lindsay asked. "Stand outside the front door and yell if she tries to go anywhere?"

"No, just keep an eye on her car every now and then."

"Honestly, I'm not the right person to help with your prison-watch plan."

"Bridewatch," Rachel corrected.

"All I'm saying is that I wouldn't be opposed to her running again. Before she came back, Luke and I had a connection."

Wow, Bailey would never have thought that she had anything in common with Lindsay Harper.

Alisha glared at Lindsay and Kayla opened her mouth, but Rachel silenced them with a hand. "No, you didn't," she said.

"Well, there was a definite spark."

Definitely a spark, Bailey thought.

"Nope, no spark. For Luke, it's always only ever been Victoria," Rachel said firmly.

Was that also true in her case? Bailey wondered. The thought was depressing. How could she have mistaken Ethan's feelings?

Lindsay huffed. "I'll make sure she is there before I go to bed, but that's all I promise to do."

"That's all I ask," Rachel said. "Thanks, ladies. Remember, any sign of cold feet or strange behavior, call or text me right away."

"And what do you plan to do?" Alisha asked, clearly not entirely on board with the idea.

"Remind her how miserable she was without the love of her life," Rachel said.

Bailey sighed. She knew the feeling.

"THANKS AGAIN FOR suggesting this, Bailey. A movie was exactly what I needed to get my mind off the wedding and all the last-minute jitters," Victoria said as they exited the theatre, which was just off Main Street and housed in the same building as the pool hall. It was quiet in that area of town since most of the residents were at the Green Gator.

"No problem." She only wished the movie had been successful in taking her mind off her own troubles. If asked, she couldn't even tell anyone what the new Brad Pitt movie had been about. "It was fun."

"I was surprised that you were free tonight," Victoria said as they walked through the gravel parking lot to their vehicles. She looked at Bailey expectantly.

Bailey sighed. She should have known she wouldn't get away without talking about it. "I couldn't do it. Does that make me a terrible person?"

"Not at all. It makes you real, your feelings real. I just still can't believe what's happened." Victoria removed her truck keys from her purse. "I mean, I know I just reappeared out of nowhere eight months ago, but at least I didn't drop a bomb on poor Luke like Emily did to Ethan. How could she not have told him before now?"

"She did try calling him…." She had no idea why she felt the need to defend Emily. Probably because she didn't blame her. How could she? She didn't blame anyone.

Victoria looked at her in amazement. "Bailey, you are too nice. If I was in your position, I think I'd still be throwing things at him."

"It's not his fault. It's no one's fault. It's just incredibly bad timing."

"Have you talked to him?"

She shook her head. Other than their run-in at the Fireside Grill, she'd been successful in avoiding Ethan. The trip to Beach Haven had helped, though it totally disproved the old saying "out of sight, out of mind." It didn't matter what she did, Ethan was always on her mind.

"Maybe you should.... I mean, once he's gone, it may be too late."

It was already too late. "I don't think I can do it, Vic. Seeing them together is hard."

"I totally understand, but I just think some-day you might wish you had been there. You two have been such good friends for years."

Bailey bit her lip, contemplating what Victoria had said. She and Ethan had been best friends for a long time, but things were so different now and they couldn't go back.

"Just think about it," Victoria said, before climbing into the truck. She rolled down the window as Bailey tossed her leg over her bike and reached for her helmet. "Just know, what-ever you decide will be the right thing."

"I SAW THAT your hand was empty and thought you could use one of these," Mark said, com-ing to stand beside Ethan near the back wall of the bar. The Green Gator was standing room only as friends and family drifted in in waves to say goodbye to him.

He accepted the beer bottle from Mark and took a swig. "Thanks, buddy."

"I can't believe she didn't show up."

Ethan nodded as he stared at the bottle in his hand. It had been the recurring thought clouding his mind all evening. He knew she was back from Beach Haven and he knew *she* knew he was leaving in the morning with Emily for Miami. The idea that she didn't want to see him before he left made it difficult to breathe. "I'm sure she has her reasons."

"Yeah, she loves you, which is exactly why she should be here," Mark said.

Ethan leaned back against the wall. "None of this is her fault. I can't believe I was such an idiot not to notice how perfect she is before now, before it was too late."

Mark punched his shoulder. "Don't beat yourself up over it—that's my job. Besides, Emily always did have a way of casting a pretty big shadow."

From across the room, Ethan watched as Emily performed an off-key version of "Girls Just Want to Have Fun" with her sister, Kimberly, on the karaoke stage. She'd always been larger than life in Brookhollow and he realized now that keeping her here had been wrong. He'd pushed her away before by making her so unhappy, making her feel trapped in a situation with him. Exactly the way he was feeling now. Would he ever feel the same way about her that he did for Bailey? Had he ever? And would the love he would, without a doubt, have for his child be enough to keep them together?

"Anyway, I think I'm going to head out," Mark said, putting his empty beer bottle on the shelf. He turned to Ethan and extended his hand. "Good luck, man. We'll miss you around here."

Ethan accepted the hand and patted Mark's arm. "Take care of the guys for me, okay?"

AN HOUR LATER, Bailey tugged against the big metal door of the Green Gator, convincing herself she was doing the right thing as she entered the crowded, dark, neon-lit bar. Small round tables were crammed to maximum capacity in the center of the room and private booths lined both walls. Locating Ethan's group was easy as they'd pushed several large tables together in front of the karaoke stage and hung a long bon voyage banner on the wall above.

Fighting every last urge to turn around and leave, Bailey made her way to the table, just as Melody Myers took the stage. Within seconds, the sound of her soft, jazzy voice singing an old Janis Joplin tune floated on the air. Bailey turned to watch, still several feet from the party, partly to enjoy the local star's beautiful voice and partly to prolong joining the group, who'd yet to notice her arrival.

"You made it," a deep voice whispered in her ear.

She turned toward Ethan, who was carrying a tray of drinks. The Green Gator staff consisted of the bartender and owner, T. J. Spencer, so there was only bar service.

Bailey forced a smile that didn't quite reach her eyes. "Wouldn't have missed it," she lied.

"Drink?" Ethan asked, studying her intently.

Yes, a strong one. "I'll get it." She really wasn't in a rush to join the others. Being around Ethan was torture. She intended to stay long enough to say she'd made an effort. Long enough to say goodbye.

"No, really. Please allow me." He leaned

closer and whispered, "Honestly, I'm trying to avoid the party. That's horrible, isn't it?"

"Yes," Bailey answered, but unexpected tears sprang to her eyes at the similar situation they found themselves in. She couldn't decide if she was happy that Ethan was feeling the same way she was or if it just made things worse. Not wanting to break down in front of him, she said, "A drink would be great, thanks." Then she reluctantly approached the table.

"Bailey!" Emily shrieked, running over to her as though she was happy to see her. Bailey wasn't buying the act. "Come on, I saved you a seat." Emily took her hand and forced her into the chair next to hers.

"Hi, Bailey," Kim greeted, glancing up from a textbook on media design.

"Can you believe it? My baby sister is going to NYU next week," Emily gushed.

Kim yawned. "Yes, and I still need to get through this book, so I'm sorry, Em, but don't count on me for a late night."

From the other end of the table, Emily's cousin Amber and her boyfriend, Chris, waved in greeting, and to her right Dwayne Adams reclaimed his seat. "Ah, just the girl I've been looking for," he said.

"Me?" Bailey asked in surprise.

"Yeah, you. I hear you need a new attacker for your self-defense class." He turned in his seat to face her.

She hadn't thought of that. One more thing Emily was taking away from her. "Yeah, I guess so."

"Well, consider the position filled. It's the least I can do to repay you for volunteering on my pit crew."

She scanned the bar for Ethan and her drink. The last thing she wanted to discuss that evening was replacing Ethan in any aspect of her life. He was standing in line at the bar, but he was staring at her. The pained look in his eyes mirrored the one in her chest.

"Excuse me for a second," she said, getting up and making her way outside. Coming here had been a bad idea.

Pushing through the heavy door, she took several deep breaths and sat down on the wooden bench on the small smokers' patio, grateful it was empty. She needed a few minutes to pull herself together. She kicked her feet free from her sandals and tucked her legs under the bench. How was she going to get through this? Loving Ethan and never being able to have him had been hard enough before, but now that she knew what it felt like to be in his arms, how his lips felt against hers, getting over him was going to be impossible. Her saving grace was that he wouldn't be in Brookhollow much longer.

The door to the bar opened and Bailey straightened.

"You okay?" Ethan asked, walking outside.

"Just needed some air. It's stuffy in there."

"Mind if I join you?"

"Where's Emily?"

"Singing with Amber," he said, sitting next to her. He leaned forward and rested his elbows on his knees. "So—"

"Don't," Bailey interrupted, glancing toward the door of the bar. The last thing she wanted was to discuss the awkward situation they found themselves in with Emily's return. Moving on and reburying their emerging feelings was the only option.

"I really think we should talk."

"About what?" Did he think this was a problem they could solve? "There's nothing to talk about, Ethan." Bailey's pained expression met his defeated one. "You're leaving… with Emily."

"But…"

"How can there possibly be a but? You are

going to be a father, you are moving to Miami to start a family. There is no *but* option." She stood and leaned against the deck railing. He was too close, sitting next to her. She needed some space. "Nothing happened and I'm just relieved that Emily came back before we did something stupid." The lie stuck in her throat and she lowered her eyes to the ground. Why couldn't he just let it go? He had to know that in time he would fall back in love with Emily as though nothing had ever happened.

Ethan stood and placed his hands on the deck railing at either side of her. He bent at the knees to look into her eyes.

"Something stupid? How about something wonderful, something amazing and real? Those are the words that come to my mind when I think of the two of us together. Which, by the way, is all the time. There's not a moment that goes by that I don't think of you, Bailey. Of what could have been."

Struggling to breathe, Bailey pushed past him and headed toward her motorcycle. She couldn't stay any longer. She'd been crazy to think she could get through the evening.

"You're leaving?"

"No, *you're* leaving. I'm just going home." Her heart ached at the hurt on his face. She hoped in time they could both push past the pain and move on. "I'm happy for you both. I just can't...you know. Tell Emily I wish her and the baby all the best." She meant that.

Ethan followed Bailey to her bike. "So that's it?"

Bailey hesitated. It no longer mattered that they'd shared a deep connection; it couldn't develop into anything more. There was no point torturing themselves with what might have been.

"That's it," she said firmly, surprising herself with the strength she heard in her voice.

"Bailey, I—"

"Don't." She put up a hand to stop the words she knew were coming. Words she longed to hear, but which would tear her apart. "Do not tell me you love me when it's followed by goodbye." Sliding her helmet on over her loose waves, Bailey put the bike in gear and sped away, fighting to see through the tears burning her eyes.

ETHAN STOOD ON the gravel, watching Bailey drive away, fighting the urge to go after her. She was right. There was no way they could be together. He refused to not be there for Emily and his baby—it just destroyed him that it was at the expense of the woman he truly loved. Running a hand through his hair, he went back inside the bar and slumped onto an empty metal stool, not ready to rejoin the others. So that was it.

"There you are," Emily said, coming up behind him. "Where's Bailey?"

"Um…she had to go."

Emily simply nodded as she climbed onto the bar stool next to him. She studied him in silence for a long moment before she said, "I'm too late, aren't I? You've moved on."

Ethan didn't know what to say. She was, but the disappointed expression on the face of the woman who'd shared so much of his past made his chest hurt. He turned and took her hands in his. Taking a deep breath, he stared into the eyes of the woman he was prepared to spend his life with.

"Look, I don't want you to worry, okay? I'm totally committed to you and this baby." He brushed a stray blond curl from her face.

"But you don't love me?"

Love. What a loaded word. He had loved her, very much. But he realized that over time that love had turned into a comfortable feeling of being safe and knowing where the future was headed. It hadn't been the gut-wrenching, insomnia-inducing passion he'd experienced with Bailey. He doubted he could ever feel that way again for Emily, but maybe once the baby was born and they'd had time to reconnect, it would be a different kind of love.

"We'll work on all that, okay?" It was the only answer he could give. Love or not, he was on a plane in the morning to Miami.

CHAPTER FOURTEEN

"WHERE ARE BRANDON and Jordan?" Bailey asked, sliding into the corner booth at Joey's across from her father the following morning. She slid her sunglasses to the top of her head, and squinted in the bright light. Lack of sleep and the countless tears she'd shed the night before made it difficult to keep her eyes open. In the kitchen, the sound of a tray of dishes crashing to the floor made her wince. That certainly didn't help her headache.

"I asked them if you and I could do breakfast just the two of us today."

"Why?" This would be the first time the boys hadn't joined them. Glancing around the crowded diner, she noticed them in a booth several feet away. "Why are they sitting over there?"

"I thought maybe you might want to talk." Ben sounded uncomfortable as he said the words.

Bailey peered at her father. "Talk? Since

when do we talk?" Hiding their true feelings and putting on a brave front was more their style.

"Just humor me, okay?"

"Sorry, Dad. I do appreciate it."

"I just want you to know that I'm here... and so are your brothers. Well, they're over there, but you get what I mean."

"I know, Dad."

Her father leaned back against the plush booth and studied her for a long moment before asking, "So you're doing okay?"

She was so far from okay she couldn't even see what okay might someday look like. "I will be."

"When does he leave?"

Bailey glanced at her watch. Two hours and forty-eight minutes from now. "Soon."

Ben nodded. "You said everything you needed to?"

Not even close, but then how could she? She wanted to tell him she loved him, beg him to stay, choose her, *choose them,* but she couldn't.

"It wouldn't change things." Picking up her coffee cup, she savored the lifesaving brew. Just about the only thing that was going to get her through the day.

Her father surprised her as he leaned forward and said, "Believe it or not, it would change a lot of things."

"How?" He couldn't possibly understand what she was facing. Loving someone and knowing there was no way they could be together. Her stomach did an involuntary flip-flop. Or just maybe he was the only one who could understand.

He sighed. "Bailey, your mom was sick for almost six months before she told me. I was so busy getting my business off the ground and working so many hours that it was too easy not to notice her gradual weight loss or her frequent naps. I never knew about the doctor's appointments...until time grew short."

She'd suspected that had been the case, but she'd assumed her mother had just kept her illness from her and the boys, not her father, as well.

"When she finally did tell me, I was angry, but her reasoning was that it wouldn't have made a difference. Me knowing wouldn't have made her better."

Bailey swallowed a lump in her throat.

"But she was wrong. Knowing would have made a big difference. Had I known, I wouldn't have worked so darn much. Time with her would have been a priority. I would have told her a million times a day how much she meant to me, how perfect she was, how much I would miss her. It wouldn't save her, but it would have made all the difference in the world. Because after she was gone, I'd have had no regrets."

"Mom knew how you felt, Dad," Bailey reassured.

Ben nodded. "I know she did because, believe it or not, the memory I hold in my mind of your mom was in her last days."

"Really? They were so awful, so full of tears and pain...." She didn't like to think of the last few weeks leading up to her mom's passing. It surprised her that her father chose to remember that time fondly.

"They were," Ben agreed. "But they were also full of love and connection. It was in those torturous days that we realized how special our love was. We knew our time together was short, but it was more valuable than any other lifetime of love could ever have been."

Bailey slumped against the booth. "Wow."

"You need to tell him how you feel and you need to hear it from him. Whether it's meant to be a lifetime love or not, you both deserve to have no regrets and to experience a moment of real connection."

Bailey hesitated. Could she do that? Could she admit to and accept love from a man as he walked away from her? Could she recover from that? She checked her watch. "His flight leaves in a little over two hours…out of Newark."

"Well, I suggest you get going."

BAILEY PUSHED AGAINST the large revolving door that was moving much too slowly for someone in a mad panic to catch the man she loved before he boarded a flight to a different life.

"Come on," she muttered, readjusting her purse on her shoulder as the door finally gave way. Long lines of passengers stood at the various airline check-in counters, dragging suitcases and carry-ons behind them. She searched the rows for Ethan, but didn't see him anywhere. Oh, please, God, she hoped she wasn't too late. Once they passed through security, there would be no chance of seeing him before he boarded the plane for Miami.

Standing on tiptoe, she moved closer to the lines, bumping into a large blue suitcase. The woman wheeling it behind her turned and shot her an irritated look.

"Sorry, excuse me," Bailey said, her shoulders sagging as her eyes searched the line a final time. They weren't there. She checked her watch. 9:45 a.m. According to the flight schedule above the United Airlines clerk, the Miami flight was scheduled to leave at 10:35 a.m. They had to have checked in already.

Swallowing the thick lump in her throat that had plagued her on the high-speed ride to the airport, she turned and scanned the hallways. The security checkpoint was several yards away to her right. It couldn't hurt to try.

Jogging, she weaved through the passengers heading in the same direction and struggled to catch her breath four minutes later when she arrived at the entry point. The lineup was even longer than the one at the ticket booth. She'd be lucky to see him at all in the sea of travelers, let alone grab his attention.

She moved along the roped corrals, looking for Ethan, ducking and leaning to see around the crowd. "Sorry, excuse me." She had to say goodbye. The right way. He couldn't leave questioning how she felt about him, even if there wasn't a thing either of them could do about it.

Then she saw him. At the front of the line, shoes in hand, removing his belt to place inside the square white bins along with his coat and carry-on.

"Ethan," she whispered. Well, he sure wouldn't hear that. "Ethan!" she called loudly, waving a hand above her head. Every face in line turned to stare at her, but all she cared about was one.

A look of wide-eyed surprise and relief spread across his face as he slowly raised his hand in a wave. Oh, thank God. Tossing his shoes into the bin, he picked it up from the conveyor belt and started toward her. Emily caught his arm with a questioning look. Bailey couldn't hear what he said, but a second later, Emily was placing her items in a bin and he was heading toward Bailey. The passengers in line shifted to the left, grumbling, but he didn't seem to hear them or care as he made his way to her.

Reaching her at last, he stood silently for a brief second before dropping the bin and wrapping her in his arms. "I'm so glad you're here," he whispered, kissing the top of her head.

Bailey nodded, hugging him tightly, but

unable to find her voice. She had so much to say, and absolutely no time, yet she was speechless. He stroked her hair and clasped her to his chest, which heaved heavily.

"I'm so glad you're here," he repeated.

"I couldn't just let you leave…." she said finally. She moved away just enough to look up at him and her heart ached at the sight of tears rimming his lower lids. "I had to see you, to tell you…I love you. And I'm not here to convince you to stay," she rushed on. "I know what you have to do and the last thing I want is to make it harder for you…or fight for you…but I never want you to doubt…me, us, what we had."

As hard as the words were to say, once they were out, it felt as though a large weight had been lifted from her chest. One she'd been carrying around for weeks. Her father was right. In that moment of sorrowful joy, she knew what real love felt like—the sacrificing unselfish act of doing what was right for another person. She had no regrets.

"I love you, Bailey," Ethan said, placing his hands on her cheeks and bending slightly to look into her eyes. "I don't want you to ever wonder about that. There is nothing that I'd like more than to stay here with you. Please believe that."

"I do." She did. She believed it wholeheart-edly.

He hugged her tight again, whispering words she couldn't decipher against her hair. It didn't matter. She closed her eyes, enjoying the feel of his arms around her, never wanting to stop holding him. In a minute, she'd have to let go and she would…for him. Drawing in one final breath of him, she clenched her jaw, forced her voice to remain steady, and backed out of his embrace.

"You have to go now."

He took her hands and nodded, bringing one at a time to his lips and kissing them softly. "I'll think of you every day," he prom-ised.

And in that moment she allowed herself to believe it, though deep down she knew in time he would move on, find happiness again with Emily and the baby. And that was what she hoped for him.

"Go." She pulled her hands away, and standing on tiptoes, she placed a final soft kiss on his lips, before turning away.

"Bye," she heard him say before the first tear slid down her cheek, followed by a hundred others. She kept walking. Away from him. Away from everything she'd always wanted.

"MA'AM, PLEASE WALK through." The security official motioned for her to pass through the metal detector, but Emily couldn't tear her gaze away from the scene happening several feet away on the other side of the glass, just beyond the long line of travelers. Ethan was holding Bailey. From where she stood, it didn't look like a hug one would give a friend, no matter how close.

"Ma'am?"

Emily glanced at him quickly, then moved aside. "Please go ahead of me," she said to the man holding a dog kennel behind her. She squinted and leaned around the people waiting behind her to see better. He was stroking her hair…and now kissing her hands. What was going on? When she saw Bailey lean forward and kiss his lips, she gasped loudly and her hand flew to her mouth.

A woman who'd been watching the scene as well patted her shoulder as she passed. "I'm sure it's nothing," she said, but her sympathetic gaze at the bulge in Emily's T-shirt said everything.

Emily nodded, her mind reeling. Ethan and Bailey? Since when? Why hadn't he said anything? And why was she here? Had she come to convince him to stay in Brookhollow? Had she somehow found out her secret?

A wave of nausea made the room spin around her, and just as her knees threatened to give way, Ethan was walking back toward her. She breathed a sigh of relief as she struggled to compose herself and stop the dizziness. He was still coming with her. Everything was going to be okay.

CHAPTER FIFTEEN

"RECALCULATING… RECALCULATING…" The woman's calm voice on the GPS system in Emily's Nissan Rogue did nothing to soothe Ethan's already frazzled nerves as he approached a stoplight on Oak Avenue and waited impatiently while the GPS adjusted his route after the last missed turnoff. "Recalculating…"

"Oh, for the love of…" he muttered as he sailed through the amber light.

Emily had said the station number two fire hall was only a few blocks from Play Hard Sports head office. But he'd been driving in circles for over a half hour now. Big-city driving was something he hated, but he would have to get used to it. He suspected the most challenging part of starting a new job with the Miami fire department would be navigating his way around the city in an emergency, and according to the chief he'd spoken to on the phone the day before, emergencies were a daily occurrence.

That was, of course, if they offered him a job. There were fourteen fire halls in Miami, and since arriving almost a week ago, he'd visited thirteen of them. None had any immediate openings, despite his experience, and station two on Oak Avenue was his last hope.

"Turn right in fifty yards," the voice said.

"Okay...." He did as instructed, waiting for the next direction.

"Destination on your left," the machine announced.

Pulling over to the side of the road, he put the car in Park and turned to look out the driver's-side window. Sure enough, there it was. Fire hall number two. Right where it had claimed to be. Two ladder trucks sat parked in front and through the open bay door, he saw three more. A group of uniformed firefighters stood around the center truck with clipboards. A shift change. He suspected the changeover in crew took more than the ten minutes it did in Brookhollow.

Grabbing his transfer paperwork from the passenger seat, he climbed out of the car, and jumped back as a large truck sped by him. That was close. The crazy traffic and less-than-courteous drivers here were going to take some getting used to. Checking both ways, he jogged across the street and entered through the open bay door.

The group turned to look at him as he entered. Wearing his own Brookhollow uniform, he couldn't help but notice the slightly different logo on the captain's crest of the man closest to him. Disappointment crept over him. Soon he would no longer be representing the Brookhollow unit.

"Hey. I'm Ethan Bishop. I'm here to see Chief Ellison."

"Chief is in his office," the young man with the captain's crest said. "Just through that door on the right and down the hall. You can't miss it."

The realization that he was both leaving the fire hall that had become a second home to him and giving up his rank hit him hard. He had worked long hours for the honor of leading the fire team in Brookhollow. He'd just have to work hard to prove himself again. "Great, thank you, Captain…?"

"O'Neil. Just call me Chris," he said, extending a bandaged hand.

Ethan stared at it for a second before noticing the other one was wrapped, as well.

"It's okay." Chris O'Neil shrugged. "The feeling still hasn't returned in them. I won't even feel your handshake."

Ethan shook his hand carefully. "What happened?"

"A chemical burn from a manufacturing plant fire last week." He pointed to the turnout suit hung on the wall behind him. The edges had melted and deteriorated along the seams. "Those things can only take the heat for so long…. I was trapped by a fallen beam for over an hour."

"I'd say you were lucky that you got out when you did," Ethan said, his gaze fixed on the damaged suit. Of course, he'd seen the damage and the danger overexposure to heat and fire could cause, but only in training. They'd been fortunate in Brookhollow never to have experienced anything so extreme.

"It had nothing to do with luck," he said with a nod toward his crew.

"Well…take care," Ethan said before heading through the doors toward the chief's office. Making his way down the hall, he took the time to look around. The first room on his right was a kitchen, fully functional with a full-size fridge, stove, microwave and dishwasher. Two long tables were set up in the center and four vending machines with pop and snacks lined the walls. A large garbage bin and a soda-bottle recycle bin sat near the doorway.

He pushed through a swinging door to his left and glanced inside. A training center. Impressive. Three treadmills stood next to a rowing machine, bike and elliptical. A full weight bench was positioned before the mirrored wall to the right and two heavy bags hung from the ceiling. Definitely a step up from the solitary treadmill and set of weights at the fire hall in Brookhollow.

Continuing down the hall, he paused to examine the photos of the crew members. Sixteen faces stared back at him. Faces he didn't recognize. Men he didn't know, hadn't trained with. Men who could be responsible for his safety in an emergency situation and he, theirs. He let out a slow, deep breath. It was a totally different ball game here in Miami. Dangers were more real, more frequent.

He turned away, and when he reached the office at the end of the hall, he tapped on the door, which was slightly ajar.

"Come in."

He pushed the door open and entered. A thin, older man sat behind a desk stacked sky-high with paperwork. He glanced up as Ethan entered.

"Chief Ellison, I'm Ethan Bishop. We spoke yesterday."

The chief stood and came around the front of his desk. "Yes, Ethan, hi." He extended a hand in greeting. "You found us okay?"

No. "Yeah, no problem."

"Great. You have your transfer papers?"

Ethan handed them to him.

"Have a seat."

Moving a large binder off the only other chair in the room, Ethan set it aside and sat as the chief leafed through the papers. "Impressive. Twelve years of service, eight of them as captain."

"Yes, sir."

"Well, unfortunately, Mr. Bishop, as I mentioned when we spoke, I don't have any ranking positions available. You'll be starting at the bottom."

Ethan nodded. He'd been prepared for that. He couldn't expect the hall to place priority on his file. The other men had served their time on staff, and in truth, they were probably more advanced than he was. Definitely more experienced, having dealt with a broader range of emergencies. "I understand."

"No, I'm not sure you do," the chief said, closing the file. "All I have right now is part-time, evening shift. Certainly with your credentials, that's not what you were looking for."

It certainly wasn't, but what choice did he have? At this point, he needed a position with a Miami fire hall. He knew he could prove himself, work hard and advance quickly... hopefully move to full-time before the baby was born. He was lucky the fire hall had any opportunities at all.

"That's fine. I'm just grateful to have work in Miami, sir."

The chief studied him for a long moment, then stood and extended a hand. "You start tomorrow at six. Come on, I'll introduce you to the team."

"WHAT EXACTLY IS THAT?" Bailey asked Friday afternoon, opening the door of the shop for Rachel Harper, who struggled to carry two baby carriers and keep an eye on her other three children running around the parking lot.

A 1948 Clipper motor home sat parked on an angle in the gravel lot. Painted neon orange with red and yellow vertical stripes down the center, it looked like something from a seventies family sitcom.

"Nathan's idea of a family road trip," Rachel said, clearly holding a different opinion as she motioned the other children inside the shop. "Please sit and don't touch anything," she said, setting the baby carriers on the floor near the counter. Abigail and Mackenzie slept soundly, undisturbed by the loud noises coming from the back of the shop.

"The noise won't wake them?" Bailey asked, bending to admire the sleeping baby girls. So precious and tiny. Maybe someday...

"Are you kidding? With three older siblings who only have one volume, loud, these babies can sleep through anything." Rachel smiled at the twin girls. "Anyway, the reason I'm here is to have you check that trailer before we go anywhere in it. Nathan bought it from his uncle Carson last week. It was a surprise." She shook her head. "Most women get flowers. I get a twelve-hour road trip to Phoenix to visit Nathan's parents once Vic and Luke return from their honeymoon."

The older couple had moved to Phoenix to escape the harsh, Eastern winters once Bill Harper retired from his longtime employment as bank manager in town last year. They'd yet to see their newest granddaughters.

"In that?"

"Yes. Nathan says because we live in a B and B, the last thing he wants to do is stay in a hotel when we travel."

"And that was his solution?" Bailey's eyes widened. Five kids in a motor home driving across the country—poor Rachel.

"I don't think the reality of the situation has kicked in yet. Screaming, fighting children, the one very tiny bathroom and the two single beds we're supposed to cram everyone into at night." She smiled as she shook her head.

"And yet you're smiling." Bailey couldn't believe Rachel was actually entertaining the idea. She was either crazy or very brave.

"As weird as it sounds, I love his offbeat ideas. I know what he was envisioning when he bought that old piece of junk—a good old Chevy Chase family vacation, and I love him for that."

Had Rachel ever seen one of those movies? Those trips never went well. Maybe she was thinking of the *Harry and the Hendersons* family road trips....

"Well, I'm just glad you brought it here to be serviced first," Bailey said. "I'll make sure it's at least safe to drive. You'll make it to Phoenix and back. Whether your sanity will… That's beyond my control." She grabbed a work order slip and wrote up a complete check of the motor home. "When do you need it?"

Rachel laughed. "Never would be soon enough…but not for a few weeks. Mid-Septemberish?" She rushed over to stop Jacob from kicking the vending machine in the hopes of shaking loose the chocolate bar that had gotten stuck. "Stop that. We're going for lunch now."

"Do you need a ride somewhere?"

"No. I have the double stroller in the back of that thing. Oh, and I also brought your shoes," Rachel said, snapping her fingers.

"Shoes?"

"Yes, your pink velvet bridesmaid shoes. I'll be right back. Kids, stay right here and behave."

Shoes? Jeez, she hadn't even thought of that. It's a good thing Rachel had.

As Rachel ran outside, little Melissa approached the counter and climbed up onto the stool, reaching for an old elastic band to tie her light brown, wispy locks away from her face. "Miss Bailey?"

"Yeah?" Bailey leaned on the counter, keeping a watchful eye on the two boys.

"How old do I have to be before I can work here with you?"

The question surprised her. "You want to work here?" How cool was that? Very few women decided on a trade for a career around here. "Well, how old are you now?"

"I'll be seven in eleven and a half months."

"So you're six?"

"Almost seven." The little girl's tone made her smile.

"Close enough, I guess. Well, you're still a little young. How does twelve sound?" At twelve she was hanging out in the shop, sweeping the warehouse floors, learning about different tools and helping Doug under cars when her tiny hands would work better than his larger ones.

"You mean I have to wait that long for a boyfriend?" The little girl pouted.

"Boyfriend?" What did that have to do with working in the shop? "I don't get it."

"Well, there's a boy I like at school, Dylan Forester...."

"Dylan Forester—isn't he like ten years old?"

"Nine and three-quarters, yeah. I like older

guys. Mom says girls mature faster and I don't want to be dating a kid," she said, rolling her eyes.

Bailey suppressed a laugh. "Of course not. Okay, well, does Dylan have something to do with you working here?" She still couldn't quite see the connection.

"The chain on his bike is always popping off. I thought if I knew how to fix it, he'd fall in love with me."

Bailey sighed. If only that was the case. If Melissa was hoping that being one of the boys would get her noticed by them, she was going to be disappointed. Bailey hesitated. Should she really arm the little girl with just enough knowledge to land her in the friend zone? She pushed the thought away. If Melissa wanted to learn how to fix a bike chain, that was a good thing, and she would encourage it.

"I'll tell you what, next week I'll stop by the inn and I'll show you how. Okay?"

The little girl's eyes lit up as she nodded.

"Show her how to do what?" Rachel asked, returning with a shoe box from Plenty of Sole, the store at the mall.

"Fix the chain on Dy...my bike," Melissa said.

"Oh, your dad will like that."

Bailey sucked in her bottom lip. Probably not, she thought, accepting the shoes from Rachel and sliding them under the counter. "Thanks. Here's your pickup slip." She handed the paper to Rachel and accepted the keys to the Clipper.

"Thanks, Bailey. If you could find something wrong with it, that would be great," Rachel joked as she led the kids outside.

ETHAN GRIPPED THE rail of the staircase leading to the tenth floor of the tall high-rise in downtown Miami. Of all days for the elevator to be out of service. Thankfully he was stopping on the tenth floor and not racing all the way to the top of the twenty-seven-story building.

He panted, struggling to catch his breath before he bounded up the last few stairs and yanked open the door to the Women's Clinic. Inside, pregnant women occupied the waiting-room chairs, while their husbands stood looking nervous behind them.

Emily sat in the corner chair near a window, folding and unfolding her legs and wiggling on the plastic seat. Her annoyed expression was clear even from across the room. Good, she hadn't been called in yet.

The last thing he wanted was to be late for this ultrasound. He'd already missed enough of this pregnancy. Letting out a deep breath, he took the empty seat next to her.

"You're late," she hissed, tossing a copy of *Vogue* back onto the table next to her.

"Traffic in this city is insane."

"You'll get used to it.... Okay, what is taking so freaking long?"

Ethan checked his watch. Her appointment had been scheduled for three o'clock.... It was 3:04 p.m. "They are only a couple of minutes behind," he said, noticing a fraction too late that some of the men nearby were frantically shaking their heads. Warning him.

Emily's eyes blazed as she swung to face him.

Uh-oh, what had he said?

"Do you realize how uncomfortable it is to try to hold your pee with a baby using your bladder as a trampoline?"

The men around him shot him sympathetic looks while the other pregnant women stared at him as though he were the most unfeeling human being ever.

"I mean, this is just cruel. They have you drink ten glasses of water, then they make you wait?"

One of the medical staff behind the desk glanced at the clock on the wall, and then grabbing a cup, she approached. Lowering her voice, she said, "Here, Mrs. Parsons, why don't you go pee a little, ease the pressure a bit. About two cupfuls shouldn't hurt."

"You can do that?"

"Will it affect the visibility of the ultrasound?" Ethan asked.

The daggers shooting from Emily's eyes spoke volumes as she disappeared down the hall, moving faster than he'd ever seen her move. He would pay for that comment later.

"Only a little…." The receptionist leaned closer. "Small price to pay for the safety of the husbands. Around here, we like to say that it helps to eliminate some of the crazy." She resumed her position behind the desk, and several other men approached asking for a cup for their wives.

Emily's face was more relaxed when she returned seconds later.

"Feel better?" Ethan asked.

"Much. Did you know you could stop peeing midstream?"

Before he could answer, the nurse called her name.

"Ready?" Emily asked him as she stood again.

About as ready as he could be given the circumstances. He nodded.

"Actually, Mr. Parsons..."

"It's Bishop," he corrected.

"We're not married," Emily said.

"Sorry, Mr. Bishop. You are welcome to wait out here just a little bit longer. The doctor just needs to take a quick look first, then we will invite you in."

"Oh. Will you be okay?" he asked Emily.

She nodded as she followed the nurse down the hall toward the last room on the right.

Ethan sat in the waiting room. He scanned the other couples waiting. Wedding bands on every hand. Were they supposed to get married now? He was in this for the long haul, but married? Seemed like an awfully big commitment for two people who didn't love one another that way anymore. Though having a baby trumped that commitment by miles. And if they didn't get married, whose last name would the baby have? Emily's, no doubt. His shoulders slumped and he rested his head in his hands. Only two weeks before, he'd been teasing Bailey about getting married. She was the one he wanted to marry.

He sat straighter and pushed the image of her smile from his mind. If he was going to be here, he had to be here fully…for Emily and the baby.

Reaching for a magazine, he flipped through the pages. The August issue of *Today's Parent* was full of parenting and pregnancy advice, and an article caught his eye. "The dad's role in D-day." D-day? *Wow, way to put an already terrified mind at ease,* he mused. He scanned the list of responsibilities for the father, all five pages of them, and when he was done, his mind reeled. How was he going to get through this? Emily would have it a lot worse, he reminded himself. It didn't help.

"Mr. Bishop? You can come in now."

Ethan stood and replaced the magazine. Immediately one of the younger fathers in the room reached for it. He shook his head. "Don't read that," he said, and the anxious-looking man dropped it.

He followed the nurse to the room. Emily lay with her knees up and bent on a small examining table, her belly exposed and covered with a clear jellylike substance. The doctor ran a wand over her bump.

Ethan had gotten an ultrasound once in

high school when his doctor had suspected he had ulcers. He was relieved to see that what Emily was enduring didn't look any worse than that. "Hi," he said, moving to the available seat next to her.

"Hi," she said with a smile.

"So, Mr. Bishop, as I told Emily, everything looks great. The heartbeat is strong, the baby's profile looks great, good position...."

She turned the screen toward them, and once he focused on the black-and-white image on the screen, Ethan didn't hear anything else she said. He reached for Emily's hand and she squeezed it, their attention glued to the monitor.

"Is that the baby's heart?" Ethan asked, pointing to a dark circle in the middle of the baby's torso.

"Yes, that's it," the doctor confirmed.

The little limbs moved and the baby began to bounce every couple of seconds. "Is he... she...okay?" he asked.

Emily laughed and the doctor nodded. "Hiccups."

"The baby gets those?" Amazing.

"All the time," Emily said. "I can always feel them, but this is the first time I've seen it."

"I'm glad I was here for it," he said.

Her smile disappeared, replaced with an expression he couldn't identify.

"Actually, that leads me to my next question. Do you want to know the sex?"

"No," Emily said.

"Yes," Ethan said at the same time.

"This happens a lot," the doctor told them. "Did you want a few minutes alone to discuss it?"

"No, I already have my mind made up. I want it to be a surprise." Emily's voice was firm, and Ethan fought the temptation to argue. Knowing would make it so much easier when planning the nursery or telling family and friends what to buy, but this was ultimately her decision. Lately, he felt very little was within his control. The feeling was foreign and he hoped once the baby arrived, things would be better.

"That's fine," he said. "Whatever you want."

Ten minutes later, after collecting the image of the ultrasound from the reception desk and slowly making their way back down the stairs, they exited the building on the side street where he'd parked her car. In a no-parking zone. She shot him a look as he opened the passenger door for her and swiped the ticket from the windshield.

"Don't worry," he said, climbing into the driver's seat. "I'll pay this." He slid the ticket into his wallet.

"So how did it go at the fire hall?"

"I start tomorrow," he said, forcing enthusiasm into his voice. This would be a good thing, he'd told himself all afternoon. A new challenge, an opportunity to push himself, prove himself again. He'd forced away every negative thought and nostalgic sentiment whenever he compared his new working environment to the hall in Brookhollow.

"That's great," Emily said through a yawn. "We can ride to work together in the morning." Her voice sounded faraway, distant, as she studied her hands.

He'd noticed how distracted she'd been since they'd left Brookhollow and he couldn't help but wonder if she'd witnessed him saying goodbye to Bailey. He missed Bailey so much. He'd only texted her once so far—to let her know that he'd gotten a job. Really, it was just an excuse to contact her…in a way that wouldn't hurt Emily. He sensed that over time, the contact would have to stop completely in order to give this second chance with Emily a fair shot…and to allow Bailey to move on. But he just wasn't quite there yet.

Right now, though, he had to make Emily feel secure. She needed to know he was there for her and always would be. "Are you okay? Do you need anything?"

She shook her head and forced herself to sit straighter. "No, I'm good. Tell me more about the job."

"Well, we won't be riding in together. My shift is an evening one. It starts at six."

Emily frowned. "Nights?"

"Evenings until 2:00 a.m."

"How will that work when the baby comes? I'm going to need your help at night." She sounded panicked.

"It was the only shift available, but it's only part-time."

"Part-time?" Her voice held an even stronger note of anguish.

"For now," he said quickly. "I need to work my way up just like anyone else, Em."

"But you were captain for eight years in Brookhollow…."

"This isn't Brookhollow." His voice took on a note of hardness that he hadn't intended. "Sorry, Em. I tried everywhere else." The opportunity they were offering at fire station two was the best he could hope for. At least for now.

She was silent for a long minute, and when he glanced toward the passenger seat, he saw the tears rolling down her cheeks.

Pulling over to the side of the road, ignoring the blaring horns as he crossed two lanes of traffic, Ethan put the car in Park. "Hey, what's wrong?" He undid his seat belt and turned to look at her.

"This isn't going to work," she whispered.

"Of course it is. Trust me, by the time the baby is born, I'll have full-time hours on day shift." He hoped. At this point, he'd do anything to make that happen.

"I don't mean the job." She wiped the tears from her cheeks.

"Well, what?"

"Us," she said, sadly.

He sighed. "Look, it's not ideal, okay? I'm not going to lie and pretend that everything is fine and that things will return to the way they were. A lot has happened—changed—but I'm here for you and our baby. No matter what," he reassured.

"But we don't love each other anymore. If it weren't for the baby, you never would have given us another chance and you hate it here."

He couldn't deny that. "The baby will bring us closer and I'll—" *What?* "—adjust," he said finally. He prayed it would happen. Either way, he was in this for the long haul. He only wished he could tell her what she wanted to hear, needed to hear, to make her feel better at that moment, but he wouldn't lie to her. He wasn't in love with her anymore. He was desperately in love with someone else.

"The baby will grow up with parents who what? Sleep in different rooms?" she continued.

He knew she was referring to his sleeping on her couch. "It's temporary. I'm not ready… and you're not ready. Emily, give it time."

She was expecting too much. He was struggling to keep his patience, but after everything in the past two weeks—finding out he was going to be a father, giving up his life in Brookhollow and the woman he loved—she had to give him some time to adjust, to get his footing.

"Time won't help. We're in love with other people. Time won't change that."

He paused. In love with other people? His gaze locked with hers. "Greg?" he guessed.

"And Bailey," she said.

His mouth gaped. She had seen them together at the airport. "That's over," he said quietly, the words ripping a hole through his chest.

"But it shouldn't be if you love her."

If only things were that simple. He wanted to argue, but he couldn't. "All that matters now is the baby. I'm willing to put everything else aside to make this work, and I need you just as committed," he said, sensing her resolve weaken.

She was still in love with Greg, so she wanted to go back to him? No way would he let that happen. He, not some other man, was going to be there for his child. Taking her hands, he pleaded, "Emily, think of the baby."

She nodded. "I am."

Relief flowed through him.

"Ethan, the baby's not yours."

Dead silence filled the air around them as he let her hands fall back to her lap. He reached for the seat beneath him. "What?" She couldn't mean that.

"The baby is Greg's."

"But you said…"

"I'm not even six months pregnant yet."

Ethan stared through the windshield of the car. "If you're saying this because you want Greg back…"

"My due date is December 26, not November."

"I don't understand." Was she seriously telling him that she'd lied to him, dragged him to Miami…?

Emily touched his arm. "I was scared, alone, I didn't know what to do. You were always so safe, strong…"

"Reliable…." he said, the realization sinking in. She'd lied. She'd used him. The baby wasn't his. "I can't believe this." In the short time he'd thought he was going to be a father, he'd embraced the idea, turned his entire life upside down to put the baby ahead of all else.

"I'm so sorry, Ethan."

"Why are you telling me now?" He'd been in Miami a week. What could possibly have happened to change her mind?

"I couldn't do this to you. Not after seeing you with Bailey. Watching you give up your job, your apartment and Brookhollow was all hard enough, but I thought maybe somewhere in your heart you still loved me. I didn't know you'd moved on. I was willing to go through with this, thinking it was ultimately something you wanted. To be with me and start a family. Not too long ago, that was something you did want."

So she was going to sacrifice her own happiness to give this baby a life she knew would be safe, secure and a home that, despite everything, would be filled with love. "This is a lot to take in, you know. I…"

"I know, and I'm truly sorry, Ethan. But I can't go through with all of this knowing that you are in love with Bailey."

"I told you that's over. I can't just leave. You're alone here." Even if the baby wasn't his, she'd come to him for support. He couldn't just leave her now. He'd been willing to make sacrifices for this child, and his or not, he was ready to follow through.

"I'm not alone. I have great friends…and I spoke to Greg today. We are going to talk. He wants to be involved.…"

"But…"

"I don't love you, Ethan."

She didn't love him. The baby wasn't his. He was free to go. Back to his life in Brookhollow. Back to the fire hall. Back to Bailey.

Still, a sense of guilt made him argue. "I'll stay, Em. If you want me to stay, I will."

"No. Go home, Ethan. I've broken your heart one too many times. I won't do it again."

BAILEY ENTERED THROUGH the front door of Dreamline Travel after work that day. She'd made up her mind. She was booking a trip to Venice. The shop's renovations were still being completed; it was the perfect time to take a few weeks off. The truth was, being in Brookhollow without Ethan was taking its toll. Every time she drove past the fire hall, she expected to see his Jeep parked out front. When she passed the football field behind the high school, she had to remind herself he wouldn't be there. A week without him felt like an eternity.

He'd texted her twice—once to say he'd gotten settled, the second time to tell her he'd gotten a new job at a Miami fire hall—but she hadn't answered either one. She was happy for him, but she couldn't bring herself to respond. As much as he claimed he was simply doing 'the right thing,' she couldn't help but wonder whether this was as tough on him as he'd said. After all, up until a month ago, he hadn't been completely over his ex.

She climbed the old wooden stairs to the second floor where the travel agency had its office and went inside.

Patricia Klein, the owner of the agency, smiled as she entered. The phone was cradled between her cheek and shoulder and she held up a finger indicating she'd just be a minute.

Bailey nodded and scanned the row of travel brochures along the wall. The beaches of the Caribbean, the magical world of Disney and the mythical appeal of the ancient ruins in Greece beckoned from the shelves, but nothing made her second-guess her decision. Years before, her mother had told her countless stories about the Venetian Isles and the beautiful scenery of the Italian city. In recent weeks, she'd been hoping that maybe she wouldn't be taking the trip alone, but now... She refused to put it off any longer. She would do Venice alone—sleep in late, stay up even later, drink fantastic wine and take in the sights at her own pace. All alone.

"Bailey, hi," Patricia said, setting the phone back on the cradle.

"Hi, did you get my message last night?"

"Yes, I did. Sorry I wasn't able to get back to you, but it's been a crazy morning. That was Victoria, confirming the details of the flight to the Bahamas...again."

The morning after the wedding the couple was headed for their two-week honeymoon in the Bahamas. Bailey suspected their vacation would have a much different feel than hers.

"No problem. I was just hoping you would

have a few minutes today to see what's available for me."

"For Venice, right?"

"Yes."

"Date of departure?" Patricia typed the search requirements into the fields on her screen.

Yesterday. "The day after tomorrow—September 3." Now that she'd made the decision to go, the only thing keeping her in Brookhollow was the wedding. Once she made it through that, she wanted to be on her way.

"Labor Day.... Hmm, that may add to the cost of travel, being a holiday and all, but let's see what comes up." She drummed her long acrylic nails on the desk as she waited. "Sorry, my computer is slow today."

"That's okay, I'm in no rush." The only other thing she had scheduled that day was the wedding rehearsal.

"Will you be attending the Mason-Dawson wedding tomorrow?" Patricia asked.

"I'm in the wedding party."

"Oh, how nice. I love weddings. I'm planning to close the office tomorrow at noon to attend the ceremony at the church. Luke and I went to Boston University together," she said, scanning the screen. "Ah, here we go. Looks like there is a flight out of New York on the third at two o'clock in the afternoon. Let's see if there's a flight to New York out of Newark…."

Bailey held her breath as she waited. At this point, she didn't care. If she had to drive to New York with her suitcase strapped to the back of the bike, she would. She just needed to get out of town to clear her head for a while.

"Wow, you are lucky."

Hardly. "There's a flight?"

Patricia nodded. "At 10:00 a.m. You have a bit of a stopover but…"

"That's fine. I'll take it," Bailey said eagerly. Reaching into her purse, she rummaged around for her ID and MasterCard to book the registration.

"Great! Number of people flying?" Patricia asked.

Her enthusiasm faltered slightly as she was forced to answer, "I'll be going alone."

"OKAY, CAN WE run through this one more time?" Victoria asked the exhausted wedding party at nine-thirty that evening. The bride-to-be was wide-eyed, unlike the rest of the group.

"Somebody take that coffee cup from her," Jim muttered, leaning back to rest his head against the second pew in the Catholic church, where the ceremony was to be held the following day at one o'clock.

Mrs. Dawson and Mrs. Mason had already decorated the pews with large white bows, and the sections were labeled "family of the groom" on the left and "family of the bride" on the right. On the altar sat large flower arrangements and the unity candle was displayed near the podium. The wedding music sat on the piano, where only an hour before Melody Myers had rehearsed with the church's pianist. The details of the forty-minute ceremony alone were overwhelming.

Bailey yawned and checked her watch. They'd been rehearsing for over two hours. She'd been under the impression that there was supposed to be food involved. After all, this had been presented to her as a rehearsal dinner.

Her stomach growled loudly. "Victoria, I think we've got it. I'm starving."

Victoria reached into her open purse on the podium, and tossed Bailey a protein bar.

"Here, try this. I've been living on them for days."

"Victoria, sweetheart, I think we have to let everyone go or we won't have a wedding party tomorrow," Luke said through his own yawn, reaching for the coffee cup and gently removing it from her hand. "And no more coffee. You need to sleep tonight."

She pouted, placing her hands on her hips. "Don't you want things to go smoothly? Whose side are you on?"

Luke kissed her forehead. "Yours. Always yours. I've learned my lesson about going up against you," he teased. "Okay, everyone. You heard Bridezilla—up on your feet."

The chorus of groans was silenced by Luke's promise of food. "One more run-through, then all you can eat at Joey's, on me."

The wedding party grumbled their way to the back of the church. Bailey took her place next to Luke's cousin Bryce, behind Jim and Rachel, the best man and the maid of honor. "Remind me again how I got roped into this. I'm not even family."

"Trust me, Luke's invite to be part of this surprised me, too," Bryce said, running a hand through his wavy dark hair.

The cousins looked a lot alike, except Luke

was fair. Bryce owned the only law firm in town, though rumors had circulated years before that he'd actually failed the bar exam twice before finally passing. However, having been the subject of inaccurate gossip herself not too long ago, Bailey was learning to turn a deaf ear to the whispers keeping the town abuzz on a daily basis.

The wedding music played, and Jim and Rachel led the way down the center aisle in the church, arm in arm, keeping time to the music. Bailey and Bryce followed. "So Bailey…"

"Shh, no talking," Victoria scolded, several feet behind them.

Eyes straight ahead, facing forward in a stiff, controlled march, Bryce lowered his voice to barely above a whisper. "So I was wondering…since we're both in the wedding party…and since Ethan's gone…"

Bailey winced. Sensitivity was not part of Bryce's character. Probably one of the reasons he was a success as a lawyer. "Yeah," she whispered.

"Well, I thought we may as well go together to the wedding."

Charming. How could a girl say no to such a heartfelt date request? Though she would have if she suspected Bryce had any real romantic feelings behind his stoic, last-minute suggestion. But she knew there was nothing to worry about. No hearts would be involved or broken after this one date. She was safe.

"Sure, sounds like fun."

"I'm not promising fun, but I'll get you home safely afterward, and I'll keep my hands to myself."

Bailey laughed for real for the first time in days. "That's the best offer I've heard in a while. Thanks, Bryce."

"Shh…" Victoria hissed behind them.

Bryce was right. Fun might be a little too much to hope for the following day. She knew for certain it would be a challenging one for her on many levels. But she had to get through it and she would.

CHAPTER SIXTEEN

THE BRIGHT MORNING sun shone through the lace curtains of Bailey's bedroom window as she rolled over, tossing the blankets aside. Checking the clock on the bedside table revealed it was just before ten o'clock. She couldn't remember the last time she'd slept in so late, but she was grateful for the restful night after the lack of sleep she'd been getting that week. Stretching, she flung her legs over the side of the bed and made her way to the bathroom, where her bridesmaid dress hung on the back of the door. The warm breeze blowing through the open window promised a perfect wedding for Victoria and Luke.

Bailey studied her reflection in the mirror. Despite how she was feeling, she had to put on a brave face. She needed to be there for her friends on one of the most important days of their lives.

Forty minutes later, showered and her hair dried and pinned in loose waves around her shoulders, she slid into the tight dress. It shouldn't have surprised her that it no longer seemed as tight. Her lack of appetite lately was at least good for something. Hurrying, she zipped the back with ease. The wedding party was meeting at the church for "before" shots with the photographer forty-five minutes before the ceremony was scheduled to start at one o'clock.

She applied a little more makeup than usual, then forced a smile on her pale pink, glossy lips as she dialed the number for the local taxi company. Bryce had left her a voice mail earlier that morning to say he was running behind and would she mind meeting him at the church. She didn't. In fact, she was starting to regret agreeing to be his date for the evening. She planned on leaving as soon as she could, still needing to pack for her trip the next day. A trip that was feeling more like an escape than an experience she'd looked forward to for years.

While she waited, she wrapped her present for the couple. An old black-and-white photo of Main Street taken in the sixties with Legend's Sporting Goods visible in the center. She'd found the photo in one of her grandmother's albums. It was one of those perfect

early-morning winter shots when no footprints
or car tracks had yet destroyed the smooth,
white dusting of snow on the ground. Everything was still and peaceful. She'd borrowed
the photo, had it restored and framed, thinking it would make a great wedding gift for
Victoria and Luke. The old store held a lot of
meaning for the couple.

The sound of the taxi's horn sounded in her
driveway a moment later through the open
living room window. Grabbing the gift, she
went to her front closet to get her shoes.

She stopped dead in her tracks.

Her shoes were still at the shop.

She groaned, checking the time on the
mantel. Twelve o'clock. She might be a little
late for the photos, but surely Victoria would
prefer that than having her bridesmaid walk
up the aisle barefoot.

The taxi horn sounded again, and grabbing
the present and her purse, Bailey dashed outside barefoot, locking her door behind her.

"I think you're forgetting something, miss,"
the taxi driver said, glancing at her feet as she
climbed into the backseat.

"I know—shoes. We're going to pick them
up now."

"ARE YOU SURE about this, Emily?" Ethan asked, as they waited in the ticket-counter line at the airport Saturday morning. "I mean, I can stay…"

"We've talked about this," Emily insisted. "You're going back to Brookhollow. And you may as well get back there today so you won't miss Luke and Victoria's wedding."

The line moved and the ticket clerk on the end waved them over. "Do you have a reservation?" she asked.

"No, but I was hoping to catch the next flight to Newark," Ethan said, excitement rising in his chest. He was going home. He was no longer committed to Emily. But one look at her nervous expression had him asking, "Seriously, are you sure?"

"Ethan, I'm not letting you back in my apartment, so unless you want to sleep on the streets tonight, and I don't recommend that in this city, you better get home."

"I may be sleeping on the street anyway. I don't have an apartment anymore, remember?"

Emily gave him a sheepish look. "I'm so sorry. I totally blame this baby brain and these uncontrollable hormones for all of this mess."

"Okay," the clerk said, "it looks like the next flight leaves in three hours. It is already full, but if you're willing to fly standby, we can get you on it if something opens up. The next one after that is tomorrow at noon."

Ethan hesitated, his gaze locked on Emily. Guilt washed over him at the relief he felt at the turn of events. While he was definitely battling disappointment that he wasn't going to be a father, he knew it would happen someday, the right way, with the woman he loved. Bailey. "I'll take the standby." He couldn't wait a second longer to get back to her.

"Wow, that was quick." Emily said.

"Emily, you…"

She cut him off with a laugh. "I'm kidding."

"Here you are, sir. Just be at gate forty-five at ten o'clock and they should know at that time if there is a seat available." The agent handed him the standby ticket.

"Thank you," Ethan said, moving away from the desk.

Slowly, he and Emily walked toward the security checkpoint. "So I've got an hour to kill. Did you want to grab a coffee or some breakfast?"

Emily shook her head, stopping in front of

the revolving doors leading out to the above-ground lot where her car was parked. "I think I'm just going to go…before I freak out again and ask you to stay."

"Em…"

"Don't worry. I won't," she reassured him, moving in to hug him quickly. "Thank you Ethan…for doing what you thought was the right thing."

"If you need anything—"

"I'll call Greg or my parents or Kim…but not you. Never again you."

BAILEY SHUT THE shop lights off just as the tow line rang. "Oh, you've got to be kidding me." She paused near the door as she contemplated ignoring it. Technically, she wasn't even supposed to be there. If she hadn't forgotten her bridesmaid's shoes at the shop, she wouldn't be. Everyone in town was either on their way to the church on Maple Street or already there. It had to be someone stuck on the highway.

The phone continued to ring and Bailey bit her lip, willing it to stop. Darn conscience. She couldn't just leave someone stranded. Struggling in the pale pink velvet high heels, she rushed to answer the phone on the fourth ring. "Bailey's Place."

"Oh, thank God. I'm stuck in the middle of nowhere," a panicked female voice said on the other end.

She'd just described everywhere within miles of Brookhollow. "Okay, just relax. Are you on the main highway?"

"Yeah, somewhere between exit forty-six and forty-seven...or forty-seven and forty-eight. I'm not sure. I'm in a real hurry. Can I talk to the tow guy, please?" the woman asked, her New York accent thick.

Bailey sighed. "I am the tow-truck guy."

"Oh," the woman said after a long pause. "Well, can you help me?"

Bailey glanced at her bridesmaid dress and stiletto shoes. She closed her eyes, took a deep breath then reached for the tow instructions pad. "Of course. Where were you heading?"

"Brookhollow for a wedding...that starts in less than an hour."

Realization dawned. "The Mason-Dawson wedding?"

"How'd you know?"

The town was too small to host more than one wedding on any given day. Obviously

Victoria's friend had never visited Brookhollow. "You're Heather from New York, right?"

"Yes, but seriously, how do you know all of that?"

"I'm Bailey. I'm a friend of Victoria's and Luke's."

"So you're…"

"Going to be late for the wedding, too."

"I CAN'T THANK you enough," Heather said, watching Bailey hook the rental car to the back of the tow truck.

Bailey stood and wiped her hands on the coveralls she wore over her dress. She'd changed into her work boots and tossed her shoes into the back of the truck. "I'm just glad I forgot my shoes at the shop, otherwise you might have been stranded for a while. The nearest tow truck is at least fifty miles away."

"You and me both." Heather checked the time on her phone. "Do you think we'll make it in time for the ceremony?" A frown crossed her perfectly smooth complexion as she paced next to the truck.

Bailey marveled at her ability to walk in the figure-hugging black dress and six-inch heels. And on gravel, no less. By now she'd have broken her ankle.

"I hope so. I'm in the wedding party and in my rush to get here, I left my cell phone at the shop and of course I never memorize phone numbers anymore." No doubt everyone in the wedding party had filled her voice mail wondering where she was by now.

"I could call Victoria's cell," Heather said.

"Not a good idea." She suspected the bride was nervous enough. "Hurry, hop in. We're all set." Bailey climbed into the truck.

Heather climbed into the passenger seat looking distraught.

"Don't worry. We'll make it. And I'm wearing the dress under these coveralls."

Heather simply nodded, staring out the window.

"If you're worried about the car, I'm sure it's nothing. I'll have it up and running in no time," Bailey reassured, turning on the safety tow lights and merging back out onto the highway.

"No, I'm not worried about that. It's just been a crappy day…week actually," Heather said, leaning back against the seat.

For you and me both, Bailey thought.

"I mean, I should have known this would happen," Heather continued. "After all, they say bad luck comes in threes, right?"

Bailey didn't believe in luck. She believed in making your own fate, good or bad, but she doubted Heather would be interested in hearing her theory. Besides, who could argue that bad luck had seemed to play a part in her current predicament? But, ever the optimist, she said, "Well, you could look on the bright side. If this was the third bad thing to happen, now you're done, right?"

"I certainly can't think of anything else that could go wrong." Heather turned in her seat. "My boyfriend and I broke up on Tuesday. He was supposed to be here with me. I was supposed to be driving with him in his BMW, not alone in that piece of junk I rented at the last minute from this shady car-rental shop in Brooklyn, where I'm staying with my sister." She cringed. "I can't afford my apartment in the city after getting fired by my ex-boyfriend—who was also my boss—on Wednesday."

That did sound like an awful week. "Sorry," Bailey said.

"That's what he said, too, after he fired me. *Sorry.* That's it. After six years with that company, giving one-hundred-and-ten percent—okay, maybe not always—but I worked hard most days." She tossed her hands up.

"You know what? It doesn't even matter. If he hadn't dumped me, my mediocre job performance wouldn't have mattered." She slumped against the seat and reached for her purse. Shaking out several painkillers, she popped them into her mouth.

"There's water in the back…."

Heather shook her head and held up a finger. She chewed the chalky tablets, swallowed hard and shivered. "I can't swallow pills. I'm terrified of choking on them." She shuddered. "Anyway, that's why I'm here alone…and jobless…and late."

ETHAN PACED THE back of St. Michael's, the Catholic church on Maple Street, checking his watch every ten seconds. Bailey had yet to arrive and worry had begun to creep into his mind. The wedding was scheduled to start in ten minutes. His worry mixing with his anticipation of seeing her made it hard to keep still.

"Any sign of her yet?" Jim asked, coming up behind him. Dressed in a black tuxedo, white shirt and pink bow tie and cummerbund, he was hardly recognizable.

Ethan couldn't help but smile as he shook his head. "Not yet, but, wow—you clean up good. Better be careful—when Jill sees you dressed like that, she may start to get ideas of her own."

Jim took in Ethan's wrinkled jeans and T-shirt, the messy, ungelled hair and five-o'clock shadow. "You, on the other hand, look terrible. Did you sleep in the airport overnight?"

Ethan ran a hand through his hair and glanced down at his clothes. It wasn't that bad, was it?

"Yeah, that didn't help. Man, you cannot see Bailey looking like that," Jim said.

"I look that rough?"

"Worse. Trust me, I know you are desperate to see her, but if you want her to forgive you and take you back, you at least need to shower and change."

"I don't even have a place to take a shower." He had nowhere to live anymore in Brookhollow and the B and B rooms had been reserved for the out-of-town wedding guests months before.

Jim reached into his pocket for his car keys. "Here, take my car. Go to my place and clean yourself up."

Ethan hesitated. He really couldn't wait to

see Bailey. She loved him; she wouldn't care what he looked like. He didn't want to wait.

"Ethan Bishop, I'm so glad you're home, but you are not coming to my wedding dressed like that," Victoria said, exiting the bridal preparation room.

Oh, for the love of... "All right, I'm going," he said throwing his hands up in defeat. Tough crowd. He would have thought they would just be happy to see him. As he jogged down the church steps, he called over his shoulder. "Not a word to Bailey. I want to surprise her."

BAILEY TOOK A sip of her champagne and shifted in her white-satin-covered chair to look toward the gazebo in the center of the yard at the Brookhollow Inn two hours later, where Victoria and Luke were about to share their first dance. The ceremony at the church had gone perfectly and she'd even managed to hold back her tears as she'd watched the couple say their vows in front of family and friends.

Her thoughts had continually returned to Ethan, but she decided that for one evening, it was okay. Okay to miss him and fantasize about what might have been.

The rest of the wedding party moved closer

to the gazebo as the couple met in the center of the covered structure and the music they'd chosen as their wedding song, "Songbird," filled the air. The couple couldn't tear their eyes from one another as Luke took Victoria into his arms, and Bailey couldn't suppress the sigh that escaped her lips.

"Didn't anyone tell you that you aren't supposed to look better than the bride?" a familiar voice whispered in her ear as she sat lost in the enchantment of the scene in front of her.

"Oh, you've got to be kidding, Victoria looks— Ethan?" Bailey swung around to find Ethan sitting in the empty seat beside her that had been occupied by Bryce just moments before.

"Hi, baby girl," he said with a smile, touching her cheek.

She rested her face against his hand, not believing her eyes. Then she straightened and scanned the backyard.

"She's not with me," he said.

"You just came for the wedding?" She knew he was off-limits and that saying goodbye to him a second time would probably kill her, but at that moment she was just so happy to see him. Dressed in a dark blue suit and white shirt unbuttoned at the neck, he looked too handsome not to touch. She rested her hands on his on his lap.

"No, I'm home, jobless with nowhere to live and wearing a borrowed suit." He chuckled.

"What about Emily? The baby?"

"The baby was never mine." He brushed a stray curl from her forehead and placed a gentle kiss there.

"I don't understand." Dare she hope what he said was true? He was home to stay... without Emily. They could be together?

"It's a long story, and all I want to do right now is stare at you for a minute, if that's okay." He took both her hands in his.

Bailey nodded, clasping her fingers tightly around his. This time she wouldn't be letting go.

"You are so beautiful," he said after a long silence. "Leaving you was the hardest thing I've ever had to do, and I wouldn't blame you if you walked away...after all the hurt."

"Ethan, stop." She placed a finger to his lips. "I'm never walking away."

"Good," he started, but she silenced him.

"Shh, I'm not done."

He clasped his mouth firmly shut.

"I mean it. I don't care if ten ex-girlfriends come out of the blue claiming they are having your child, I'm not letting you go again."

"Well, that's not something we have to worry about, I can assure you." He lowered his head and rested his forehead against hers. "But I am homeless...and broke and everything I own is still in Miami."

"I don't care. I love you, Ethan."

"I love you more."

"I loved you first," she teased.

"About that... Don't worry. I plan to spend the rest of my life making it up to you, starting right now."

Realization hit her and she groaned.

"That wasn't exactly the response I was hoping for...,"

"I'm leaving tomorrow," she said. Of all the bad timing. She tightened her grasp around his fingers. For years she'd been dying to take this trip, and now all she wanted to do was cancel it. She wondered if it was too late.

"Leaving for where?"

"Venice. I finally decided I needed to do it." She let out a deep sigh. He was home and she was leaving for two weeks. How was she supposed to enjoy Venice when the whole time she'd be wishing she was back in Brook-hollow, back in his arms?

"You were planning to go alone?"

"With only thoughts of you occupying my mind and heart," she whispered.

Ethan touched her chin, tilting her face toward him. "Well, what if I came with you?"

"You want to come with me?"

"Bailey, I had to say goodbye to you once. I don't plan on ever doing it again."

"So I'm finally getting what I've always wanted?" It seemed too good to be true.

"Yes, baby girl, you are…and so am I," Ethan said, before softly kissing her lips.

* * * * *

REQUEST YOUR FREE BOOKS!
2 FREE WHOLESOME ROMANCE NOVELS
IN LARGER PRINT
PLUS 2
FREE
MYSTERY GIFTS

🌟🌟🌟🌟🌟🌟🌟🌟🌟🌟🌟🌟🌟🌟🌟🌟🌟🌟🌟

HEARTWARMING™

🌟🌟🌟🌟🌟🌟🌟🌟🌟🌟🌟🌟🌟🌟🌟🌟🌟🌟🌟

Wholesome, tender romances

YES! Please send me 2 FREE Harlequin® Heartwarming Larger-Print novels and my 2 FREE mystery gifts (gifts worth about $10). After receiving them, if I don't wish to receive any more books, I can return the shipping statement marked "cancel." If I don't cancel, I will receive 4 brand-new larger-print novels every month and be billed just $4.99 per book in the U.S. or $5.74 per book in Canada. That's a savings of at least 23% off the cover price. It's quite a bargain! Shipping and handling is just 50¢ per book in the U.S. and 75¢ per book in Canada.* I understand that accepting the 2 free books and gifts places me under no obligation to buy anything. I can always return a shipment and cancel at any time. Even if I never buy another book, the two free books and gifts are mine to keep forever.

161/361 IDN F47N

Name	(PLEASE PRINT)
Address	Apt. #
City	State/Prov. Zip/Postal Code

Signature (if under 18, a parent or guardian must sign)

Mail to the Harlequin® Reader Service:
IN U.S.A.: P.O. Box 1867, Buffalo, NY 14240-1867
IN CANADA: P.O. Box 609, Fort Erie, Ontario L2A 5X3

* Terms and prices subject to change without notice. Prices do not include applicable taxes. Sales tax applicable in N.Y. Canadian residents will be charged applicable taxes. Offer not valid in Quebec. This offer is limited to one order per household. Not valid for current subscribers to Harlequin Heartwarming larger-print books. All orders subject to credit approval. Credit or debit balances in a customer's account(s) may be offset by any other outstanding balance owed by or to the customer. Please allow 4 to 6 weeks for delivery. Offer available while quantities last.

Your Privacy—The Harlequin® Reader Service is committed to protecting your privacy. Our Privacy Policy is available online at www.ReaderService.com or upon request from the Harlequin Reader Service.

We make a portion of our mailing list available to reputable third parties that offer products we believe may interest you. If you prefer that we not exchange your name with third parties, or if you wish to clarify or modify your communication preferences, please visit us at www.ReaderService.com/consumerschoice or write to us at Harlequin Reader Service Preference Service, P.O. Box 9062, Buffalo, NY 14269. Include your complete name and address.

HWDIR13R

LARGER-PRINT BOOKS!

GET 2 FREE
LARGER-PRINT NOVELS
PLUS 2 FREE
MYSTERY GIFTS

Love Inspired®

Larger-print novels are now available...

LILPDIR13R

REQUEST YOUR FREE BOOKS!

2 FREE CHRISTIAN NOVELS
PLUS 2
FREE
MYSTERY GIFTS

HEARTSONG
PRESENTS